CONVOY COVER

DANA DUTHIE

Matchstick Literary
1-888-306-8885
orders@matchliterary.com

PREFACE

"This is GOD on Guard. Last one out, turn off the lights."

That was the radio call heard at noon on the 15th of August, 1973 in the skies over Cambodia. The U.S. air war in Cambodia was over. Air Force and Navy fighter aircraft had flown their last sorties and were returning to their ships at sea or air bases in Thailand. B-52s had dropped their last bombs and were returning to their base at Utapao, Thailand, or Anderson on Guam. The Nail FACs (Forward Air Controllers) of the Air Force had just crossed the border northbound toward their temporary duty base of Ubon, Thailand. Nobody knew for sure who made the radio call, but the scuttlebutt was it was the Nail's squadron commander, Lt. Colonel Howie Parsons. "Guard" is the emergency radio frequency all aircraft, military and civilian, monitor and use in case of an airborne emergency. For that reason it was not normally used for gag radio calls, but then Howie Parsons was not a normal guy.

The U.S. had supported the Cambodian government and military since 1970 when the Khmer Rouge, communist insurgence backed by North Vietnam, had moved in and were battling for control of the country. Over 250,000 tons of bombs had been dropped by the Air Force and Navy, most from the big B-52 and FB-111 bombers, but a significant amount was delivered by fighter bombers under forward air control in a close air support role, providing support for the Cambodian army. The FACs were from the 23rd Tactical Air Support Squadron (23rd TASS) flying the OV-10 Bronco, mostly from Ubon Air Base, which was the closest base to the Cambodian border. The FACs were home based in Nakhon Phanom Air Base in northeast Thailand, close to the Laotian border. Nakhon Phanom, or NKP as it was known, was home to the 56th Special Operations Wing (SOW). Earlier in the Southeast Asian conflict the 56th SOW flew A1-E Skyraiders, AC-119 and AC-130 gunships, as well as rescue helicopters, and the earlier aircraft flown by the FACs - O-1 Birddogs, and O-2 Skymasters.

The air war over Cambodia was mostly a joke, thousands of tons of bombs, mostly blowing down banana trees. There was significant combat happening on the ground, but the rules of engagement (ROE) imposed by the U.S. administration and Pentagon limited the bombers to high altitudes for fear of losing more aircraft to surface to air missiles and anti-aircraft fire. The FACs were supposedly limited to a minimum of 10,000 feet. But from that altitude it was nearly impossible to detect any activity in the jungle below. The pilots would have radio contact with a Cambodian ground commander and he would scream for help. All the FACs carried were white phosphorus (Willie Pete) smoke rockets to mark the targets. If delivered above 10,000 feet, with the manual aiming capabilities of the Bronco, and wind effect on the Willie Pete, the FAC would be lucky to put his mark within a click (kilometer) of the target. Most of the FACs disregarded the 10,000 foot restriction. The Khmer Rouge had a few SA-7 shoulder fired heat seeker missiles, but not much in the way of anti-aircraft weapons. Basically, whereas the 23 TASS had lost many OV-10s and pilot's in Vietnam, there was only one recorded shoot down over Cambodia. So the Nails got down lower where they could at least aim at something. Hopefully the ground commander would see the Willie Pete go off and could give the FAC the corrections to be made. The FAC would pass it on to the flight of bombers waiting overhead. The bomb sights in the F-4, F-105, A-7, A-6 and A-4 jets were quite a bit more sophisticated than what the Bronco had, and they usually could put their bombs close to where directed. The Air Force fighter pilots also had altitude restrictions, and sometimes they would actually stick to them. That usually meant that if the FAC had a flight of Air Force F-4s or A-7s holding above, along with a flight of Navy A-7s or A-4s, he'd put the Navy in first with the better hope of bombs on target. Most of the time however, the pilots would have to take the word of the ground commander if they were on target. Banana trees don't make much of a secondary explosion.

Cambodia is probably the most kicked around country on the Indochinese peninsula. It was a prosperous Khmer Empire centuries ago, and somewhere around the 12th century the magnificent Angkor Wat temple was built in the northwest part of the country. It is to this day Cambodia's number one tourist attraction, and luckily was spared (for the most part) any damage by various conflicts in the country. The empire fizzled in the 1800s and the French colonized the country, holding it until WWII when the Japanese occupied Cambodia. Independence was declared after the war, with Cambodia becoming a Kingdom again.

The Khmer Rouge communist insurgents occupied much of the north and eastern part of the country in the 1960s, backed by North Vietnam and the Viet Cong. In 1970 Prince Sihanouk was deposed and a pro - U.S. government was formed as the Khmer Republic. The U.S. interest was to enable its withdrawal from Southeast Asia, but by hopefully keeping Cambodia from going communist. However, the Americans only supported the regime by dropping tons of bombs, and providing a handful of military "trainers" to help the Republic's rag tag army. That all came to a halt in 1973 when the U.S. bailed out and later, by 1975, the Khmer Rouge had taken over. Cambodia became a killing field with Pol Pot in charge. His atrocities put Hitler to shame and his terror regime lasted until the 1990s. Today Cambodia is a typical third world country closely aligned with Vietnam, but basically peaceful.

Chapter One

WELCOME TO SOUTHEAST ASIA

I arrived at Nakhon Phanom Royal Thai Air Force Base (RTAFB) in June of 1973 as a young captain eager to stick my nose in the fight and get some combat time. I'm Captain Brad Mitchell, a wannabe fighter pilot, thankful to get the next best thing for an assignment as a Forward Air Controller (FAC). After graduating from pilot training in 1969, I "plowed back" to pilot training as a primary jet instructor at Laughlin AFB, Del Rio, Texas. I did ok there, and I rose through the instructor roles to flight examiner, or check pilot - flying mostly with other instructors, administering their check rides. I must have impressed somebody, because in early 1973, when the entire wing got only one assignment to a cockpit for all of its instructors due to rotate, I was selected for this FAC assignment. The war in Southeast Asia was winding down and the Air Force was going through one of its "gluttony" times, realizing it had too many pilots. The solution was something called "rated supplement," where pilots were offered non-flying jobs in locations of their choice (or close), and the "promise" of their choice of assignment next time around. It was a voluntary program, although the word was you either volunteer or "you'll get what we give you and suck it up." I decided I was not going to volunteer, and if they were going to take me out of the cockpit, it was with my heels dragging. I got real lucky.

So here I was, stepping off the "Klong" at NKP along with my buddy Pete Trask. The "Klong" was the moniker given the C-130 aircraft that made the rounds of all the U.S. bases in Thailand once or twice a week, bringing in new folks, and taking out the "old heads" ready to fly back to the good ol' U.S. of A. The Klong also brought in the mail, and here I was thinking the revelry and "happy to see ya" reception Pete and I got was for real. Shoot! As we were to find out, getting mail was the highlight of one's week at NKP. That's what they were celebrating.

Pete and I met in OV-10 training at Hurlburt AFB, Florida earlier in the spring. We had similar backgrounds. He came from pilot training as an instructor as well, though he was in Columbus, Mississippi. We hit it off early on, got to know each other well at Hurlburt, and went through basic survival training and jungle survival school together on our way into the country.

I shouldn't really complain that the welcome we got wasn't real. In fact, though most of the the 23rd Tactical Air Support Squadron (TASS) was down at Ubon RTAFB flying in the war, there were a few of the guys at NKP flying new-guy orientations, check rides, etc. One of the squadron flight commanders and two of the newest lieutenants met us at the ramp in a golf cart adorned with the squadron flag and a host of paraphernalia - not to mention a cold beer (or three?). They scooped up our gear, and then drove us all around the base on an introductory tour, blowing a horn and hootin' and hollerin' "Nails are Shit Hot!" "Nail" is the call sign of the 23rd TASS pilots. We would soon get our "Nail numbers" and be full fledged, "shit hot" Nails. I became Nail

32 and Pete was Nail 48. As we saw on that base tour, and came to understand throughout our year at NKP, the Nails were the closest thing to fighter pilots on the base, and we were "expected" to play the role - playing hard and generally making a nuisance of ourselves to the rest of the base. By that time, only the rescue helicopter squadron, the "Jollies," were there flying along with a few C-130s and other miscellaneous aircraft on base.

We ended up our tour around the base at the Nail hooches - two long barracks buildings, one story, about 2 dozen two-man rooms in each with a communal toilet and shower room in the middle of the building. The rooms opened toward the "courtyard" with the "Nail Hole" in the middle. The Nail Hole was the most important building on base - the squadron bar where we were introduced to Nou Paul, our squadron bartender and all around good guy. There was one empty room in our hootch, so Pete and I moved in, and fortunately (I think), it was the closest room to the entrance of the Nail Hole. Fortunately because it wasn't too far to crawl after a night of over doing it, but maybe unfortunately because we heard all the noise of the revelry after we had turned in.

Anyway, we unpacked and went directly to the Nail Hole for our first night in country. We heard all the stories and looked forward to our time flyin' and fightin,' and joining the camaraderie. After a couple of beers, we sloshed over to the Officers Club for dinner and then back to the Nail Hole for a scotch or two. It was then that I took some time to reminisce and think about the last few months.

Chapter Two

WATER SURVIVAL SCHOOL

I was sent to Homestead AFB, Florida from my home base in Texas in January of '73 for water survival training. What a boondoggle! I wondered at the time why they didn't just send me there on my way to or from OV-10 FAC training. Would have made a lot more sense logistically. As it was, I flew into Miami, caught a shuttle down to Homestead, played around in the ocean for 10 days (with only 6 days of actual training), then flew back to Del Rio. Then I sat around for a week or two before heading out to Hurlburt Field, back in Florida, for my longer training stint.

Water Survival consisted of 4-6 hour days. There was a little bit of academics on the use of the various bits of equipment carried in Air Force aircraft that was supposed to help you survive a ditching or over water bailout. We had hands on training as well, and I got to play with all kinds of stuff I'd never see - like 12 man life rafts, and shipborne life rings and preservers. I did learn how to deploy the one man life raft that would be attached to my butt if I ever bailed out of the OV-10, as well as the flares and other signal devices that would be found in my survival kit.

The only nerve racking part of the training was when we were sent up to the high dive platform of the swimming pool on base in full flight gear and boots. Probably a strange thing for a pilot to say, but I'm afraid of heights. I'd never dived or jumped off a high dive in my life, but I managed to do it once at Homestead. There was a fully opened parachute spread out in the water below us. We had to jump in feet first beside it, swim with all our gear on over to the parachute, and then pull our way under it to the other side. The idea was to teach us how to get out from under our chute if we bailed out over water and the chute floated down on top of us. The technique was to turn onto your back and then reaching back over your head, grab a handful of parachute and pull it down to your knees. Hopefully it would only take 6-10 of these strokes to get out from under. Then we had to take off our flight suits, tie knots in the arms and legs towards the ends, and then blow air into them, creating a makeshift life preserver in case the one we were issued didn't work. That was only hard part for me. I got the flight suit off down to my ankles when I realized I needed to get my size 14 boots off first. I thrashed around like a fish on a hook for a minute or so before I was able to join the rest of my classmates who were floating around watching and laughing at me.

The final day of water survival we went para-sailing. This was in 1973. Para-sailing wasn't known as a tourist attraction yet - at least not at any beach I ever went to. But it obviously became quite the money maker for entrepreneurs who owned a boat, a rope and a para-sail later. Our para-sail was actually a full blown parachute, not the tailored down version used for tourists. As a result, it was big and heavy to get airborne and we didn't get too high. The trainee would hold on to the parachute harness as he was pulled up into the air. Then, when the chute made it to the maximum altitude, the guys in the tow boat released the line. For a few seconds then we were hanging in our chute as if we had bailed out over the warm Atlantic. The trick was to release the fanny pack that held your survival kit and life raft so that it would dangle beneath you on a rope. Then we assumed the position - feet together, knees slightly bent, hands on the quick releases, and eyes on the horizon. As soon as our feet hit the water, the trick was to quick-disconnect the chute so it wouldn't come down on top of you. The idea also was to not quick-disconnect too soon so you don't go "splat" on the ocean. One of my classmates did that and the trainers had to pull him out gingerly. He had gotten tangled up in the line that held his life raft and hit the water in a belly flop. He ended up with two broken ribs.

After we had successfully jettisoned our chute, we had to pull our raft over, and invariably it hadn't self inflated like it was supposed to. So we had to go through the process of blowing up the raft, then crawl in and open the survival kit. We got to shoot off a flare, turn off the emergency beacon that was going off since the "ejection," use the signal mirror to show the tow boat where we were (of course they were just sitting there having a good time watching us struggle), and talk on the radio to guide them in to our rescue position. Once we had all gone through this exercise we were herded around in a group of one man survival rafts and one of us had to signal and talk in a rescue helicopter to hover over our position. Then a PJ (Para-jumper) would jump in with us and the extraction hoist would be dropped down for us to climb on and be hoisted up into the chopper. Exercise over.

I spent a couple extra days in Miami Beach eating as much seafood as I could and drooling at all the scenery walking around in skimpy bikinis. Needless to say we didn't get much seafood in

Del Rio, Texas, and there were only a few good looking girls - mostly all married to other instructors or students.

I had almost two weeks before I was supposed to report to Hurlburt, so I hung around Del Rio with not much to do. I had been officially signed out of the squadron so I couldn't fly, and that didn't bother me too much. By then I had over 1700 hours in the T-37 trainer and I was ready to move on. So I spent about ten days out on Lake Amistad in my new sailboat before it was time to load it up and drive away.

Amistad was created by a new dam on the Rio Grande just up river from Del Rio. The dam had been dedicated the year before I got to Laughlin AFB in 1969, and the lake slowly grew so that at that time it was the largest man made lake in the U.S. At first it was great for fishing and water skiing. The lake was mostly down in the west Texas canyons with good wind protection and it had been stocked with small mouth bass. I bought a 16 foot Glastron boat with a 65 HP Evinrude engine and did a lot of fishing, water skiing, and just plain partying with my squadron mates for a couple of years. Then, as the lake got so big it outgrew the canyons, the wind protection was gone. We had to motor a ways to find a canyon to ski in, because the wind in west Texas blows hard all the time.

One of my squadron mates was originally from southern California and he had done a lot of sailing. As Amistad grew there were quite a few sailboats out and about. Roger had bought a Ranger 23 - a twenty three foot sloop that would uncomfortably sleep four, had a porta-potti, a stove, a sink, and an icebox. It also had 1500 pounds of lead in a fixed keel, so it was a great boat in strong winds. I had never even been on a sailboat before, but I went out with Roger and actually crewed for him in a couple informal races. I was hooked after my third "cruise" and I immediately sold my "stinkpot" (sailor talk for a power boat), and ordered my own Ranger 23. It took a month or so to arrive, and in that month I spent every day I could out on the lake with Roger, learning the ropes (or is it sheets and halyards?).

I found that sailing was my second love - after flying, and once my boat arrived I spent all my free time on Lake Amistad. That was about six months before I got orders to leave. I took most of my squadron mates out and narrowed it down to two "shipmates" as my crew whenever there was a race. Of course, as far as I was concerned, if there was another sailboat on the water, it was a race. He might not think so, but I sure did. The beauty of the Ranger was that with that substantial ballast she could point high into the wind. For you land lubbers, the ability to point high into the wind meant that you didn't have to fall off as far when sailing into the wind and you would always arrive at your upwind destination before the other guy. That was big advantage in a race. I really got to learn that well when I got to Hurlburt and put my boat in the bay at Ft. Walton Beach.

The west Texas winds and weather almost blew me away one day on the lake. Roger had his boat out as well and it was beautiful day. We had sailed up to a point a few miles north of our marina and tied up to have a picnic. We were sitting there on the rocks enjoying our third or fourth beer with our backs to the north, when what is known in those parts as a "dry norther" came through. The wind went from light and variable to 30 plus knots out of the north in a matter of seconds. No weather associated with it, just a lot of dust. We sat there for a few minutes hoping it would blow out as fast as it came in. Bad decision. It got worse. Later reports said the winds got up to 78 knots. I had no idea what to do. I knew we didn't want to have much sail up and even our heavy lead keel wouldn't help much in what amounted to a cyclone.

Roger had all the experience so he decided to go first. He loaded his wife and kids aboard and shoved off. At first he just raised his main sail about half way, but when he got about 100 yards off shore he took a gust from abeam and was knocked flat. By releasing the boom the keel righted his boat right away, and fortunately the wife and kids were tied in. He lowered his sail and disappeared around the next downwind bend. Now it was my turn. I had one of our other flight members and his wife with me. We all put on the life preservers and Rob tethered his wife to a cleat. We pushed off and I basically "bare poled" it down wind and downstream toward the marina - no sails. I was sitting at the helm steering as best I could and Rob's wife was screaming and pointing behind us. I looked back and we were basically surfing on waves that were at least ten feet high. The marina was in an inlet just upstream of the main highway bridge that crosses the lake. We wanted to make the marina, because it we missed it, my mast would not fit under that bridge.

We came roaring around the bend in toward the marina and lo and behold - the marina was gone! The winds and water had ripped the floating docks loose and every boat that was tied up that day was at the bottom of the lake. After I squirmed to readjust my underwear, I saw the mast of Roger's boat further into the inlet, up against the rocks. He was on shore waving me in. He had found a small inlet on the inlet that gave him a little wind protection and he had beached his boat up on the rocks. I had learned to be able to sail into the marina or other landing spot by turning into the wind and letting loose of all the sails, thereby eventually coming to a stop. But this was something different. I had no sails to let loose so I went blowing by as close as I could stand it to the rocks and then cranked the tiller to turn us into the gale. It almost worked. I had gone too far before coming about, but Roger was there to throw us a line and he pulled us in beside his boat. We battened everything down and then spent the rest of that day and the next helping folks get their boats off the bottom and out of the water.

So I spent my last couple of weeks just sailing and cruising and drinking and eating. One of our favorite combinations on Lake Amistad was Annie Green Springs wine and Philadelphia Cream Cheese with picante sauce on crackers. I did in a few bottles of Annie and then it was time to pull my boat out of the water. This was quite a feat, since a boat with a fixed keel about 4 feet long is not normally trailerable. But I was bound and determined to take her with me to Florida. I had kept the cradle that she was delivered on off a flatbed semi. I went out and bought a used flatbed trailer with dual axles, got help lifting the cradle onto it, and towed it downtown to a Mexican guy who was a welder and jack-of-all-trades. He basically bolted and welded the cradle onto the trailer and I was ready to go. Almost!

I had to step the mast - take it down. I nestled up beside the biggest sailboat in the marina, a Balboa 26 that had a mast a little taller than mine. We rigged a halyard off his mast to the top of mine, and then with four guys at the end of lines to keep it straight, we lifted my mast out of its housing. Then we laid it down on the boat, securing it to the tiller in the stern and the bow pulpit up forward. Then came the tricky part.

Because the cradle has supports across the width of the boat we couldn't pull the boat onto the trailer like most captains do. We had to submerge the trailer and cradle, move the boat in from the side, and then very slowly pull the trailer and boat out together to get her to rest where she had to on the cradle cross pieces. It took a few tries and a whole case of Lonestar beer, but we got 'er done.

I had gone out and bought the biggest Pontiac Catalina station wagon I could find, got my Mexican amigo to mount a heavy duty hitch and wire it for brakes, and hooked up for my trek across country. I had one problem though. With the mast laying on the bow pulpit, the boat and mast sat 11'3" high, which meant I had to really pay attention to underpasses and most of all, gas station roofs. As you might imagine, I think I only got about 8 miles to the gallon on the trip. Or maybe it was 8 gallons to the mile.

The trip wasn't too bad. I only had one near miss. That was in Biloxi, Mississippi when a little old lady in front of me decided to stop on a yellow light with me too close behind her. I honked on the brakes and felt the whole back end shudder. I looked in my side mirror and it looked like the trailer and boat were coming my way - sideways. Fortunately we stayed hooked up, and although there were lots of shudders and weaves back there from then on, I just took it slow and limped into Fort Walton Beach to a marina with a bunch of sailors scratching their heads and wondering what this cowboy with Texas plates was up to. That marina had one of those huge machines that lifts boats and wheels them all over, and they were able to float my boat in a New York minute. They even mounted the mast for me and I was ready for the next chapter of my flying and sailing adventures.

Chapter Three

HURLBURT FIELD
- FAC TRAINING

After settling my boat in for the stay, I checked in for my three months of training at Hurlburt Field, a satellite base of the larger Eglin AFB complex. Eglin sits on the north coast of the Choctawhatchee Bay in Fort Walton, Florida, and Hurlburt is just down the highway to the west. The Air Force has a large presence in the Ft. Walton area. They even own miles of beautiful white sand beach just east of town, all the way to the Destin pass, where the bay empties into the Gulf of Mexico. In those days the town of Destin was little more than a couple of restaurants, a bait store, and a boat ramp.

FAC training was relaxed to put it mildly. We seldom worked an eight hour day, and took Fridays off about every other week. It was a dream assignment for the permanent party instructors. Lots of home time and recreation. Our training started off with a little academics. The OV-10 is not a real complex airplane, so the classes we took about the aircraft and emergencies were fairly short and tests were easy. We also took courses on intelligence gathering and what we could expect when we got in theater. The FAC business had been going strong all through the Southeast Asia war, but a lot of the intel training was really no longer valid for us going through the course in 1973. Our theater of operation was going to be Cambodia, and with very restrictive rules of engagement. About the only real issue was being able to tell a banana tree from a palm tree.

Our flying training consisted of 30 sorties, starting off with basic aircraft operations and instrument flying. We each took a basic instrument and "contact" check ride, and then we launched into the FAC training itself. A "contact check" consisted of stall recoveries, some aerobatics, and landings. We had be proficient in single engine landings, as well as short field take offs and landings.

The OV-10 Bronco is a very good airplane for the FAC business, although it wasn't designed for that. It was originally built for the Marines to use for close air support and perimeter defense. By the time it was produced, the Marines didn't want it and the Air Force picked it up to replace the O-2 Skymaster in use as a FAC platform. The Bronco had twin turboprop engines that were on the front of twin booms off the high wing. The glass cockpit sat in the nose of the aircraft body with tandem ejection seats and very good visibility. The plexiglass extended down to the pilot's hips, and he was completely glassed in up and over the top. Behind the second seat was a substantial cargo area with a large door in the tail that swung open for loading. Although we never used it, if the door was detached and the second seat removed, the compartment would accommodate five fully dressed and equipped paratroopers. There was even a red and green jump light back there, activated by the pilot. The Air Force flew with the seat installed and the door closed, and about all the cargo space was used for was to haul cases of Coors beer back to Hurlburt from Colorado, or lobsters from Maine for the next squadron party.

The Bronco could carry up to 3200 pounds of bombs on the centerline pylon assembly and if installed, wing pylons. It also had 4 X 7.62 mm machine guns on the centerline assembly, able to deliver 2000 rounds per minute. As FACs we carried rocket pods on the wing pylons to shoot white phosphorous (Willie Pete) rockets to mark the target for our support bombers. The Eglin AFB complex included several gunnery ranges and there were others within the general area. We usually would fly to one of the ranges and expend our rockets and strafe with the guns. Typical of the micro-management of the Southeast Asia war though, it was ordered that the guns in the OV-10s in theater would be removed to keep us from getting too low to strafe targets. Heaven forbid if we should actually do some ground commander under siege any good by strafing his enemy. The same rationale existed when it came to defending ourselves with heat seeking air to air missiles. The OV-10 could carry two AIM-9 Sidewinder missiles on the wingtips, but the powers wouldn't have any of that either. After all, we might try to defend ourselves if attacked by a MIG. The "fighter mafia" running the Air Force at the time would never let some lowly FAC shoot down a MIG. There weren't enough MIGs to go around and the fighter jocks got what action there was.

The OV-10 was fully equipped in the cockpit with all the up to date navigation and communications equipment. We had 5 radios and we were fully instrumented for flying in weather or at night. We sometimes carried flares to drop for night fighting as well, though night sorties were limited in theater by the time Pete and I got there. A few of the aircraft in theater were outfitted with smart bomb targeting systems, known as Pave Spot. Navigators, or Weapons Systems Operators, (WSOs) as they liked to be called, were assigned to the 23 TASS to fly on Pave Nail missions. A targeting pod was loaded on the aircraft and the WSO would "designate" the target with the laser from the pod. Fighters carrying "smart bombs" would deliver their 500 - 2000 pound laser guided bombs into a "basket" close to parameters, and the bombs would glom on to the laser and ride it down to the target. This technology was developed within the fighter bomber force itself later so they could laser guide their own bombs.

Our typical training mission consisted of a four ship formation with 2 or 3 trainees and four instructors initially. Later we would go up with just two instructors and we would fly solo. We would fly out to one of the ranges, and the first FAC trainee would pull out of the formation and go and seek a "target" to use for his scenario. The other three aircraft would simulate the fighter bombers. Sometimes, but very seldom, we actually had real fighters from Eglin or MacDill AFB (Tampa), or some Navy guys from Jacksonville to FAC. Like I said though, it was very seldom. I think I got one sortie with the real thing. The FAC would simulate talking to the commander on the ground and then brief up the fighters on the target and scenario. Then he would roll in and "mark" the target with a Willie Pete smoke rocket, give the bombers corrections from that smoke, and standby while they rolled in and simulated dropping their bombs by shooting their own rockets. Each flight of "bombers" would make 3 or four passes, correcting as per the FAC's directions. Then we would switch roles, so by the end of the time on the range, each trainee had a turn playing FAC. The instructors would often throw a wrench in the scenario by coming up with another target or simulating anti-aircraft fire, anything to complicate the mission. As I was to find out later in theater, complicating the mission was the norm rather than a rarity.

The trick to FACing was being able to fly, look through binoculars, talk on five different radios, write down the ordnance the bombers had to offer, direct and deconflict multiple flights of bombers, and navigate with your lap full of maps. One of the great things about the OV-10 was all that plexiglass. We would fly with grease pencils and would write down the fighters' call signs, their bomb load, and time on the scene, on the plexiglass. Writing down anything on a knee pad inside was difficult when you had a big map displayed there. Besides it meant you spent too much time "heads down" when you needed to be heads up and looking outside. We would often come back from a real mission in theater with grease pencil marks all over both sides of the cockpit. Some guys actually learned to write with their opposite hand to give them that much more room to write. Our crew chiefs weren't too happy when we shut down and they had to clean off the canopy for the next mission.

Flying with one hand on the stick, the other holding binoculars up to your eyes, and the third writing down coordinates, bomb loads, etc. was a real trick. Especially since most of us only had two hands. The airplane didn't have an autopilot of any sort to be able to hold a bank and an altitude, so it took constant corrections and a good trim technique. I can't count the number of times I dropped the binoculars on the floor after putting them in my lap to make a correction. I soon learned to put a tether on the binocs and tie the other end to my wrist.

As I said, we had five radios on board. We had an Ultra High Frequency (UHF) radio that we used to talk to the bombers as well as air traffic control, the tower, etc. for basic flight. We had a Very High Frequency (VHF) that we used to talk to the airborne command post, usually a C-130 tasked with command

and control of the war. We had two FM radios - one to talk to the ground commander, and one used as "squadron common" to talk to each other. We also had a High Frequency (HF) radio that we used for other tasks in the area or for long distance discussions. The HF became our way to talk to home after the war. We would night fly when the airwaves were most conducive, climb to about 15,000 feet, and with the HF radio, call up some Ham operator somewhere in the states (usually on the west coast). He would then dial the phone for us and get our wives, sweethearts, or folks on the line. Then we would relay the mushy stuff, assuming we didn't mind the HAM operator listening in. It went like this: "Hello honey. Can you hear me? Over!" She would then say "Yes I can hear you but weak. Over!" My turn - "I love you. Over!" Hopefully followed by "I love you too. Over!" And so it went. Contact with the real world.

Our training at Hurlburt ended with a big staggered launch of every OV-10 we could get airborne. All the trainees (there were 12 of us) and most of the instructors flew. We would take turns and control the skies with airplanes all around us, stacked at different altitudes. The scenario was complicated and ever evolving. We actually were lucky and a flight of A-4s from the Navy stopped by, and we worked them into the fray as well. We expended lots of white phosphorous, shot lots of bullets, and managed not to run into one another. After it was over we had a big party with Coors beer, Apalachicola oysters, and Maine lobsters. Training was complete. We were sufficiently FACked.

Chapter Four

SAILING

I spent most all of my free time at Hurlburt either on the beach admiring (and chasing a few) bikinis or sailing on my boat The apartment complex we stayed in (Pete and Linda Trask had a flat there too) had its own dock and a couple of slips right on the Intracoastal Waterway about a mile west from where it empties into Choctawhatchee Bay. It was a bit tricky to get in and out of because only a narrow channel in from the middle of the Waterway had been dredged. I had a small outboard engine I mounted on the boat's transom, and usually I'd have to drop sails out in the middle and motor into my slip. Every once in a while though, if the wind was out of the west, I'd sail in on the beam from the middle of the Waterway, turn downwind toward the dock, release the jib or Genoa (front sail) and let it flutter and blow by the dock under main sail alone. Then, if I was good enough, I'd briskly bring her about pointed into the wind, release the main, and cozy right up the pylons. If I came about too late, and the wind was too strong, and I couldn't make it back to the dock, I'd have to scramble and start the engine to keep from running aground downwind. One time I had Pete on board and I guess I hadn't briefed him well enough on what I was doing. He was up at the bow and as we approached the dock to go by under sail he jumped off with a line and pulled us toward the pylon. With the main sail full we plowed into the dock with a "crunch." Nothing hurt or damaged, but not the graceful approach I was looking for.

We'd often go out for the afternoon after getting home from flying, and tool around a bit in the bay, with me racing every boat I saw, whether he wanted to race or not. Then approaching the cocktail hour, we'd sail into one of the shoreside restaurants or bars, tie up in their adjoining marina, and go in for some libations and great seafood. Sometimes the sail home afterwards in the dark was a bit shaky, but we made it every time. I learned the hard way on one of those return trips about right of way rules on the waterway. I knew that sailboats had the right of way over power boats, and I guess I just assumed that because the tugs pushing the huge barges down the waterway were under power, then I would have right of way over them. Not so! One night I had sailed up the waterway to abeam our dock and was about to turn in when I realized there was a huge barge full of gravel plowing down the middle. Since I thought I had the right of way, I turned right in front of him to cross. Obviously those things can't stop on a dime, and the tug captain back at the rear pushing it could only see my mast anyway. He blew his horn and I turned to parallel the barge just in time, and subsequently missed our entry channel. I waited until the barge had passed, endured all the foul language you would expect out of a sailor (the barge captain), and then slinked on home, tail between my legs.

I sailed in several informal races on the bay, taking Pete or some of my other FAC classmates on as crew. One day I had six aboard as my "crew," although they were much better at drinking beer than playing sailor boy. We raced another boat down the bay to the Destin Pass, and then because the other boat went out through the pass, we did too. That was the one and only time

I sailed her outside the bay in the Gulf of Mexico. Suffice it to say the waves were a lot bigger out there, and although the boat handled them well, and we did fine sailing just by reefing the sails, it was a rough ride. Four of my six crew mates got sick and started calling "RALPH" over the side. Anyway, we made it back to the pass without losing anyone overboard into the puke infested Gulf, and attempted to re-enter the Choctawhatchee Bay. Now someone once told me (after this adventure) that the Destin Pass is the fastest moving water in the country, creating a venturi effect when the tide is coming in or out. In this case the tide was coming out. I should have realized it when we flew through the Pass on the way out to the Gulf. Even with wind on the beam and all my sails full we couldn't overcome the tide coming out and had to fall off the attempt twice. My little putsy-putsy engine wouldn't do any good either. So we pulled into an inlet outside the Pass and waited until the tide changed to come in. That was about four hours and a lot of beer later. To be sure we had enough beer, two of the guys hoofed it over the dunes to the highway and up to the bait store to buy a couple more cases. I think we pulled into my slip at the dock a little after midnight to the welcoming of a lot of pissed off wives and girl friends. Hey - I had fun!

Most of the races that went on in the bay were informal. There was always a race on Saturday and Sunday. Someone would set a course, float some buoys, and away we'd go. But there was one big race a couple weeks before we left Hurlburt. It was the Billy Bowlegs Regatta. Billy Bowlegs was a pirate who use to terrorize the coast in that area back in the 1700 time frame, and Ft. Walton Beach put on a huge festival every May to celebrate him. There was a carnival, a parade, a costume ball, and a big sailboat race. So I signed up. We had to sail over to the Ft. Walton Yacht Club in an inlet off the Bay at the west end. I had outfitted my crew (Pete and Linda Trask and me, the stalwart Captain) with Tee Shirts - gold color with the name of the boat embroidered - "Shenandoah."

We sailed into the Yacht Club marina, tied her down, and walked in to register. Everyone was gawking at us. "Whoa! Who are these ringers with uniforms and all?" Right away we had them all on the defensive. Right! Anyway I went up to the registration table and paid my entry fee. The lady there asked me "What's your handicap?" Huh! Handicap! I guess sailboats are handicapped in the unlimited class of sailing based on hull length, square footage of sail, etc. I had no clue what the handicap of a Ranger 23 was, so I simply looked at Pete and then back at the lady and said "My handicap? Him?" while pointing at Pete. That got a laugh out of everyone else around but not from Broomhilda the registrar. She looked at me with a sneer and said she would simply assign me a generic handicap. I found out later she socked it to us and we lost more time than we probably should have on the race.

The race started and finished right out in front of the Yacht Club. The start and finish line was formed by a man on the shore with a couple of flags and a bullhorn, and a boat moored in the inlet about 60 yards out. Now there are those that say a sailboat race must be really dull and boring. It might be to watch, but when you're in the middle of a gaggle of boats from 20 to 45 feet long, weighing up to several tons, all circling around in a small area, jockeying for position to be at the line when the horn goes off, it gets tense and very exciting. You had to know the under sail right of way rules, but in my case, when some of the boats were twice my size, my having the right of way didn't mean much.

I used my pilot prowess for a technique to set up for my timing. Much like we did flying in a holding pattern prior to commencing an instrument approach at a designated time, I set up a holding pattern with the wind directly off my beam. We'd sail outbound with the wind off our port side (left), time the leg, time the turn about, and sail inbound with the wind off the starboard (right). If it was a direct beam, hopefully the leg times would be the same. All the captains had a time hack off the starter before the race, so I timed my last outbound leg to give me the inbound leg that arrived at the starting line right within a few seconds of the "Hack" time. I got there about three seconds early so I turned to parallel the line and then came about right on time at the starter's horn. We were off in first place, and the captain was smiling.

The outbound leg was a long up wind haul all the way down to abeam Destin Pass (about 8 miles). It meant a lot of beating into the wind, coming about when it was strategically appropriate and pointing as high as possible. As I mentioned before, the Ranger with her 1500 pounds of lead in the keel, is an outstanding pointer. We increased our lead over the rest of the fleet by several minutes. We were "smokin'" and the Captain was ecstatic.

The next leg was a short beam run of about a mile, just to deconflict with the boats coming home from those still plugging along on the first leg. I had my 150% Genoa up, and with the boom at about 45 degrees we were moving. We didn't gain anymore space on that leg, but we didn't lose any either. By the way, a "Genoa" is a foresail that is larger than a standard "Jib" sail. A Jib usually would take up 110% of the space between the fore "stay" where it attaches and the mast. A "Genoa" would take up more than that. My "Genny" was a 150, taking up 150% of the space. They come as large as 175%.

The third leg was an 8 mile downwind run back to just outside the inlet where the finish line is. We turned for home and went "wing and wing." That means we let the main out all the way on one side and pulled the Genny over to the other side, propping it out with another pole. That way we got as much sail to the wind as possible and road the waves home. As I looked back behind me my big Cheshire cat grin faded to "aw shit!" Every one of the boats back there was popping a big, colorful spinnaker. The spinnaker is a balloon style sail that one raises out in front of the main and Genny, and it provides a great mount of speed. Trouble was, I didn't have a spinnaker. They weren't cheap and I never needed one in Texas. So, one by one these bigger boats with their beautiful sails plowed by with their crew looking at us and scratching their heads - like "What did I know that they didn't?" I couldn't take it for long so I thought I'd be sneaky and fall off a bit to the inland side of the bay, trying to shorten the leg. Big mistake!

We were going along lickety split in our wing and wing configuration with the competition off to our 8 o'clock, when all of a sudden the water turned color to a murky brown. I recognized it right away, but not soon enough. I brought us about more to port and tried to get on a beam reach so the boat would heal over and avoid what was about to happen. CRUNCH! And we came to an abrupt halt. We had just run aground. Insult to injury, it spilled my beer too. We were hung up there for what seemed like forever. It was in fact only a few minutes. By tightening up the sails on the beam we were able to lean her over, though rather uncomfortably so for Linda. I then jumped in and was able to stand on the sand bar and push her along until we burst free of the bottom. "Burst free" was the right description too. With the sails full tight and the wind off the beam, Shenandoah wanted to fly, so she did, with me standing on the bottom watching her go. Fortunately we had prepared for this and Pete threw me a line. He had sailed with me enough to also know to bring her about into the wind, release the sails, and come to a stop while I pulled myself aboard. So, we were back in the fight.

Half of the fleet was now ahead of us and we still had about a mile of downwind to go, wishing I had a spinnaker. But the last short leg was back into the wind again to the finish line. I was able to pass up a few of the boats ahead, but overall we came in 8th out of 38. Not bad until Broomhilda's generic handicap knocked us back to 14th. Oh well. We had a good story to tell and the after race party was loaded with good food and more beer. They even gave me a prize at the awards ceremony. It was a photo of one of the America's Cup racers with a big, beautiful spinnaker out front. Someone had written on the border of the photo - "It's all about the equipment!" Hah! Hah! Funny!

The next week I sailed over to the big Marina where I had floated the boat earlier. They hoisted her out and set her gently on her cradle on my trailer. We stepped the mast and tied it down, and I spent a couple days cleaning the bottom, oiling the teak, and packing things up. Then I hauled it up to the property of one of our OV-10 instructors, parked her next to a tree in his back yard, and chained her down. He wasn't a sailor, but he said he'd watch over her for me. Then I sold my wreck of a Pontiac, packed up my gear, and flew out with Pete to Fairchild AFB, Washington for basic survival school.

Chapter Five

AIR FORCE BASIC SURVIVAL SCHOOL

We flew into Spokane, Washington and were taken to Fairchild AFB by "Blue Goose" (a basic school bus painted blue). Fairchild was a Strategic Air Command base with B-52 bombers on board. It also housed the Air Force's Basic Survival School, base within the base. It had barracks and classrooms and a full blown prisoner of war camp, a dining hall, and various training devices for para rescue and survival training. We were housed in the barracks. Most trainees at Fairchild were aircrew members - pilots, navigators, etc, so most were officers. There were some enlisted folks in each class as well. They were aircrew members of bomber, transport and helicopters that because they might fly over enemy territory, stood the chance of being shot down. Regardless, the barracks were pretty standard. Captains and below shared a room with one other. Majors and above had their own rooms. This was great! …. for a few days.

We started off with academics that included use of rescue equipment, survival techniques, political classes on the Southeast Asia countries, and personal stories of previous POWs. Our American POWs had been released from Hanoi earlier in the year of 1973. They weren't quite ready to talk about it to new guys, but a few did give interviews to the staff of the survival school. Later I understand several of our previous POWs made the trek up to Fairchild to tell their stories to trainees. We got a pretty good cross section of experiences though, and I was in awe of what our POWs went through and how they communicated and survived.

Our prisoners communicated with what was called the "tap code," words relayed by tapping on the pipes, even blinking if the other person could see your face. There was even an enlisted Navy guy who literally fell off the boat in Haiphong Harbor and was scooped up by the North Vietnamese. Because the guards and officers of the Hanoi Hilton thought he was harmless - I mean, who falls off your ship in enemy territory? - they actually gave him the job of sweeping up around the camp. By using the tap code with his broom he was able to gather and memorize the names of dozens of prisoners in the camp, and then, when he was released early, he passed on the names to his superiors when he got home. That way, dozens of wives and families of fliers previously thought to be Missing In Action (MIA) and probably deceased, found out that their loved ones were actually alive in the Hanoi Hilton as POWs.

After four days of academics and practice using the various survival equipment our time as respected Air Forces officers and airmen was over. We were herded together and loaded onto two large helicopters. There were 22 in our class so the choppers each took eleven and launched off into a wooded area southwest of the base. Pete and I were on the same chopper and we had a pretty good idea of what was coming. They landed in a clearing several miles from the base where we unloaded. We were given a canteen of water, a standard issue survival knife, a compass, a map of the area (much like we would have if flying over the area), and a mirror. Then the helicopter took off. Our mission was to navigate in twos using the compass and map. Each pair and the one trio was given a different point to navigate to. Supposedly, once we got there we would be given a survival radio and instructions on how to guide in a rescue helicopter.

Since there were five groups from our chopper alone we often ran across another pair or trio, but we were to treat everyone as the enemy and avoid detection. To enhance that theory we were all given a book of chits. The idea was that if you discovered another pair or trio of evaders they would have to give you one of their chits. Supposedly the chits would bring you benefits later. Since we all knew that at the end of this exercise was the POW camp, we assumed the chits might bring an extra serving of rations, or a shower, or …. whatever. Anyway, it was best to avoid each other and not be detected, because who knew for sure who saw whom first.

They inserted us into the area about 1600 hours, so we didn't have a whole lot of daylight to travel in. We had no flashlights and it was very dark out there in the forest. Pete and I went about as far as we could using our map and compass, and realized we were going to have to bed down for the night. We had moved into some pretty rough terrain - lots of ups, downs and rocks, and we didn't want to fall in the dark. We found a makeshift cave and settled in for what we thought would be a restful night. Not so fast!

It must have been about 0200 when I woke to a ruckus and a very bright light in my eyes. "Get up, American dog!" an oriental looking guy in black pajamas yelled at me. He prodded me with his rifle and kicked me in the butt. I sat up and saw that they already had Pete in handcuffs with a hood over his head. Turns out he had thought he heard something earlier and got up and walked right into this not so friendly gook and his buddies.

"Stand up!" My antagonist yelled. I stumbled over to where they were holding Pete and they quickly tied my hands behind my back and threw a hood over my head.

"Thank you." I said. "That light was awfully bright." I thought I was being funny.

"Oh, you be Yankee Smart ass." Black pajamas said. "You think you velly funny? We see how funny velly soon." And he pushed us out onto what we remembered coming in there was a very faint trail. They kept pushing us and we kept stumbling around. One time I took a pretty good tumble and with my hands behind my back couldn't protect myself very well. I crunched my knee and banged my head on a rock. About this time I was concerned that we were really in danger, and almost to the point of thinking this wasn't make believe - this was the real thing.

After a few minutes we must have come to some sort of clearing because there was a truck of some sort in front of us. Black PJs prodded us again and yelled for us to get in the back of the truck. It must have been some sort of panel truck, so we clamored in and lied down, soon to realize we weren't alone. There were at least two other bodies in there. Pete tried to ask who was there, but PJs yelled "You shut up! You no talk." But by squirming around and touching one another, and getting in a quiet whisper here and there we ascertained that there were two pairs and the one trio of so called evaders in the truck.

We bounced along on what must have been not much more than a mountain trail for what seemed like forever. In reality I guess it was about an hour and we pulled into a stop. We were not so softly unloaded and then herded into a group in an area with very bright lights. I could tell that much through the hood. We were held there in a group, not allowed to talk, while more and more of our ranks grew. I had to take a leak real bad so I asked if I could and I was told to just pee down my leg. So I did. Couldn't help it. I'm glad I didn't have to take a dump at least.

Finally after about another hour, they took our hoods off and untied ur hands. We were in the middle of the Fairchild Prisoner of War Camp. Bright lights illuminated the compound and we were told to get in ranks and stand at attention facing a flagpole with the North Vietnamese flag flying. All of the guys with guns looked to be oriental. Most were camouflaged in "war paint," so they could have been from anywhere. But the officer who came out of the building behind the flagpole looked for real. He looked to be Vietnamese and he wore the uniform and hat of a North Vietnamese major.

"Ah, welcome to your new home Yankee dogs." He said with a definite accent. "You are now guests of the Peoples Republic of Vietnam. Most of you will be tried for crimes of violence against the people of Vietnam and will be dealt with accordingly. You will all do as you are told, only what you are told, and maybe you will survive. However, be advised if it were up to me and most of my guards, you would all be shot right now." He threatened, and I really felt threatened. This was a nightmare.

"Now, turn around. You see that building over there?" He pointed to a low building with open window shutters and a few lights. "That is your new home. You will go there now. You will be told what to do and when to do it. I will be seeing each of you individually in the coming weeks and months. Now - GO!" He ordered and the guards prodded and pushed us toward what was a make shift barracks.

The building had a couple rows of bed frames - wooden planks, no mattresses. We each got a blanket and a canteen cup for drinking. There was a trough in the middle of the building where we were to urinate. To take a dump there were two outhouses out back. There was one sink and a shower that didn't work. We all fanned out and selected a bunk. The rest of the camp included what looked to be a classroom, a stage where we were forced to listen to the history of Ho Chi Minh and communist propaganda, and two rows of low concrete structures with about a dozen doors 2-3 feet apart. We found out what that was later. There were loud speakers throughout the camp with constant loud oriental music and heavy metal rock blaring. The whole camp was encircled by two rows of concertina wire, and there were three guard towers.

We were able to communicate when the guards weren't in the building with us. We discovered we had one Lt. Colonel in our ranks. John Younger. He actually was one of the FAC trainees in our class at Hurlburt, and was on his way to Thailand as well. Colonel Younger took command (or what there was of command) of the group. He reiterated that we were U.S. POWs and should act as such. That meant not breaking under any interrogation and attempting to escape whenever we could. That actually was something the camp staff instructed us on in part of our early academics. We were even given hints as to what to look for in the way of weaknesses in any POW camp we might be unfortunate enough to inhabit. We all knew this was a training exercise, but a few of the guys (me included) had our doubts and we all played the roles expected of us, if for no other reason than to lighten the load of shit the guards dumped on us.

We were fed twice a day - rice and fish or rice and some nasty looking vegetables. But we ate it. We weren't supposed to be in there all that long, but we knew we had to keep our energy up. The rice was gooey and it's a good thing because we were given no utensils. The interesting thing was it didn't seem like the guards ate much better, although I think it was just for show. I marveled at how they could sit on their haunches and ball up a glom of rice and pop it in their mouths just like a native. I was impressed at how many "just like natives" there were on the Survival School staff.

Over the next two days, one by one we were bound up, hooded, and marched off to be interrogated by Major Whatshisname. They marched us into a room with a table and two chairs and a very harsh light pointed directly in the face of the "prisoner." We were hit with questions like "How many airplanes in your squadron? What kind of bombs does your airplane carry? What is the plan for America to save Cambodia?" Some questions we knew the answers to and some we didn't, but to all the answer was "name, rank, and serial number." Of course that just pissed off the major more and he would yell and threaten. Fortunately in this training scenario there was no physical abuse. But they had really done their homework and did a good job in the psyops part of things.

In my case he started asking questions about the girl I had almost married back before pilot training, my mother, and the fact she had cancer, even questions about my father that I couldn't talk about and I was surprised he knew anything about. My father worked for the government - that's all I ever told anyone. But the Major knew our family had a tour in Indonesia right after they kicked the Dutch out of their country. The U.S. interest at the time was to try and keep Indonesia from joining the communist camp, and my dad was an integral part of that. Suffice it to say I didn't answer any of those questions and the Major didn't pursue it. But it made me wonder - if I ever was shot down and interrogated in a real POW camp, what kind of questions would I get about my father's occupation.

The night of the fourth day in camp Pete and I and three other guys made a break for it. The camp was set up for it and they expected us to try. We figured out where there was a blind spot between the guard towers, and lo and behold, there was a break in the fence. All we had to do was get skinny and shinny under the concertina. Four of us got through just fine, but the fifth guy was a little "portly." He got his shirt caught on the barbed wire and was stuck. We went back to try to help him but it was a lost cause and he knew it. He wasn't going to squeeze under, so he voluntarily snuck back in and we took off. Turns out there were several more "escapes" over the next two nights so about half of us made a run for it one way or another. One guy actually crawled up in the back of a truck owned by one of the guards, and managed to squeeze into a large equipment box. He had emptied all of the equipment and hidden it and just sat there - fat, dumb, and happy until shift change. He made it all the way to downtown Spokane and was one of the very few completely successful escapees of Fairchild's POW camp. He voluntarily turned himself in the day of our "graduation," and was celebrated and graduated with us without having to go through the hell that the rest of us had.

Pete and I and our two partners ran like hell for the rest of the night, found a decent place to hide out during the next day, and lit out further east. We were hoping to make the Idaho state line. We knew there were a couple bars and even a strip joint there, although we doubted that they would take us in looking like we were - escaped prisoners. About sundown the next day we came upon a gas station out in the middle of the boonies. There were a couple homes around too, but we stayed away from them. We had a couple of bucks between the four of us so we drew straws and the short straw cleaned himself up a little, took the money, and went into the store to buy some food. We hadn't eaten in a couple days and that was just rice and fish. We were starving. All he could come up with was a couple Snickers bars, but they were like heaven to us, and we sat leaning up against a tree across from the gas station and enjoyed the moment.

A moment was all we got too, because pretty quick a military jeep with a big red star on it came screaming up and two guards got out and leveled their guns at us. We were caught. It seems the owner of the gas station has a deal with the folks at the base. For every survival school escapee he turns in he gets a half hour of use of the base firing range to practice his gunnery skills. Son of a bitch!

They stuffed all four of us in the back of their jeep, and when we came through the base gate they stopped and put the ever present hoods over our heads. We drove for a little more to what obviously was the POW camp. The music was blaring loud and clear. They stopped and pulled us all out of the jeep and put us one by one into what was the solitary confinement area. Those were the low, concrete structures we had seen before. After shoving me in, the guard took off my hood and slammed the door shut in my face. I was in a room that was about 3 feet by 5 feet and 6 feet high. Being 6'4" certainly didn't help me here. There were no windows. It was pitch dark in there. I did manage to spot what looked like a coffee can in one corner. That's what we were to use to relieve ourselves in. I found out at mealtime there was a sliding door type access in the bottom of the main door. They would raise it and slide our meal in to us. Meals now were about half the quantity as before. I guess they figured that because we couldn't move around and get any exercise, we wouldn't be very hungry. That Snickers bar didn't last very long with me.

We were in these cells for what seemed like an eternity. I guess it was only about 24 hours, but it sure seemed longer. I was able to determine there were others on both sides of me. The walls were fairly thin and we could actually whisper, as long as the guards didn't hear us. I determined that Colonel Younger was on one side of me. An airman I hadn't really met was on the other. I remember him telling us he was an Air Force PJ (para-rescue jumper) - a hero in my book. Anyway, we were able to communicate enough to find out that all but one escapee had been found and that those who hadn't tried to escape were still in the main barracks. I found out later that as a "reward" for not trying to escape they were put through physical hell - sit ups, push ups, burpees, distance runs, and no sleep. At least I could scrunch down in my little cell and catch some Zees. I suppose it was the camp's way of telling the prisoners who stayed home they should have tried to escape.

Twenty four hours later the gook-like Major came over the loud speaker and announced that the war was over and the Americans were coming to rescue us. I could hear cheering up and down the building, but the loudest came from me. Then the doors to our spaces were all sprung at once and there were three or four of the main school officers in U.S. uniforms there to welcome us. We were ushered back to our original barracks outside the POW camp, where we showered changed, and then enjoyed a magnificent steak dinner. We could even get wine. Survival training was over. At least that portion.

Pete and I and a few others of us going to the front, flew down to San Francisco where we had three days of R&R before hopping on a charter jet to the Philippines. We cruised Fisherman's Wharf and China Town, rode the trolley, and even took in an X-rated movie - "Deep Throat" with Linda Lovelace. Wow! That woman had talent!

Chapter Six

CLARK AIR BASE AND JUNGLE SCHOOL

The "Freedom Bird," as the contract carrier planes were often called, deposited us at Clark Air Base in the Philippines. There it picked up a couple hundred warriors whose tours in SEA were over and they were going home to "freedom." Clark was a large, sprawling base with a couple of long runways and plenty of aircraft parking space. There were no permanent forces stationed there, but B-52s often turned at Clark from one bombing sortie to the next, and it was a good stopping off place for attrition aircraft coming through from the States. Otherwise it was a good rest and relaxation (R&R) location for mid-tour time off.

Clark had a very nice golf course, a large Base Exchange (BX), and the typical "A Town" that most U.S. bases in the Pacific had. Clark's "A Town" was a complex of bars, restaurants, and whore houses just off base, well staffed by pretty Filipino girls and some shady characters looking to take advantage of the horny GIs and airmen. Beer was cheap, although not very good. The most popular (cheapest) brand was San Miguel, which in the Philippines was laced with formaldehyde. The Clark Officers

Club was a large facility that sported a Filipino Big Bands brass band, and the original Mongolian Barbecue set up.

Pete and I and a couple of our FAC mates had a week at Clark, with three days of it taken up by Jungle Survival School. The rest of the time we played golf, hung out at the O' Club, and tried out "A Town." We also took a day trip up to Baguio, in the mountains. Baguio was at 4000 feet elevation, so it wasn't as hot and humid as the rest of the country. It was the hangout of the Filipino President when he wasn't in residence in Manila, and it had a U.S. forces recreation center with the funkiest golf course I ever played.

The Baguio golf course was 18 holes with lots of terrain features in the mountains. One par three hole was about 300 yards long, but 200 yards of that was straight down. You stood on the tee box and looked over the edge to a small green way below you. Club selection was a trick. The strangest hole though was a 120 yard par 4. It was just the opposite. The green was way above and completely out of sight. The "fairway" between the tee box and green consisted of a mountain with several terraces on it, side to side. The idea was to take your loftiest club and hit it as hard as you could. It would plug into the side of the hill and fall down onto one of the terraces. Then you would grab on to a rope tow at the side of the fairway. It towed you up to where you were abeam of your ball on the terrace. You let go there, trudged out to your ball and hit it again, hoping to get over the top. Back to the rope tow to the top, and look for your ball somewhere around the green.

Thursday night was Mongolian Barbecue night at the Clark O'Club. This was the first time I had ever had Mongo BBQ, and the rumor was that it was actually started by the chef at the Clark club. They had several large round caldron-like grills - a solid iron sheet over a big tub where the chef for that grill kept a fire going to keep the grill sizzling hot. You selected your meat, added all the veggies you might want, loaded your bowl up with several different oils (some of which were real spicy), and gave it to the chef. While he's grilling it up you went and got a plate of rice. When your food was done, the chef would scoop it onto your plate and you were off to chow. Nowadays I know sometimes your food is weighed before it is cooked and you pay by the weight. At Clark in 1973, Mongo BBQ was $6.50 for all you could eat, plus whatever tip you added to the chef's coffers.

Jungle survival was sort of a boondoggle compared to our Basic Survival experience. We had one day of academics, rehearsing the use of all the equipment we had trained on twice already (Water and Basic Survival). The new take though was demonstration and practice of how to get out of a parachute that was hung up high in the jungle trees. Inevitably, if a pilot went down in the jungle, he most likely wouldn't make it to the ground. We hoped to make it though, and the position to assume when approaching the trees was to keep your feet and knees together and cross your arms in front of your head and face. You also had to release the life raft and survival kit that was dangling below you from some aircraft. The idea was to be as streamlined as possible while plunging through the foliage, and with the raft and kit attached, you could find yourself upside down with it caught higher in the trees. Assuming you didn't make it all the way through, now you had to get out of the harness and lower yourself to the ground. Some guys carried a length of rope in their pocket, but some of those trees are 100+ feet tall. That's a lot of rope. If you had time to pull in your survival kit and raft before you turned it loose, you could cut off that much rope. Otherwise the technique was to disconnect from one (of two) risers first, and hope to then swing over to grab the tree.

Worst case scenario, one simply disconnected from the risers and assumed the position again, slightly bent at the knees to be able to land and roll on contact with the ground.

The finishing exercise to the jungle school was another escape and evasion event. They took us out into the jungle and turned us loose to trek only about a mile to a pick up point in a clearing where a helicopter could land. The only problem was we were turned loose about 1700 hours and wouldn't be picked up until 0800 the next morning. There were Filipino Negritos (natives) in the jungle looking for us. Our job was to remain undetected. If we were discovered, we were to give the Negrito our chit and he turned it in for pay. Then we were to sit tight until daylight and make it to the pickup point.

I found a great hiding place - I thought. I climbed a huge banyan tree to about 50 feet off the ground and covered myself with big "elephant ear" leaves from the tree next door. I was completely covered and comfortable enough that I could lie back and sleep without fear of falling. I was there about 45 minutes when "tap tap." I jumped a foot in the air and looked around to see the face of a grinning Negrito who'd just tapped me on the shoulder. He only had about 6 teeth in his shit eating grin, and he had his hand out for my chit. Oh well. I stayed up there and got some good shuteye until about midnight when it started raining. It poured. Even with the jungle canopy over me, it didn't take long to get soaked through. The rest of the night was miserable, but at least after we were "rescued" and graduated from the school that morning, it was Thursday - Mongolian Barbecue night.

After our week of golfing, eating, drinking, and playing in the jungle, there were 5 of us who boarded a C-141 Starlifter cargo plane to Korat Royal Thai Air Force Base, a little north of Bangkok, Thailand. There we transferred to the "Klong," the C-130 that made the rounds of the different bases, and eventually dropped us off at NKP.

Chapter Seven

NEW NAIL FACS

We got three sorties at NKP to start off our tour. The first one was in the back seat with an instructor up front so he could show us the area. Then we had two with the IP in the back, confirming that we could demonstrate proficiency in flying and accomplishing all the other tasks involved with a FAC mission. The IP provided scenarios and simulated targets and we went through the motions. Then we were sent down to Ubon RTAFB to join the rest of the squadron. Ubon was closer to the Cambodian border, but even at that it often took an hour or so to fly down into the location where the war was going on. We met our squadron mates, were bedded down in barracks that were more like regular Air Force facilities - three floors of double and single rooms. The first night at the Ubon bar we were formally welcomed in with songs and hijinks that usually meant we bought the bar.

At that time there were five major bases in Thailand where the Air Force operated from. There was NKP that had very little activity directly in the war. The C-130s flew from there, but even the rescue helicopters forward deployed to Ubon. There was Udorn, more in the middle of Thailand with F-4s and the RF-4 (reconnaissance) squadron. Korat was closer to Bangkok, also operating F-4s, and Takhli was nearby with the F-111 bombers. Then there was Utapao down south in the long peninsula of

Thailand. B-52s flew from there and it was also an R&R stop, being next to Pattaya Beach, where the US had a good size recreation presence.

Ubon had the most action, being the closest to the fight. It also was the home of the Wolfpack, the 8th Tactical Fighter Wing, flying F-4s. The Wolfpack had previously been commanded for two years by one of the Air Forces famous Aces - Robin Olds. He was a "triple Ace," having shot down 17 enemy aircraft over three wars - WWII, Korea, and Vietnam. He shot down two Mig 17s and two Mig-21s in Nam, two of them on one mission. A colonel when he left the theater, he was as famous for his hard play as his hard work. He had left his command of the Wolfpack a couple years earlier, but the traditions he instilled in his fighter pilots were alive and well. They partied hard, singing filthy songs, saying "Ice" and throwing "Fuck."

Olds was a maverick to say the least, and because of that he was not endeared by his superiors. He had a big handlebar mustache when mustaches were barely legal, and if you had one, it was supposed to look like Hitler's - A little dinky strip of fuzz. Olds blew that off and tolerated his boys fudging the rules a bit as well. He was also a hard drinker - borderline alcoholic. When it was time for him to leave, the Air Force had little choice but to promote him to Brigadier General. He was too popular in the press. So before he retired, they pinned a star on him and sent him around the country on speaking tours - good PR.

I first met General Olds when I was an instructor pilot in Del Rio, Texas in 1972. He had come to Laughlin AFB to be the speaker at our wing Dining In. A Dining In is a formal affair, usually stag (or without wives and hubbies), where the attendees wore their formal Mess Dress uniform. There are many traditions involved, and one of the junior officers (Mr. Vice) usually honchos the tradition based hijinks, with the local Commander as the Mess President. On this occasion, Mr. Vice was our youngest lieutenant instructor. He had a small table out on the floor, equipped with the Grog Bowl. The grog was usually some vile alcoholic mixture that was the "refreshment" whomever Mr. Vice targeted for "heinous" breaches of tradition had to imbibe in. Well, Mr. Vice evidently was on some powerful cold medication and he had a lot to drink. Out of the blue he piped up with "General Olds, is that your stomach or has the Air Force stamped Good Year on your butt and sent you around the country?" General Olds had gained a few pounds lately.

There was a deadly silence in the crowd. Everyone looked at the head table. The Wing Commander, an ex-bomber pilot, had buried his head in his hands and was about to slide under the table. General Olds was pissed. He stood up, threw his napkin on the table and announced "I don't have to take this shit." and marched out of the room to the bar.

The first thing the Wing King did was have the Lieutenant arrested and confined to his quarters, then he spent about 15 minutes sending notes back to the bar asking Olds to return and accept our humblest apologies. But the weak dick didn't have the balls to go to the bar and talk with Olds face to face. After about 20 minutes, General Olds came up on the club PA system with "I'm not coming back to your damn Dining In, but if any of you ass holes in there aspire to be fighter pilots, come on back to the bar. Booze is on me." The room emptied in a heart beat and those of us who had always wanted to fly fighters, along with several who had done so already in previous tours, stood around at the bar listening to one of the country's top Aces tell war stories over rounds of whiskey and tequila. That night stuck with me forever.

Anyway, that was the atmosphere still permeating the Ubon Officers Club. It was open 24 hours a day to accommodate all the night fliers as well. It was not unusual to stumble in for breakfast at 0600 prior to our day missions and share a table with a bunch of guys downing beers after their recent night sorties.

Chapter Eight

CAMBODIA

Pete and I each got 6 or 7 combat sorties before August 15th. We started off in the back seat of an instructor's aircraft to basically learn the local area and the process. No amount of make believe training in north Florida can prepare you for the real thing. What got to me the most was the constant chatter on the five radios. That is one of the hardest things for a FAC - realizing which radio he wants to talk on and make the switch changes. My first ride was with one of the seasoned guys who was actually on his third tour. He had flown the O-1 and the 0-2 as a Covey and Nail FAC. Coveys were a different squadron that had been disbanded by the time we got there.

The next two missions were with the instructor in the back. One was basically a training mission with me making all the decisions and him critiquing me. The third mission was my actual combat check ride, after which I was cleared solo and a full up, combat ready FAC. That particular mission was probably the most exciting one of my half dozen combat sorties. We were tasked for river convoy support, providing cover and support for a convoy of barges making deliveries up the Mekong River to Phnom Penh. The Khmer Rouge were along the river bank lobbing mortar shells at the barges. My job was to talk with the Cambodia army guys that were along the river as well, trying to keep the convoy free of conflict. I controlled four flights of fighter bombers, three flights of Air Force F-4s and one flight of Navy A-7s. I couldn't really see any of the bad guys in the jungle. Every once in a while I spotted what I guess was a mortar muzzle flash, but I had to go by what the ground commander was telling me, lay down a smoke rocket, and then take his corrections from there.

The Navy won that particular mission. They got down low with their 500 pounders and strung them along the river bank. They must have hit some sort of weapons cache, because all of a sudden there was a "WHUMP!!" that I could even hear, and definitely feel up at about 8000 feet. A cloud of debris and dust and fire and gunpowder spiraled up out of the jungle almost as high as I was flying. The ground commander was ecstatic. "Oh my Nail. My Nail 32, velly good bomb. Choo got him. Choo got him good." He yelled over the radio. I passed on the good news to the A-7 boys in a BDA (Battle Damage Assessment) report that they could take back to debrief their intel folks.

The rest of my missions were not all that exciting combat wise, just blowing down a bunch of trees and probably killing a bunch of monkeys. Pete and I both though got a very important mission just before the end. Every day the squadron would send 3 or 4 FACs down to work their morning mission, then land, refuel, and rearm at Phnom Penh International Airport. That's a bit of a misnomer - the airport consisted of two runways with a lot of bombed buildings and one or two still standing. From those one or two the Cambodian Air Force flew their missions in T-28s and T-34s that the U.S. had provided them. But the key to this mission was we would land, eat lunch, and take off for another mission on the way back to Ubon. The important thing was the lunch. We had to eat what they gave us, witnessed by another FAC who was there, and then you could get the coveted "Phnom Penh for

Lunch Bunch" patch for your party suit. We all had party suits in Southeast Asia. Basically it was a coverall, or "flight suit" with lots of patches and pins. The Nail party suit was black and the PP for Lunch Patch was front and center over the left breast.

The "lunch" we were served was what they called barbecued chicken, a banana, a piece of French bread, and a Coke in a bottle. The Coke was good, the banana wasn't bad, and the French bread was ok once you removed any "movers" (little white wormy things) that might be in it. After all - Cambodia used to be a French territory - they should know how to bake bread. It was the chicken that was suspect. They were scrawny chickens - dubbed "yard birds." Not much meat on them and the sauce they had on them was pretty raunchy - also very spicy. I managed to eat mine, but regretted it a couple hours later.

I managed to get through my afternoon mission with no problems. Towards the end I handed off my coverage area to an AC-130 gunship that was to be out there most of the night, lighting up the sky with some awesome firepower. I was about half way home to Ubon when it hit me. I was in trouble. Now the OV-10 cockpit is fairly large, but we still had the control stick between our legs. Down there also was a relief tube that we could (and usually did) use to take a leak. The only thing to worry about there, assuming you were able to fish out your warrior from your flight suit and undies, was whether or not the wise ass crew chiefs might have stuck a wad of gum an inch or two down the tube.

The use of the relief tube wasn't my problem. I had to take a dump, and soon. The OV-10 does not have an auto pilot, so I trimmed it up for straight and level flight the best I could, and went through the contortions of getting out of my flight suit. First I had to take off my boots, then I got the suit off and folded it up on the side console. Then I pulled out one of the maps of the extreme northeast part of Cambodia where we never flew, spread it out under me and let 'er rip! Aaaah, that felt good! But stink? Whewee! I wadded the map up carefully so as not to spill any, and took about another twenty minutes to get re-dressed. Then I rearmed the ejection seat. Before doing all this I had disarmed it. I wanted to be sure I wasn't blown through the canopy in my all together, not attached to my parachute.

So now what? How was I going to get rid of my cargo without somebody knowing? It was dusk when I arrived back at Ubon and I requested a short field landing. The OV-10 is an excellent STOL (short takeoff and landing) aircraft and we practiced both quite often. I came down with a hard "plunk," rammed the engines into reverse and came down hard on the brakes. Soon as I came to a stop I opened the left canopy exit and tossed out my prized map full of lunch. Then I quietly snuck into parking and thought I was the cat's pajamas, and had gotten away with it. About that time an airfield operator in a "Follow Me" truck pulled up in front as I was de-planing, went around to the bed of his truck, and with two fingers, very daintily held up my wadded up map. "Captain, did you lose this?" He broadcast so the whole ramp could hear him. I was toast.

Neither Pete nor I got to fly on the last day of the war. All of the "old heads" got in on the fray that day and I understand between the Air Force and the Navy we dumped more bombs in six hours than we had for the whole two days prior. Lots of rotting bananas out there. Anyway, those of us that didn't fly welcomed the warriors home to a big party at the Ubon Officers Club. A lot of beer, whiskey, lies, and one or two war stories were put away that night. The brass gave us an extra day to sober up, dry out, and pack up, and we flew back to NKP to another big party the next day. The war was over! We thought.

Chapter Nine

THE WAR'S OVER.
NOW WHAT?

The first two or three weeks after we all got back to NKP were rather hectic. About a dozen of the pilots who had been around the longest were packing up to go back to the land of the big BX. That was one of the endearing labels we gave to the good old USA. They had all extended their tours so they could get in on the last couple months of the war, or because they hated the next assignments the personnel system had in store for them. So, every night there was a going away party for one or two of the old guys, or a welcome for the newbys. About the only flying we did was a checkout for new guys or a "fini-flight" for the "short" guys. "Short" being short-timer.

A fini-flight was his last sortie, in most cases not only the last one in theater, but the last one in the OV-10. It was usually a two ship formation flight and they would go out and harass the countryside for an hour or so, then come back and beat up the traffic pattern. The OV-10 had a smoke generator, much like that you see from the various aerobatic teams. The rationale for the FAC being able to stream smoke was to help the fighters he was controlling see him so they could keep from running him over.

Anyway, we made sure the smoke generators were fully and armed on fini flights. That way the departee could be sure and announce his presence in the traffic pattern and when pulling into parking.

The rest of the squadron would be there waiting when he shut down, ready to douse him with a firehose and pop a cork on a bottle of cheap champagne. Then we would parade him around the base in the back of our trusty golf cart, blowing horns and ringing bells - basically making complete ass holes of ourselves. Obviously the tour ended up at the Nail Hole for a good party. This went on for a couple weeks until the squadron was back to normal personnel strength, and settled down to training. We actually had been significantly overmanned for wartime operations. During the war we flew at least 30 sorties a day, seven days a week. We needed lots of pilots to do that. During peace time though, we only flew 18-20 sorties a day, five days a week. So the departure of the old heads was a relief for us new guys who wanted chance to fly.

We also had welcoming parties for all the new guys. Pete and I were still considered "new guys" because we hadn't been "Hammered" yet. Every Nail had to be "Hammered," and there weren't enough folks around when we first got to NKP. So when the squadron returned, we had "Hammering" parties about every night. The Nail was called up to the front of the bar by the boss and handed a huge mug of the vilest concoction I ever drank. Someone said it was grain alcohol and Creme d Menthe. I just know it was green and tasted awful. But, we had to drink it all in a chugalug with the whole squadron singing "Ya ziggy ziggy ziggy zumba zumba, ya ziggy ziggy ziggy zumba yay!" until either the grog was gone or the Nail puked. Having passed that test, the Nail was then rewarded with a big chrome coated nail of about 10 inches long. We cherished it forever.

Our lead party monger, was our combat leader - our squadron commander, Lt. Colonel Howard Parsons. He was a great guy and the type of leader we would follow anywhere. Sometimes that got all of us in trouble, especially when on the base struttin' our stuff. Howie Parsons was about 6'5" and probably weighed 250. He hadn't a hair on his head and some often called him Mr. Clean. I don't think he liked that name so much, so we didn't use it much. He loved to gamble and there was a dice game going almost every night in the Nail Hole with Howie at the helm. Not sure how much money he lost over his tour, but suffice it to say he was way behind. Part of that was because he imbibed heavily during the games, and later in the night he would often lead us on some wild and crazy tours of the base.

One of our late night escapades got Howie in trouble with the brass and all of us on the hot seat. There was an A1-E Skyraider aircraft on a pedestal on base. NKP was the home to the squadrons that flew that great aircraft during the war. It was a single engine turboprop that could carry a good load of bombs. The pilots flew it down in the weeds and did a lot of damage when they did. It was the plane that one of America's greatest Medal of Honor winners flew on one almost unbelievable day. Captain Bernie Fidler was flying on a mission in Vietnam when his wingman was hit and went down near a large clearing in the jungle. The Viet Cong had surrounded and were approaching the downed pilot fast and Fidler knew there was no time to wait for rescue choppers to come in to extract him. Bernie actually landed his A-1E in the field, dodging rocks and craters and taxied up beside his comrade. He popped open the canopy and the pilot dove into the cockpit in the space behind the seat. Bernie closed the canopy and managed to actually take off, taking round after round of ground fire, and brought his wingman home.

Anyway, Howie Parsons had allowed as how the A-1E on the pedestal was "mis-labeled," and maybe we should do something about it. It seems that our current wing commander had his name stenciled on the side of the cockpit as the pilot. He had never flown the airplane, and in fact was an airlift pilot by trade. So around 2 AM about 6-8 of us marched up to the static display aircraft with a can of paint and some duct tape. Wonderful stuff that duct tape. Anyway, we sprayed over the good Colonel's name and mounted 8 big banana trees that we cut down from a nice garden display nearby on the pylons under the wings of the plane, so it looked like it was on a banana tree delivery mission.

Well, it seems the wing king didn't like that too much and although there were no witnesses, he assumed correctly that the rowdy Nails had done the dirty deed. He had our fearless leader on his carpet in his dress blue uniform to get a dressing down, and as a result, those of us who had participated got to go and de-arm the A-1E, and paint over our black covering of the Colonel's name. At least he realized the significance of our displeasure and didn't require his name re-painted on. In fact, he got word of our real wishes and he had Bernie Fidler's name applied to the canopy.

Another exploit that got us in trouble sometimes was the "war" we used to have with the Jollies and their hooch across the street. The Jollies were the rescue helicopter squadron - great guys and often our heroes. But, because they were the only other real operators on the base, there was always some good competition between us. Their hooch was about 60 yards away from ours, so we devised a "cannon" by taping five regular coffee cans together, opening both ends to four of them, and punching a small hole in the bottom of the first one. Then we would "load" with a full roll of toilet paper, squirt a bunch of lighter fluid down the barrel onto the "load," and then hold a lighter to the hole in the end, with the "cannon" pointed at the Jollies hooch. Actually we had to use a lot of elevation calculations. The aerodynamics of a flaming roll of toilet paper were not published in our armament books, so it was a lot of trial and error. "Whump!" and a flaming roll of TP made the arcing flight to the Jollies' roof. Anyway, one night we had to call the fire department. We were too accurate with our shot and the hooch roof caught fire. Fortunately Howie Parsons had departed by then and the new commander had a rude welcome to his responsibilities.

Our most fun during our off time - which there seemed to be a lot of after the war - was carrier landings on the USS Nail FAC. The guys had built a platform about 25 feet long, by 5 feet wide and 18 inches off the ground. It was well anchored into the ground and at one end was a large pit about 10 feet long, five feet wide and 18" deep. The platform was topped in strong plywood and then covered with a canvas of some sort that got slippery when wet. This was the USS Nail FAC, an aircraft carrier, complete with a tail hook arrester when she was operational. The process was easy. Soak the deck down with a little water and a lot of beer, fill the pit with a lot of water and enough beer to build up a head, and then man the "hook arrester" with two flight commanders attached to a fire hose. There was also a landing control officer (LCO), usually a lieutenant armed with two ping pong paddles. Hopefully you're getting the idea by now. No? Well, OK!

The landing Nail on the USS Nail Fac was usually a few sheets to the wind, hopefully not too much though. He had to get a good running start and approach the carrier as fast as he could, flop down onto the deck on his belly, raise his legs up behind him, and hope that the LCO liked his approach and didn't "wave him off" with the paddles. If the LCO liked the approach, the signal would go to the barrier crews and the fire hose would slap down on the back of the legs enough to arrest the approach and keep the Nail from overshooting into the pit. HOWEVER, if the LCO didn't like the approach, or if the barrier crew were too slow, off the end the "aircraft" went into the slimy, muddy and raunchy pit. Good Fun! Pete and I got pretty good at carrier landings. We even made formation landings side by side, but we also got real muddy, wet, and smelled like Pabst Blue Ribbon. Unfortunately there were a few casualties during carrier landings. Every once in a while the approach was too low and the Nail would head first into the ship BELOW the deck. Other times there was not enough strength left in the nose gear of the approach and the chin would hit the deck hard. If the barrier crew was too zealous there could be some pretty good welts left on the pilots tail hook. But.... like I said - good fun!

Perhaps our greatest prank though was played on one of our own. Lt. Rowdy Harrington was one of the more senior guys in theater. He was slated to leave on a Saturday by way of Thai Airways to Bangkok where he was to get married to a beautiful Pan Am stewardess he had met on a few R&R trips. Then the two of them were headed home to the states via a honeymoon in Hawaii. We had the mandatory bachelor party for Rowdy Friday night in the Nail Hole. We made sure he got completely plastered, but he made us promise to get him to the plane out on time Saturday. Thai Airways ran a rinky dink operation from the various towns a couple times a week to Bangkok. They flew a small twin engine prop job that held about a dozen passengers and all kinds of cargo from suitcases to live chickens and pigs.

Anyway - we got Rowdy lathered up, figuratively with lots of booze and literally with soap and shaving cream. After he had passed out, a couple of the guys took him to his room, lathered him up, and then our flight surgeon (also three or four sheets to the wind) shaved him bald all over and put him into a full body cast. Then we let him sleep it off.

Rowdy woke up about 0630 for his 0800 flight and discovered his dilemma. He started screaming and using every raunchy word in the book. Not to fear though, at about 0740 the flight surgeon (and a couple guys to protect the flight surgeon from a pissed off lieutenant) came in, cut Rowdy out of the cast, and then helped him get dressed, and delivered him to the plane right on time. Rowdy was livid. He was really pissed about losing all the hair around his manhood, but he didn't know the full extent of it until that night in Bangkok after the wedding, and when he and his young bride were in the Chao Piya Hotel. His new wife started laughing her ass off when she saw his ass. Unbeknownst to Rowdy, the guys had used indelible magic marker-like implements and wrote "I LOVE MARY" across his buns. The trouble was, Rowdy's new wife's name was Jennifer.

We actually did do a little work during those first couple months after the war ended, although it was arguably very little. The bottom line was the Air Force didn't know for a while what they wanted to do with the OV-10. Some were recently stationed in Germany where their use would be a complete joke and disaster. The threat that the Soviet bloc countries held over NATO countries would completely annihilate a slow moving, low altitude aircraft like the OV-10 in a close air support role in the East Germany/Czech environment.

The fighting force in Thailand had been thinned down quite a bit. B-52s were pulled out of Utapao right away. The F-111s from

Takhli were brought home, along with the F-4s from Korat. There were still F-4s at Udorn and about half the 8th TFW was still at Ubon. All were slated to leave soon though. They all had places to go. Stateside units had been badly depleted of flyable jets during the war, so that those units in theater could field a formidable force. Now the returning jets could fill out the squadrons at home, in Europe, and in Korea. So, we pretty much had Thailand to ourselves, but without a mission.

Chapter Ten

CHANDY RANGE

We did have a gunnery range we could use in the middle of Thailand. It was Chandy (pronounced "Shandy") Range. Unfortunately it was too far from NKP for us to get much use. That actually became fortunate, because it meant we went TDY (Temporary Duty) to Korat or Tahkli to fly from there on the range. I say "fortunate" because Korat and Tahkli were much nicer bases with a lot of amenities. The Korat Officers Club had a great swimming pool with a roving daiquiri man. He was a Thai bartender who pushed a good size cart armed with two blenders (and a generator), all kinds of fresh fruit, some frozen fruit like blueberries, lots of rum, and ice. He'd come by while we were working on our he-man tans and make us a great frozen daiquiri. My favorite was a mango/banana daiquiri. Hmmm, Hmmm! The Korat club had also been a pretty good fighter bar, so there were a few left over bar flies we had our choices of.

Tahkli was a different story. Being an FB-111 base it wasn't as "fighterish," and the club was very quiet. But it was also the closest base to Bangkok, so we could get some good in-country R&R with a couple days of leave. Tahkli had one claim to fame though that was not so much fun. It was called the "Cobra Capitol of the World." No shit - there were cobras all over the place. Our crew chiefs would have to approach the aircraft very carefully each morning because the snakes liked to spend the night up in the wheel wells. One of our squadron mates had a helluva experience one morning. He was sleeping in the bottom bunk of his two-man room with one of the more experienced guys up top. The Thais decided to run a practice anti-aircraft drill at 6 AM that morning. The Whump! Whump! Bam! Bam! of the guns going off woke everyone up. The "old head" in the top bunk who had been through "Incoming!" drills for real in a previous tour in Vietnam, came flying off the bunk and slid underneath the bottom bunk thinking it was a real attack, yelling "Incoming!" About two seconds later he came sliding and screaming out on the floor yelling "SNAKE!" Soon after him a cobra slithered out with its unmistakable cloak in full display. Holy shit! Both guys got the day off.

Bangkok was, and probably still is, the oriental "sin city." The Thais got real smart in the latter years of the Southeast Asia war and realized that they had the nearby and lucrative R&R center of the region and could make a lot of money off the American GIs on leave. There were huge, beautiful, classy hotels. The kind where you can sneak off with one of their bathrobes, and get chocolates on your pillow at night. There were very good restaurants. The best Kobe steak I ever had was at a restaurant called Nick's #1. It was great. I liked it a lot better before someone told me it was not really steak as we know it, but water buffalo. It tasted great anyway. Bangkok also had every decadent and deviant establishment you could think of to get your sex urge satisfied. There were whorehouses that basically were large establishments with a lot of small rooms upstairs and with what we called a "fish bowl" downstairs. You walked in, paid your cover charge and then got to chose your "fish" who was sitting on a tiered set of stands behind a glass partition with all her friends in the complete all together. Each one had a number around her neck. You told the "maitre d" what number you wanted, he gave you a room number, you went up to that room, and lo and behold, in walked your fish.

There was one place in Bangkok called Caesars Palace. Not exactly like the one we knew about in Vegas, at least I don't think so. This one had seven floors. Each floor for a different fantasy or fetish. If you like little boys, there was a floor for that. If you like big boys, there was a floor for that. if you just wanted to watch, there was a floor for that. No thanks! I stayed away from that place. I can't imagine it's still there.

Utapao was the other R&R base in Thailand. It sits down on the long skinny peninsula next to Pattaya Beach, one of the nicest beach areas in the world. Since we had B-52s there through the war, it had a lot of the necessities for the GIs - rooms, food, etc. This was Pattaya before it got as big as it did later as a huge tourist attraction. So it really was a rest and relaxation location. There were a couple hotels of decent size and a few good restaurants, but mostly it was just a place to go and unwind with a few froo-froo drinks - you know, the kind that come with little umbrellas and a slice of pineapple - and catch a few rays. I had actually been to Pattaya for a few weeks back in the summer of '65. My father worked for our government and the family was posted to Bangkok for a couple years back then. I went over to visit them between my freshman and sophomore years at the Virginia Military Institute. Dad pulled some strings and got me a job as a life guard at the budding U.S. recreation center at Pattaya Beach. It had your basic diner type snack bar for hotdogs and burgers that had a small room in the back. That was my room - complete with a cot, a toilet, a sink, and a chair. I used the public showers that all the bathers used to wash the salt off their sun burned bodies. My real tough job was to rake the beach each morning to clean up trash and seaweed, and then to sit on a lifeguard chair admiring the bikinis all day. The water was very shallow for almost 500 yards out to an outer reef. It was pretty hard for anyone to drown. I remember I had one "interesting" save one day when a drunk GI fell face first into the water about 18" deep. I saw him fall and then waited a bit for him to get up. He was slow in trying and kept stumbling back in. I finally went out and escorted him in to his buddies.

Our flights on Chandy Range were a good use of flight time. It was a well equipped range with plenty of targets to shoot our white phosphorous rockets at, so we all got pretty good at hitting our targets from deliveries of anything from 30 to 90 degrees of dive. We really didn't have a mission to train for, but we had a good time doing it. We were probably better at actually hitting our target than the guys who had to do it for real just a couple months before. Otherwise our training flights from NKP consisted of two ship formations, picking out simulated targets, and practicing controlling the fighters who were represented by our own wingman. We had one big rocky area not too far from base that we got permission from the Thai government to live fire our Willie Petes on. We had to make a couple low passes first each time to be sure there wasn't some wayward Thai wandering around down there looking for his flock of sheep, or pigs, or water buffalo. On those missions we invariably saved one rocket for when we returned to the NKP traffic pattern. We would approach the turn onto "initial," the first leg of an overhead visual landing pattern that flew on runway heading, and because the NKP runway was situated parallel the river and border with Laos, and because it was only about a mile west of the border, just before we made our turn, we'd launch our last Willie Pete off into Laos. I guess we were hoping to scare up some action or something. It wasn't a real smart move, but there's nothing worse for a fighter pilot than peacetime, and "smart moves" seemed few and far between.

By a month after the war ended we were back to normal manning, we had a new squadron commander, and Pete and I were considered the "old heads" - experienced combat veterans. Just about everyone else was new - lots of lieutenants and young captains. Because of our seniority, we were each made flight commanders, responsible for 6-8 pilots and one or two weapons systems officers (WSOs). The rather boring flying and the always exciting partying went on for what was to be months - we thought.

Chapter Eleven

MEANWHILE, BACK AT THE RANCH

Phnom Penh was under siege. It had been for most of the war, but with the American help and a concerted effort by the Cambodian government forces, the Khmer Rouge had been held out of the city for the most part. However, within a matter of days after the August 15th termination of U.S. participation, the KR moved in and took over the Phnom Penh International Airport. The Cambodian Air Force that was operating there was able to evacuate about half of their aircraft to other bases. The other half was secured by the KR and intelligence suggested they were working on some sort of training to learn to fly. The North Vietnamese were rumored to have sent a few pilots into Phnom Penh to instruct the KR wannabe pilots. This could be a death blow to the Cambodian's defense of their country. Already the presence of a few North Vietnam MIGs in the area was aiding the KR in getting a strong hold on many areas of the country. However, at least for the immediate future, the army still had control of their anti-aircraft artillery around the city, so any attacks by the aging T-28s and T-34s flown by novice KR pilots would be facing significant defenses of the city. The question was how long could this last? With the airport in enemy hands the people of Phnom Penh were all but cut off from the rest of the world and deliveries of food and aid. The only real solution they had were the regular river convoys bringing food and supplies up the Mekong River.

The convoys came under fire from shore batteries of mortars almost continuously. Fortunately though, the Mekong is almost a mile wide in most places and mortars didn't have the range to do much damage. There were a few choke points where the river narrows, but the army had beefed up its presence in those areas. Again the intelligence and rumor mill activity indicated that North Vietnam was going to supply gunboats to the KR. River convoys were about to become sitting ducks.

On September 18th, 1973 all hell broke loose. There was a large infusion of KR troops around the city of Phnom Penh. They had brought mortars into the airport and had completely taken it over. They were indiscriminately shelling the surrounding neighborhoods. The American Embassy was inside the range of the mortars, and several direct hits were pounding the compound. There were about 40 personnel in the Embassy, protected by a dozen Marine guards. All of the dependents were long gone. Phnom Penh had been decried a war zone and the few personnel that were there were staying on the embassy grounds, and were well armed. Their duties were to coordinate with the Cambodian government, but when the U.S. pulled out on August 15, communications were short and not so sweet with the local government. The Ambassador spent his time apologizing for deserting the Cambodians. We did maintain an intelligence presence and shared what we could with the army to help them survive.

The largest convoy of relief packages, including some arms and ammo was about 15 miles downriver when it was attacked by mortars and gunboats. The tugs were either destroyed and sunk or raided and commandeered by KR "sailors." They steered the barges to the shore and proceeded to torch everything that was of no value to them. Obviously food and military gear were valuable assets to have. This was the largest convoy to sail up the river in a month, and its loss was a devastating blow to the inhabitants of Phnom Penh. Their food supply had dwindled down to where there was rationing throughout the city. With the siege from the surrounding countryside, no deliveries from local farmers made it through. In short, the people of Phnom Penh - close to 500,000 - were starving, and the government was teetering on falling. Martial law had already been declared weeks earlier and there was a surging threat from communist sympathizers to take over the government. The Americans and other foreigners in the city were in jeopardy. The American Ambassador had put out an SOS to his bosses in the State Department and the CIA.

All this was basically happening in a vacuum to us at NKP. We got some news through the Armed Forces radio network, and certainly the intel folks on base that worked with JUSMAG (Joint U.S. Military Assistance Group) were up to speed on what was going on, but those matters hadn't filtered down to the basic operators. At least not yet. As far as we knew, what was happening in Cambodia was going to stay in Cambodia, and logically our people will be pulled out when necessary. We didn't expect any of it would involve us.

The first we heard of any activity on the part of the U.S. came when two squadrons of F-4s that were set to deploy out to the States were put on hold. At the same time, the Jollies held off on their schedule to send out 4 of their choppers. Two had already been packaged and wrapped up and were sitting on the ramp, awaiting a big C-5 to come in and airlift them out. The next and biggest indication to us that something was up was when Lt. Colonel Howie Parsons stepped off the Klong, unannounced. Needless to say we were glad to see him back, but also very curious.

Parsons moved into one of the VIP hooches, so he didn't uproot our current squadron commander who had replaced him. Lt. Colonel Louis Bastione had come to us from the JUSMAG staff and had just completed his basic upgrade rides in the OV-10. Parsons called us all together for a briefing the next day.

"Sit down guys" Parsons decried when he came into the room of about 50 pilots, WSOs, and others attached to the squadron, all standing at attention. "Let me say first that I'm glad to be back. I really didn't make it too far. I was still in Hawaii, enjoying the beach, the babes, and the big city. As you know, I wasn't real thrilled about going to a staff job in the Pentagon anyway, so when my boss came a knockin', I raised my hand immediately.

"I really can't tell you much. I really don't KNOW that much. Things are heating up down in Phnom Penh. The city is under siege, the people are starving and the Khmer Rouge have taken over the airport. They also stopped and commandeered a large convoy on the Mekong and have it completely under their control - or else they've sunk it by now.

"My task, as far as I know it, is to command a large rescue package to potentially rescue the Cambodians and our embassy personnel." Parsons went on. "For now all we can do is get ready. Lou, I want you to deploy 6-8 Broncos to Korat and maintain a rotating schedule to get every pilot enough sorties to be highly proficient in rocketry." He addressed our Squadron Commander. "Other than that I'd say we need some intense target area study along the Mekong and around the outskirts of Phnom Penh. More to come when I know it. Dismissed!" Parsons left and we all stood around scratching our heads. Pete Trask and I, being the "old heads" and flight commanders, took over the task of organizing groups to split up the target areas for study, and we worked with the schedulers for the deployment list for Korat. I took the first group down and Pete would relieve me in a week. The squadron supervisors - Commander, Operations Officer, Assistant OPs, were split up for adult supervision. We were all eager to do something worthwhile for a change.

Chapter Twelve

WASHINGTON - WHITE HOUSE SITUATION ROOM

"Be seated" President Richard Gatewater said as he walked into the room, followed closely by his White House Chief of Staff, Gary Larson. His National Security team had been called together for an emergency meeting. The only one absent was the Vice President, Spiro Agnost. He was on a goodwill tour of South America. The team consisted of Henry Crittendon, who was both the Secretary of State and the National Security Advisor; Harold Schlesser, the Secretary of Defense; Charles Butler, Director of the CIA; and Admiral John McLean, the Chairman of the Joint Chiefs. The different Chiefs themselves were held out of this meeting.

The President sat in his customary seat at the head of a large table. "All right Henry, what is so pressing that we need this meeting?" He addressed Secretary Crittendon.

"Mr. President, as you know, things have gotten worse in Cambodia." Crittendon responded in his guttural German accent. "I was able to get through to our Ambassador Robert Mondavi this morning for a little while, and then our connection was lost. I have not been able to reach him since."

"I also have not been able to reach our Chief of Station" Charles Butler of the CIA added.

"The Khmer Rouge have taken over the airport. The only flying in or out has been the military aircraft the Cambodian Air Force left behind." Crittendon continued, not real happy the CIA Director had butted in. "We have significant intelligence that indicates those aircraft were being flown by North Vietnamese instructors and Khmer Rouge trainees."

"That doesn't sound good." The President remarked. "What happened to our agreement with the Vietnamese that they would stay out of Cambodia?"

"Apparently they have overlooked that issue sir, and I need not tell you that even though their aircraft are old and slow, they could do major damage and the only opposition would be the CAF in the same type aircraft." Crittendon responded.

"In fact sir, if the KR doesn't change the paint scheme on these aircraft, the CAF wouldn't know who's the enemy and who's their wingmen." Admiral McLean spoke up.

"The other major issue is the fate of the river convoys that have been bringing much needed supplies - food, medical supplies, and arms to the city." Crittendon went on. "The latest convoy was hijacked yesterday about 15 miles down river on the Mekong. Several barges were destroyed and the rest were beached here on the north shore of the river" He went to the large map display on a screen in front of the room and pointed out the resting place of the convoy. "The Khmer Rouge obviously got a large cache of food, supplies and ammunition. Suffice it to say they are well equipped for a long haul."

"So what do we do about this?" the President threw it out to the group. "What CAN we do about this with all the agreements we have in place and our own stated resolve to disengage from Southeast Asia?"

It was the Chairman of the Joint Chiefs who spoke up first. "Mr. President about our only recourse would be to mount a large scale airborne invasion to retake the Phnom Penh airport and bring in food by airlift, while at the same time pulling our embassy personnel out. As long as the Vietnamese stay out of it, we should be able to pull it off without too much resistance."

"Mr. President, I would strongly advise against such an attack." Crittendon responded. "We made it very clear when we stopped hostilities in August that we would not be back with a physical force. I believe anything we do militarily will stir up the hornets' nest of the North Vietnamese, the Viet Cong, and the Khmer Rouge. Right now it seems that the North has all its eggs in the basket of South Vietnam. We don't want them to take Cambodia as well and pose a direct threat to Thailand." He pointed to the western border of Cambodia which is a shared border with Thailand. "I think any military action will start something I don't think we want to finish."

"Sir, with all due respect to the Secretary," McLean reacted, "We can't just let those people at our embassy be taken. These are 52 American souls, not to mention the hundreds of thousands of starving Cambodians."

"Mr. President, I think I have to agree with Secretary Crittendon on this one, and you know I am known as a relative "hawk" on issues like this." It was CIA Director Butler. "Our intelligence contacts in the area confirm that though the North Vietnamese are only lending their support, and evidently their instructor pilots, to the Khmer cause, we don't think it would take much to escalate into a full blown invasion of Cambodia from the north."

"Gentlemen, we seem to be between a rock and a hard place here." The President said after pondering the issue for a while. "I agree with the Secretary that we cannot start another extension of the war down there. Our people are already demonstrating and near rioting about our involvement in Vietnam. I don't want to give them more cause to riot, and I definitely don't want to give my opponents more ammunition to use in our upcoming election. Having said that though, I agree with the Chairman - we cannot leave American sheep to be slaughtered by Khmer Rouge wolves. We need to come up with a smaller scale excursion to get our folks out, and hopefully help the Republic stay in power. Have we heard anything from them - the Cambodian government?" He looked again at Secretary Crittendon.

"No sir. Ever since they threw Prince Sihanouk overboard, there hasn't been any one spokesman for the Khmer Republic." The Secretary responded. "It seems to be a different general in charge every week. Before I lost contact with Ambassador Mondavi, he was constantly complaining about the lack of communication, much less cooperation with the ruling junta."

"That's probably my fault for appointing a wine maker to an ambassadorial position." The President said mostly in jest. "But he donated a lot of money to our cause, and back then things were going along relatively smoothly in Phnom Penh. I thought it a relatively harmless post.

"Ok - let's come up with a plan gentlemen. Admiral, since this will be mostly a military operation, you take the lead. However, run your plan through your cohorts here. Time is of the essence. Do we even have an estimate on how long the city, and especially our embassy, can hold out?" The President aimed his first directive at the Chairman, but looked at everyone for input to his question."

"Mr. President, we talked bout this." Secretary Crittendon answered. "The embassy and its staff can probably last a month or so as long as the shelling and the overall situation doesn't get worse. However, the people in the city are already starving, and with apparently no adult leadership there's no telling how long before they try to take over the government."

"I think a coup is probably only a remote possibility sir" Director Butler chimed in. "Our experience in Phnom Penh, and the whole country for that matter, is that there is no structure - no organization that could rise up in a coordinated insurrection. What is probably more likely is that one by one, or neighborhood by neighborhood, the inhabitants of Phnom Penh will capitulate with the Khmer Rouge who occupy the airport. Basically, as long as the KR has food and offers it to the neighbors, their dominated area around the airport will simply grow. The embassy is only a mile or so from the airport. It could be crawling with rebels in a matter of days."

"That's a sobering thought Charles, but I see your point. Starvation is a potent weapon. All right gentlemen, get back to me with a plan. Let's get back together here in 24 hours. Until then, no one outside of this room is to be read in on any potential action we might take. I don't want to read about this in the Post." The President rose to leave the room. Everyone else stood as well.

"Mr. President, I'll need to at least read in the service chiefs of any forces we might use." Admiral McLean stated.

"I understand. Just keep this subject to those with a need to know. Goodnight."

Chapter Thirteen

THAILAND - BRING IT ON!

I took six Broncos and 12 pilots to Korat and set up the first contingent of training. We got 6 hours of range time on Chandy Range every day, and we made the best of it. We loaded up with two rocket pods per aircraft, made sure the smoke generators were always armed, and did a lot of coordinating with the various fighter squadrons around.

A typical mission would be about 2 - 3 hours long with two ship formation flights and both seats filled in each aircraft. We would get to the range and split up, flying a large circle around the range at about 6000 feet. The second aircraft would usually fly on the opposite side of the circle and maintain altitude deconfliction in case we lost sight of each other. That was pretty regular, because once the fighters showed up, there was no need for the FAC to normally worry about a second FAC in the fight. Our combat mission was always "alone and unafraid." But during this training scenario the second FAC would play the role of the ground commander, or river boat captain. He would come up with a scenario and pass it to the FAC in charge, who would in turn pass it to the fighters that were in orbits nearby.

The back seater in the lead FAC's plane would play the roll of the Airborne Command and Controller (usually a C-130) typically far from the action, and centered so he had contact with all players from when they took off until they returned to their base. This guy's job in our training scenario was just to keep the radio chatter constant to present a bigger challenge for the FAC. The fighters were F-4s from either Ubon or Udorn RTAFBs in Thailand, or A-7s and A-4s off the carrier Enterprise that was in the South China Sea just south of Thailand. The FAC would stack his fighters in orbits with de-conflicting altitudes to keep them from running into each other, and peel them off from the bottom of the stack to use against his target.

There were a few tactical targets on the range - tanks, jeeps, a couple well bombed out buildings, and of course, the conventional target, which was a well destroyed tank in the middle of an array of concentric circles of plowed ground and whitewashed rocks. We had created a ground and river scenario that had the make believe river flowing through the range with a few of the targets simulating mortar sites or gunboats. We had passed the simulated scenario to both the Ubon and Udorn wings and the Navy, so they had a general idea of what we meant when we said "see that barge down there?"

Chandy Range was not a live fire range, except for our Willie Pete rockets. The fighters carried BDU-33s, 25 pound iron "bombs," shaped like bombs and with close to the aerodynamic characteristics of a 500 pound Mark 82 bomb. The BDUs had a smoke charge that indicates where they hit. The fighters also had their "hot" guns, albeit with training/tracer rounds. We tried to get the brass to re-install our 7.62 mm guns as well in our OV-10s, but no such luck. After all - we were not fighter pilots. We were lowly FACs and we were to leave the real fighting to the real men! Excuse me a minute while I puke.

A typical mission would go something like this. On the way to the range the lead back seater would simulate a call to the FAC, passing him the situation and coordinates of a river convoy in distress along the Mekong. The FAC would get on target, set up an orbit and call the ground commander on the shore, looking for Khmer Rouge mortar teams, or the river boat captain who was taking incoming mortar rounds. Those roles were played by the other FAC. The fighters would check in either as two or four ship flights and brief the FAC on their simulated ordinance and how much "play time" they had (based on their fuel state). The FAC would roll in and mark a target or two with his rockets and the ground commander would give him corrections. The FAC would pass that to the fighters and then clear them in to drop their bombs. Each of us would control one or two flights of fighters and then we would switch roles. It all took a lot of imagination, but the bottom line was that both the FACs and the fighter jocks were getting a lot of target practice with constant chatter going off in their ears. That night we'd party down at the Korat Club or do a few rounds of frozen daiquiris at the pool.

At the end of that first week, each of the line pilots had at least 6 missions as the primary FAC. The wing staff and squadron supervisors would get two or three sorties. Pete came down with 6 new Broncos and 12 new pilots and replaced us for a week of the same. Back in NKP we took care of a lot of housekeeping. Check rides, check outs for new guys, target study, and intel briefings. I put together a new roster of guys for the third week. It included anyone who hadn't been to Korat yet this time around and those from the first week who I thought could use some more practice.

We launched off from NKP on a Sunday, a month after the airport in Phnom Penh fell.

Half way to Korat I got a call through the HF radio that I authenticated and acknowledged. We were diverted to Ubon, the closest base to Cambodia and the base we had operated from during the war. Pete's contingent came in a couple hours later, and 6 more Broncos were flown down from NKP with whomever had been left up there in the squadron. A special C-130 was diverted into NKP to pick up all our maintenance guys and all the personal gear we thought we might need for a month or two. The maintenance folks from our detachment at Korat came in the next day, and we had a full up, ready to fight squadron. Now we waited.

The rest of the U.S. forces in Thailand ramped up their readiness as well. It was deemed by the higher ups that no units or aircraft that had rotated back to the states, or at least out of country, would return. I guess that would be an indicator that something was up. Of course, anyone curious only had to listen to the news to know that things were going to Hell in a hand basket in Cambodia. The F-4 units at Ubon and Udorn went into the full combat mode. Leaves and rotations back to the states were cancelled, and personal and next of kin information was updated. So we had two full squadrons of F-4s at Ubon, and one at Udorn. There was also a small detachment of 6 RF-4 reconnaissance birds at Udorn. They hadn't left town early enough on their squadron deployment to Korea. There were a few extra C-130s brought into NKP and Utapao to keep a constant airborne supply chain going, and a total of 5 AC-130 gunships came in to reside at Ubon. The Jollies from NKP also came down to Ubon to be closer to the action.

And we waited.

Chapter Fourteen

WASHINGTON

It was the next day in D.C. The Joint Chiefs and CIA Director of Southeast Asia operations had been meeting in the Pentagon for about 14 hours. They had brought several more "players" into the fold. CIA Chief of Southeast Asian Operations David Wong had been present for the duration. Commander in Chief of Pacific Forces (CINCPAC) Admiral Mike McMaster, Commander in Chief of Pacific Air Forces (CINCPACAF) General Curtis LeCroix, Commander of the Navy's Seventh Fleet, Admiral Steve "Rock" Ages, and Commander of the Joint United States Military Assistance Group (JUSMAG), General Timothy O'Reilly were all in on the planning by phone, mainly for their local expertise. The main planning was headed up by Navy CNO, Admiral Albert Zumer and General Bob Black, AF Chief of Staff. Those that were in D.C. were in the Situation Room. The others were linked in by phone. The President arrived and he was informed of who the new players were and why their expertise was needed.

"Ok. Fine gentlemen, but let me be clear. None of this planning or the operation itself is to be broadcast around. I do not want to hear from the New York Times or the Washington Post." The President said, then "Sit, and let's hear it"

Chairman McLean went to the podium and a large map of Cambodia was displayed on the screen. There were smaller inset maps strategically placed where needed. "Mr. President, before we get started and in keeping with your guidance, I believe we need to clear the room of anyone without the need to know." McLean looked at Gary Larson, the White House Chief of Staff.

"I agree." The President said as he looked around. "Who's here that doesn't need to be?"

"Since he's eye-balling me, I assume the Admiral is wanting to boot me off the posse." Larson said. "I highly disagree gentlemen. Whatever the President knows and the information he gets always comes through me. I have all the appropriate clearances, and Mr. President, I think I need to be here to watch your back."

"Sir, obviously it is your decision. I just feel that this is a military operation, not a political one, and…" McLean started.

"So if this is all about the military, what is the Secretary of State and the CIA doing here?" Larson butted in.

"I'll speak to that if I may sir." Secretary Crittendon spoke up. The President nodded and SECSTATE went on. "Our input is paramount because we are talking about an operation where State Department and CIA personnel are Involved. As the Admiral said, this is not a political show, and…"

"All right gentlemen, I get it." The President said. "Gary why don't you sit this one out? I think I can hold my own hand here." He nodded for Larson to leave the room.

"Sir, I must disagree. Whatever you decide here could bring dire consequences down the road with Congress and the American people." Larson complained.

"I get it Gary, and I got it from here. You've surely got enough on your plate to keep you busy." The President said firmly. Larson got up and left, not saying a word, but if looks could kill, Admiral McLean was toast.

"So - let's hear it gentlemen." President Gatewater said.

"Sir, we believe we can rescue the Americans at the embassy and provide significant relief to the people of Phnom Penh using one of the regularly scheduled river convoys. Although as you know, the last convoy was halted and hijacked, we believe we have a plan for that as well. First, a quick geography lesson." The admiral took a pointer and approached the map.

"There are four rivers which are spawned by the Mekong as it winds down the peninsula. Shortly after the Mekong flows into South Vietnam the Son Wau river branches off near the town of Cho Vam. Then, farther downstream and closer to the delta two other rivers, the Co Chiel and the Ham Luong branch off and form their own deltas. The Mekong itself flows on and its delta is situated the farthest north and close to Saigon. All of these rivers are navigable, and in fact for the last couple of years, the river convoys that have been plying up the Mekong to Phnom Penh actually originate at the Co Chiel port of Cau Ngong." The Admiral pointed out all of the rivers and towns as he went along. "The reason for that is that Can Ngong is still in the hands of the South Vietnamese and the aid has been introduced under the radar."

"Sir, I must interject here." Secretary Crittendon came in. "We have no doubt that the North Vietnamese and the Viet Cong know all about the convoys, but they have maintained a low profile up until now, mainly because Cambodia has not been of primary interest as they have been fighting for control of South Vietnam. We also have no doubt that stance will change if they hear about our operation, and in fact, very likely is changing as we speak - witness the hijacking of the last convoy."

"So the North Vietnamese have been letting Cambodia survive out of the goodness of their hearts?" The President said with a chuckle. "Ok. Go on."

"The Son Wan river here is the key to our success." The Chairman went on. "It joins the Mekong here at Cho Vam, but there is another branch of the Son Wan that comes down through Chau Doc, a fairly large town just south of the Cambodian border. Mr. Wong, the CIA Chief of the Southeast Asian branch, has made contact with an agent of South Vietnamese intelligence who currently stationed in Chau Doc. He believes he can get us a barge and a tug that we can load up and join the convoy when it passes through Cho Vam. Historically these convoys start off in South Vietnam early in the mornings, so that by the time they pass into Cambodia it is night time the next day and dark, providing a degree of safety from the Khmer Rouge mortars. If we have a barge and tug here where the river branches off to join the Mekong, we hope to be able to join the parade in the dark."

"Ok. So what are you proposing to put on the barge, monkeys and bananas? You're a hundred miles inland from the Cambodian coast in Apache territory." The President noted.

"That's where it gets sticky sir." the Chairman went on. There is a road that parallels the Cambodian/Vietnam border all along this stretch." He pointed to the border from the coast inland to Chau Doc. The Secretary has been vehement that we cannot encroach on Vietnam territory to bring our equipment on board."

Crittendon barged in. "Mr. President, I'm sure you understand that with the tenuous agreements we have with the Vietnamese, and our need to disengage from the area, we cannot be driving on Vietnamese roads a convoy of trucks full of equipment to be used to fight against their allies, the Khmer Rouge."

"I absolutely agree. No action that could be seen as hostile when all we want to do is cease all hostilities. I assume you have a work around Admiral?" The President confirmed his SECSTATE's position.

"Yes sir, we do. First of all, we propose to low level extract four large Army M-819 trucks from two C-141s in the middle of the night next Monday night. The extraction is a new method the Air Force has developed whereby the C-141 comes in low and slow over the beach here north of Ha Tien. A parachute is deployed out the open bay doors of the plane and it pulls the truck out on a pallet where a larger chute is deployed and the truck gets one swing under canopy and makes a hard landing on the beach. Tests show that the pallets are built to absorb the shock and actually have shock absorbers in them. We have successfully delivered even Abrams tanks this way. Anyway, the C-141s will each make one pass and deliver their cargo of four trucks. Just prior to that a SEAL team and some army truck drivers will be delivered by the submarine Virginia to the waters just off the coast. They will have two Zodiac fast boats and all their gear, and will have landed on shore ahead of the trucks.

"These trucks will be loaded with food, medical supplies, arms, ammunition. There will be enough to sustain our embassy personnel and these troops for a month if necessary. The convoy itself will be loaded with almost all food and supplies for the people of Phnom Penh. Our mission is to join that convoy and make sure it makes it to its destination.

"Since we cannot use the road near the border in Vietnamese territory we propose to use the rough access road that parallels the fence for maintenance of the fence purposes. It is a rough dirt and rocky road. In many places that you can see here and here (He pointed to areas along the border fence), the terrain is rough and steep. These trucks are sturdy and their big diesel engines should be able to hang in there to get to just across the border here from Chau Doc. We should be in place there by about 0200 hours Wednesday morning. Mr. Wong's contact on the ground promises to meet us there. We are still working out the details on how to make a border crossing there and travel the five miles to where we hope to have a barge waiting. This is where we will have to break the rule about use of Vietnamese territory. There simply is no other way short of parachuting down on Chau Doc, and Secretary Crittendon assures us that would never be an option.

"The plan from there will be to drive the trucks onto the barge, cover them, and shove off back down the Son Wau River, and over to Cho Vam to meet the convoy coming north. We'll merge in with the convoy or tag along behind. The SEALs will set up shop on the barge with their own mortars and light artillery to blast the shore as needed. They will also re-launch two of their Zodiac boats and act as escorts to protect the convoy from gunboats.

"During all of this we will have Forward Air Controllers airborne with fighter/bomber support for convoy cover. There will also be a few F-4s designated for air escort to maintain air superiority against any threat the Khmer Rouge or the Vietnamese might launch. Forces currently stationed in Thailand and on the carrier Enterprise will be available for these missions. We will have C-130 Command and Control aircraft up, as well as AC-130 gunships at night."

"Well, that's certainly a complex plan." The President said. "What kind of chance for success do you predict Admiral? And what happens when the convoy arrives in Phnom Penh?"

"Sir, to be honest with you I think we probably have overall success odds of about 75%." The Chairman replied. "The short pole in the tent is landing those trucks and moving them up and through Chau Doc to the barge undetected by the Khmer Rouge or the Vietnamese. Once we get on board the barge I think we will have a good chance of making it to Phnom Penh with the whole convoy. Of course that depends on the air support from the FACs and the fighters. And as soon as the first bomb is dropped it will be obvious to the world that we are back in the skies over Cambodia. I know that is something you want to avoid, but it is our opinion that without air support this convoy will meet the same fate as the last one, and at that point we will even have more Americans in enemy hands."

"Ok. Supposing I'm supportive of that premise, what happens when you land at the port in Phnom Penh?" The President repeated.

"Sir, I'll talk to that." SECSTATE Crittendon jumped in. "Assuming I can get in contact with Ambassador Mondavi, he will have an escort of marine guards meet the SEALs and trucks when they are off loaded. They will make their way to the embassy and get ready for the next phase of operation. We'll leave the off loading of food and supplies for the city to the Cambodian government."

"And if you can't reach Mondavi?" The President played devil's advocate.

"The the SEALS and truck drivers will simply barge through to the embassy themselves." The Chairman said. "The area of the city between the port and the embassy is not currently under KR control."

"Ok. Now what? What is your next phase of operation?" The President asked.

"Sir, assuming all goes well, we plan to have all forces in the embassy and ready to go out on Saturday night. The plan is to use the SEALs and marines to fight our way into the airport and take it over, setting up a perimeter of about a mile out and controlling all flights. Again we will have air support by way of forward air controllers and F-4 and A-7 close air support. Once we have established a cordon around the airport, 24 hour air support will be maintained. On Sunday morning we will bring in two C-130s escorted by F-4s to land at the airport and upload the entire embassy staff, SEALs, truck drivers, and any other American in the city who needs a ride out. They will be evacuated out to Utapao here in Thailand." The Chairman again referred to the map.

"Well gentlemen," The President observed, "you certainly have put in a lot of work in on this, but I'm not sure I like it. Henry, this seems like an awful lot of incursions into places we said we were not going to go again." He looked at the SECSTATE.

"Ye sir, it is." Crittendon responded. "And I don't like it much either, but short of an all out invasion of Phnom Penh, the Chairman and his Joint Chiefs assure me there is really no other way without putting many more Americans at risk."

"Mr. President, I too understand your concern, but Henry is correct. Removing 52 people from deep within hostile territory is no easy task." The Chairman defended his plan. "We will be doing this only with forces that are already there in Thailand or on the Enterprise. Certainly the SEALs and army truck drivers are an addition, and their mission could easily expose our plan, but I think we have to take that risk. One more very important point sir. We have to maintain complete secrecy about this. If the word gets out in the press or otherwise to the Vietnamese, or even the Cambodian government, our cover would likely be blown and our forces put in jeopardy."

"I agree with that. I will not inform Congress or anyone else about this, and I urge you all ..... strike that. I demand that you all keep a lid on this until it's over, and even then, because of the sensitivity of what we are about to do, I want to be informed of any need to release any information." The President looked hard at everyone in the room.

"Now Admiral, I know you all are fond of naming your little exercises and operations. What do you plan on calling this one."

Admiral McLean smiled and nodded. "Yes sir, we've decided on the name.....

DRAGON SAVIOR

Chapter Fifteen

UBON RTAFB - TUESDAY

We were at breakfast at the Ubon Officers Club when Lt. Colonel Bastione, our squadron commander, came in and joined us. He announced that there would be a meeting in the 497th Tactical Fighter Squadron building of key players of a coming operation at 1300 hours. He designated Pete and I and the other flight commanders, as well as our Operations Officer, as "key personnel." He didn't know what it was all about, but he'd gotten the word from Lt. Col. Parsons. We were to contact the rest of the squadron mates to standby in quarters or at our operations building. We would probably have a squadron meeting later in the day.

At 1300 hours we were all seated or standing in the 497th main briefing room. There were representatives there from each of the squadrons on base, the squadrons in Udorn, the C-130 and AC-130 folks, the Jollies, and even the Air Boss from the Enterprise had flown in. There was a lot of speculation, but more shoulder shrugging than anything else. We had no clue why we were there. At five after the hour the doors swung open and someone yelled "Room, TenHut." In walked the PACAF Commander in Chief General Curtis LeCroix, 7th Fleet Commander Admiral "Rock" Ages, JUSMAG Commander General Tim O'Reilly, and 7th Air Force Commander Lt. General Larry Tobin, followed by the 8th

TFW commander and a slew of horse holders (general's aides). They marched up to the front of the room and General LeCroix took to the podium. He was a gruff old guy. Not so old I guess, but he looked much older than other generals I had seen. He wasn't a big guy, but built like fireplug. He always had a half chewed up cigar in his mouth. I'm told he actually lit it once in a while.

"Be seated." the General ordered in a deep gruff voice. "Ladies and gentlemen let me first say it's good to be here. As you can imagine, being cooped up on the Hawaiian Islands like I am is no fun." He paused while we all laughed at that one. "Well, ok maybe it is more fun than here at Ubon, but at least you all have a mission to accomplish."

Someone in the back of the room had the balls to say a little too loud, "Yeah, the mission of sitting on our asses." That brought a few chuckles, but mostly concern as to what the general's reaction might be.

Fortunately he laughed and said "Ok. I get it. Sitting around here with no war to fight and wondering when you're going home to whatever is next is no fun. But we're here to bring you something to do. You all have been preparing in some way to be able to react to what's going on in Cambodia, specifically Phnom Penh. That preparation is about to be put to the test." Lots of mumbles and a few "All Rights!"

"Now before I go any further I need you to cull the herd. This will be a very sensitive mission and we cannot afford any leaks. So, look around you. If there is someone in here who will not be specifically involved in flying or preparing their pilots to fly, I need them to clear the room. That includes you lady and gentlemen." He looked directly at his own aide de camp as well as the other straphangers who had come in with him and the other generals. One was a drop dead gorgeous female first lieutenant who was General O'Reilly's aid. They all reluctantly, but obediently got up and left the room.

"Now let's get down to it. Lt. Colonel Parsons - front and center." LeCroix ordered and Howie Parsons stepped up to the podium. "Because all of what you are about to embark on involves close air support, the FACs will be center stage, and I have selected Colonel Parsons as the operational commander of operation Dragon Savior. Howie, the podium is yours."

"Thank you General," Parsons responded and then he looked out over the room. "It will be an honor to work with all of you and as you shall soon see, cooperation and communication will be paramount. To that end, do we have Master Chief Johnson on the horn?" He looked towards a speaker on the wall.

"Yes sir and greetings from the USS Virginia and the South China Sea." a voice said from the loudspeaker.

"Good to hear from you Master Chief," Parsons said, "and for the rest of you, Master Chief Johnson is the leader of SEAL Team Five and a few army special ops guys who will be our truck drivers. They will be the players on the ground during this operation."

Parsons proceeded to brief us on Operation Dragon Savior and how we will all be impacted. We all took copious notes and a few had questions, but most of the details had been worked out. "The first on station will be the gunships at 0200 tonight." Parsons said. "I want you in an orbit near the coast near Ha Tien for when the C-141s come in to deliver the trucks on the beach. In addition, I want a flight of four F-4s configured for support and air to air for the SEAL landing, and around the clock for the next five days. You'll be augmented by others as the mission progresses, but I want primarily two flights of two, mainly for air to air support, constantly airborne. Udorn, you let me know if you need more than just your units to man the caps (combat air patrols). We'll task the Wolfpack units if necessary."

"I think we can handle it in house sir." The Udorn wing commander responded.

"Good! Now then Spectres, you will continue to monitor the trucks as they make it along the border until daylight when replaced by the first FAC in an OV-10." Parsons directed to the AC-130 representative. "Any issues there?"

"No sir. We can do that with two aircraft operating out of Utapao." The gunshipper responded.

"Ok, and then I need you airborne all night, every night until Sunday morning when hopefully we have taken the airport and the airlift is underway." Parsons added.

"Can do sir."

"All right, Nail FACs." Parsons looked directly at Trask and me. "We'll need you on station continuously starting tomorrow morning an hour before sunrise and everyday until you hand the action off to the Spectres, and through Sunday when the C-130s have departed with their precious cargo. Keep in contact with Master Chief Johnson and his folks. Chief you still with us?" He hailed the loudspeaker. "Aye sir, reading you loud and clear." the SEAL responded. "Ok FACs, 'men on the scene.' Any problems there?" We waited for our squadron commander to speak up, but when he didn't, our Ops Officer responded "We got it sir."

"We will put out a FRAG order each evening starting this evening for fighter bomber close air support." FRAG is the acronym given to an attack operation in detail. It includes what units, which aircraft, what bomb load, time on target, everything needed to fly the mission. It is basically the order to kill someone, which is the true definition of 'FRAG.' "We'll start off in the morning with just Wolfpack F-4s until the Enterprise can get in a little closer." Parsons went on. "CAG can you pick it up in the afternoon with at least two fourships of A-7s a day?" He asked the Navy's Commander of the Air Group of the Enterprise.

"Aye Colonel. We can easily do twice that if you wish. We're pushing into the Gulf of Thailand now from the South China Sea, and we should be within 100 miles of the Cambodian coast by tonight." The Navy Captain replied.

"Ok, I'll plan on that and it will free up more of Ubon's F-4s to help out with the escort and air superiority role. The plan for you bombers is for a mix of 500 pounders and CBU (Cluster Bomb Units), if anything, heavier on the CBU. If we spread those little critters all up and down the river banks, the mortar gunners should have to keep their heads down." Cluster bomb units are just like they sound - canisters full of dozens of small bomblets, each about the size of a baseball, filled with ball bearings and nails that open above the surface and spread death and destruction along a wide swath. They are deadly on troops and small vehicles, and would probably do a number on a gunboat as well.

"Once the convoy docks in Phnom Penh, Nails keep in contact with the SEALs and hopefully the marines from the embassy and provide air support for the trucks until they get inside the embassy. Then help them out when they attack the airport with perimeter defense and close air support.

"I have set up a command center here at the Ubon Command Post" Parsons went on. "I need as many of your intel folks and targeteers as you can spare from your fighter squadrons. Have them report directly to me. I guess that's all I have for now sir." Parsons gave up the podium to General LeCroix.

"All right Howie, sounds like a good plan." LeCroix said as he walked to the front of the room. "There's only one more thing left to do. General Tobin?" General LeCroix motioned for the 7th Air Force commander to join him at the podium.

"Don't go anywhere Colonel Parsons. The rest of you, on your feet." LeCroix commanded. We all stood at attention. Lt. General Tobin read from a certificate.

"By order of the President of the United States, Lieutenant Colonel Howard S. Parsons is hereby promoted to the rank of full colonel, effective this date, October 16th, 1973." At that he handed one of the shiny silver eagles to General LeCroix and they both pinned an eagle on a very surprised Howie Parsons' shoulders. The Nails in the room all yelled and whooped and hollered, and everyone else applauded.

"This is what's called a spot promotion, or a field promotion," General LeCroix announced. "It's not used much anymore, but in this case, considering the fantastic combat background Colonel Parsons has, and the position he is about to assume, it is a well deserved honor. Congratulations Howie." The General and the new Colonel exchanged salutes and LeCroix commanded. "Take your seats." and he went back to the podium.

"Men, I need not tell you how important this mission is. There are 52 American men and women stuck in the embassy in Phnom Penh. They are in the middle of a powder keg that is due to explode any day now. Our mission is to rescue them and to do so as quietly as possible, that is to say without blabbing it all over the press and even your friends and neighbors. If the mission is compromised, Master Chief Johnson and his team will be in real harm's way and chances are the embassy would be besieged in a heart beat.

"By God I wish I was going with you. We haven't had a mission worth a damn in this part of the world in years. Yes, it will be a complicated mission with many opportunities to fail, but I have faith in you and your leaders. So go out there and kick some Khmer Rouge butt. As you were." With that the generals, Admiral, and Colonel Parsons departed.

Lt. Colonel Bastione looked like he was a fish out of water, so I piped up with some suggestions. "We need to get the squadron together and get the first couple of flights into crew rest sir. They're going to have to take off by 0330 in the morning to be on scene before sunrise tomorrow. Then we need to get everyone on the same page and doing some target study. We probably need to come up with a schedule that covers the whole period of time so we know who's on deck and who needs to prepare for what part of the route." I said. Pete and the other flight commanders nodded and LTC Majors, our Ops Officer agreed. Bastione simply backed off, knowing this was all out of his league as a new guy to the mission, the job, and the OV-10. "Mike, you got the squadron stick on this." he said to Colonel Majors. "I'll ride top cover for you if you need any help with the brass, but you and these guys run the show." He indicated to us. "Let's call for a squadron meeting in 30 minutes."

Pete and I hit the road running.

Chapter Sixteen

23RD TASS DEPLOYED OPERATIONS BUILDING

Pete immediately selected one of his flight guys as a spare for tomorrow morning and they went to quarters to get close to 12 hours of crew rest before showing up the next morning at 0230 hours. He was to take off at 0330 to be on station over Chau Doc at 0500. He would take over the mission from the Spectre AC-130 on station and stay until 0700. I was to be there to relieve him by 0645, taking off from Ubon at 0515 to make that.

We set up a schedule so that an OV-10 departed Ubon every hour and 45 minutes for the hour and a half flight to the target area, two hours on station, and an hour and a half return. We would hand off the duty back to the Spectres around 1915 hours. We could actually make the schedule by turning a few of the Broncos that had landed early, but our maintenance chief wanted to at least try to do it with 16 different planes. We made it harder on him though by requiring one spare aircraft cocked and ready for each takeoff should something go wrong at start up. As long as that spare wasn't used, it could be ready to go for the next flight or two as well.

Each of our four flight commanders, the Squadron Operations Officer, and the Assistant Ops Officer flew six of the daily missions. We rotated the other two amongst the most senior and most experienced guys in the squadron. Our plan was to keep that rotation going each of the four days the operation was supposed to last. That meant that about half the pilots got at least one mission. We also worked two of our Pave Nail aircraft into the schedule in the middle of the day missions with our Pave Spot qualified WSOs (Weapons Systems Officers) in the rear cockpit. We coordinated with Colonel Parsons and his mission planners at the Command Center on that, in case they wanted to task some of the fighters at those times with "smart" bombs.

The pilots not on the schedule for each day were to do all the mission planning and map preparation for the missions. They were also used to preflight all the aircraft and "hot cock" the spares - basically allowing a pilot to jump out of his lame aircraft in the chocks and start up and go with the spare in minimum time. For every take off we had a running spare of a well qualified FAC who could take off ASAP if one of us had a maintenance problem early in the mission. We actually had to use that spare twice during the four day ordeal.

We briefed the squadron on the mission at 1530 Tuesday afternoon. Everyone was there except Pete and his spare and me and my guy. I was to take the second

flight in the morning and had to be in crew rest as well. Since Pete and I had been in on the earlier briefing by Colonel Parsons, we figured we wouldn't miss much, and in fact LTC Majors came over to our hooch later on and briefed us in on the latest poop.

Our maintenance folks were scrambling. We had 18 Broncos on the deck at Ubon. Sixteen of them were mission ready. One of the others needed an engine change and the last one had a hydraulic problem. They were working hard to get that one up and ready in time so that they could fill every mission with a new aircraft and have plenty to spare. The engine change would have to wait until we could get a spare engine delivered from NKP. Each plane had two full rocket pods of 12 each and full smoke generators. The Pave Spot pods were hung on four aircraft and checked to see if they worked.

The complete schedule for the four days was up on the scheduling board at the Ops desk. Pete and I had the first two launches of each day. We had picked the best and most experienced for the rest of the missions. The Nails were ready for war again.

Chapter Seventeen

WASHINGTON D.C.

Gary Larson, the White House Chief of Staff was having a hissy fit. The Chairman of the Joint Chiefs had been in to see the President twice since the meeting he was kicked out of, and he was summarily dismissed again. He didn't like it. He wanted to have his finger on the pulse of everything that goes on in "HIS" White House. He had asked the President about it, but was told it was no big thing and it all would come out shortly. While cleaning up the President's desk one evening after the boss had retired to his quarters, Larson came across the name "Dragon Savior" written on a note pad. He assumed it had something to do with an operation around Cambodia. He had been in on the briefings enough to know that was the center of whatever operation was being cooked up.

On a hunch, Larson put in a call to CINCPAC, Admiral McMaster. The Admiral's aide de camp answered the phone. Larson identified himself as the President's Chief of Staff and said that the President wanted an update on the preparations for Dragon Savior. The young Navy Lieutenant on the other end of the phone was in a fluster. He didn't know anything himself, because he too had been shooed from the room anytime the mission was discussed. The trouble was though that the Admiral was not available. He was at the hospital visiting his wife who was dying of cancer.

"It's a real tenuous situation right now sir, but do you want me to interrupt the Admiral for the President?" The aide said.

"No, no. Just tell me what you know and I'll brief the President." Larson responded. "If he wants any more information, we'll call back."

"Well, I don't know much myself." The Lieutenant said. "The aides were dismissed from the room when we were in Ubon for the mission briefing. There were lots of folks there - even a Captain from the USS Enterprise, and I know they talked to a Navy SEAL who's on the submarine Virginia. I don't know any specifics of the upcoming operation, but I do know a Colonel Howard Parsons was given a field promotion and named the commander of the operation. That's about all I know sir, but I'll tell Admiral McMaster you called."

"No. No. Don't do that. The Admiral has plenty on his plate right now. Just give him the President's best wishes and we'll be praying for Mrs. McMaster." Larson back pedaled. "Tell me this though Lieutenant. Do we know when this is all going to happen?"

"I don't know for sure the timing sir, but I know it will be soon - in the next few days."

With that Larson ended the call, finished cleaning up, and left the White House for his favorite watering hole - the bar at the Mayflower Hotel.

Larson was sitting at the bar nursing his second double Black Jack when Washington Post reported Bob Woodall came in. The

Mayflower was a favorite haunt of Woodall's. He knew that a lot of the Washington political establishment frequented the bar and it was always a source for a juicy story. He spotted Larson and saddled up beside him at the bar.

"Hey Gary. How ya doing?" Woodall sprang. "You look like you've lost your best friend. Are the underlings in the White House not paying enough attention to their real leader?" Larson had a reputation for eating White House staffers for lunch. Most of them avoided him whenever they could.

"Oh. Hi Bob. No, it's just that we've got a lot going on right now and I'm fighting a communications gap that's hard to breach." Larson responded.

"It wouldn't have anything to do with Cambodia, would it?" Woodall asked and Larson about choked on his drink.

"Where'd you hear anything about that Bob?" Larson reacted. "That's not for public dissemination."

"Oh. I don't know anything. There was just a Reuters report that came across the wire earlier about a river convoy that was hijacked and destroyed on its way up the Mekong to Phnom Penh." Woodall explained. "They say that the city is under siege and the people are starving. Don't we have some Americans there at the embassy? Is the U.S. going to ride to the rescue of another Southeast Asian country?"

"I can guarantee you we are not going back in there to fight their war for them again, but I can tell you we won't abandon American citizens either." Larson said, then realized he probably said too much. "I can't tell you any specifics Bob, and I'd appreciate it if you'd let it ride until we come out with an official statement."

"Sure Gary. Sure. I don't have much to go on anyway. But how about an exclusive when you can? The President needs some friends at the Post." Woodall said and got up to leave.

"Yeah, I understand. I'll keep it in mind and if or when we plan anything, I'll let you know. Good night." Larson finished his third double and signaled the bar tender for his bill.

"No tab Mr.Larson. Mr. Woodall picked it up." The bartender said.

Damn! Larson thought to himself. I hate owing that guy something.

Chapter Eighteen

WHITE HOUSE - WEDNESDAY MORNING

Larson came in to the White House with a bit of a hangover, but nothing he hadn't experienced before. He got his first cup of coffee and then sat down to scan the eight newspapers he edited for the President every morning. The Washington Post, New York Times, Wall Street Journal, Chicago Tribune, Los Angeles Times, Denver Post, Miami Herald, and the London Times were all lined up for him. He would highlight any story he thought the President needed to see and hand them over to the staff to cut and paste for the President's perusal. The first front page he saw hit him like a ton of bricks.

The headline on the Washington Post read "U.S. Launching Rescue Mission for Phnom Penh Embassy." It was Bob Woodall's byline and his story basically said the Air Force and Navy were putting together a plan to invade Phnom Penh and rescue all Americans at the embassy. He went on the describe the convoy that was originally hijacked and destroyed, and listed all the Air Force and Navy units nearby. He even quoted a Chinese source that said they witnessed the USS Enterprise and her armada enter the Gulf of Thailand from the South China Sea. The story didn't release anything that was classified, other than the location of the Enterprise, and that obviously was not classified enough to keep Chineses eyes off her. But the story alluded to a pending operation, and the President was not going to be happy. Fortunately Woodall did not cite any specific source.

Larson couldn't keep the story from the President. He was going to hear about it anyway, but he had the staffers put that story last in the coverage. Maybe the President would get tired of the news by then and skip it. No such luck!

The first one to react was Admiral McLean and he was on the phone about the time Larson put down the Post article. "What in God's name is this all about Larson?" McLean yelled. Larson could tell he was really pissed because he used Gary's last name instead of Mr. Larson - Chief of Staff. Gary sincerely believed that his status in the administration was above the Joint Chiefs - he didn't care if they wore four stars or not. They were his subordinates.

"I assume you are talking about the Post article this morning Admiral?" Larson reacted. "I assure you, I know nothing about it because I have not been privy to any of your planning or conversations. Perhaps if I had been, I could have headed off any blunder like this."

"Be that as it may Gary, suffice it to say we have a leak, and it's a very dangerous one with many American lives at stake. Find out what you can on your end. If you find anything, let me know. We'll be doing the same from the Pentagon and SECSTATE houses. Let the President know we are looking for our leaker." The Chairman hung up.

"Yes sir. I'll put a man right on it." "You fucking ASS HOLE!" Larson yelled into the muted phone. Who the fuck does he think he's dealing with?

Predictably the President was livid. Gary assured him he knew nothing about the issue and that he is questioning his staff to ascertain if anyone in the White House is culpable. He also told the President about the Chairman's call.

"Ok. Get the Chairman, Crittendon, Schlesser, and Director Butler in here as soon as possible and clear my calendar for whenever you set it up." The President ordered. "God DAMNIT!"

SECSTATE, SECDEF, CIA, and the Chairman all arrived a little before 8 AM. They also brought with them FBI Director Andy Anderson. Larson escorted them into the Oval Office, and then before leaving he quietly left a pocket recorder in the "record" position in a plant on a side table. Larson left them alone.

"So how much damage have we got here?" The President asked. "And do we have a clue where this story came from?"

"Sir, first things first." The Chairman started. "It's just about too late to derail the train now. The SEAL:s will be put ashore off Ha Tien at midnight tonight. The convoy has already left its port on the Co Chien River, and our contact has obtained a barge for our use at Chau Doc. We could call everything off, but we would not get another chance like this for a couple weeks with the next convoy."

"I had a discussion with Ambassador Mondavi this morning sir. He is losing it. The man is cowering in his office." SECSTATE Crittendon said. Charles is trying to get in touch with his Station

Chief to see if she can run a "coup" and get the embassy staff under control." He nodded toward CIA Director Butler.

"Yes sir." Butler added. "My station Chief has indicated in the past her lack of faith in the Ambassador, and evidently the entire staff is of the same persuasion. If I can get through to her, I'll tell her to take over."

"Right. Tell her to lock that God damn wino in a closet and to not let him out until it's time to evacuate. In fact I have half a mind to leave him there." The President said. "Ok. let's press on. Tell me again the timetable."

The Chairman outlined the schedule of the SEAL landing, the truck delivery by the C-141s, the gunship and FAC on-station schedule, the convoy forecast, and the plans to take the airport.

"Ok. Let's keep going." President Gatewater decried. "Now, Andy - what do you have for us?" He looked at the FBI Director.

"Sir, as soon as I saw the Post story this morning I did some digging. Since I wasn't privy to the planning, I wasn't sure what was going on, but I was certain whatever Woodall was putting out there was damaging." Director Anderson replied. "As you know, at your direction, we have had a tail on Bob Woodall and Larry Berngarten for some time now. Last night we followed Woodall into the bar at the Mayflower Hotel. He sat at the bar and had a long conversation with your Chief of Staff, Mr. Larson. We don't know what was said, but Woodall left an hour or so later and went straight to the Post's office. He stayed there a while and then went home. Is it possible that Mr. Larson is our leak?"

"Christ! I don't know. I suppose it's possible, but Gary has not been in on any of our meetings about Dragon Savior. I don't know how much he really knows." The President responded. "You have my permission to ask him about it though. We can't afford for any more specifics to get out about this. There are lives at stake."

The meeting adjourned. Director Anderson stopped by Larson's office and made an appointment to see him at 11 O'Clock.

Larson entered the Oval Office and brought the President the brief on his next meeting, a state visit with the Prime Minister of Australia.

"Thanks Gary. Say, you have any luck tracking down who may have leaked the story to Woodall at the Post?"

"No sir. I've asked just about everyone who might remotely have any business in or around the situation room and our comm people. No luck with anyone." Larson said as he went about cleaning up coffee cups and dishes from the earlier meeting. He retrieved his tape recorder from the plant when the President wasn't looking.

"All right. But keep looking." The President said. "This could be a potential disaster."

Chapter Nineteen

PHNOM PENH - AMERICAN EMBASSY

CIA Station Chief Liz Montgomery was in her office at the Phnom Penh embassy when she was delivered an encrypted message from CIA Headquarters. She broke open her "cookie" - daily code breaker - and read the message twice. Then she went to her safe, pulled out her sidearm, and went to collect a couple of her agents. They then went down to the Marine Guard station and enlisted two Marines to accompany them to the Ambassador's office.

Ambassador Robert Mondavi was in his office busily writing in a diary. He was recording everything that had happened in the last few days, trying to make sure his 6 o'clock was covered. He was bound and determined that whatever went down would not be on him. He was also scared shitless. Mortar strikes had come close to nailing him once already and he had several wounded staffers on his hands. Secretary Crittendon had tried to brief him on a pending rescue, but Mondavi thought it all too risky. He wanted to turn the embassy over to the rebels and appeal to their honor and mercy to let the staff leave the country.

"Mr. Ambassador, Ms. Montgomery is here to see you." His secretary announced through his intercom.

"Tell her I'm busy right now. I'll call her when I can talk." The Ambassador responded. As soon as he released the intercom button, his office door was busted open. Two huge Marines came in first, followed by Liz Montgomery and two of her agents.

"Mr. Ambassador, we're here to put you into safe custody. The Secretary of State is worried about your safety and ordered me to keep you in a safe place. Please come with us." Liz said.

"Oh thank God." The Ambassador whined. "Thank you Liz. I'll be in your debt. Marsha, will you cancel all my appointments and close up the office?" He directed his secretary.

The Ambassador was taken to his quarters and although the door was not locked, the Marines were directed not to let him out. Liz Montgomery went back to the Ambassador's office, and with Marsha's help, set up house. She was now the acting U.S. Ambassador to Cambodia. Her first action was to put in a call to Director Butler and SECSTATE Crittendon. She was briefed in on Operation Dragon Savior and directed to form an escort team to meet the trucks off the convoy and to prepare the staff for evacuation Sunday morning.

Chapter Twenty

WASHINGTON D.C.

Gary Larson locked himself in his office and listened to the tape. He was amazed at what his boss and the military were about to do. He had always thought the U.S. should have just gone into Cambodia with carpet bombs and napalm and turned the whole country into a parking lot. This political posturing and pandering to the North Vietnamese over the last few months was disgusting. He knew it was all about politics and the President's need to appease the masses by withdrawing from Southeast Asia, but it basically meant the country is turning tail and running. This operation though at least had some balls to it. He wondered what Bob Woodall would be willing to pay for this tape. He put it in a drawer and locked it.

At 11 AM sharp FBI Director Anderson and one of his special agents appeared at Larson's door. Gary invited them in, wondering though who the special agent was and why he was here.

"Mr. Larson, this is Special Agent Mike Malloy. He has been on special assignment for the past several weeks, keeping tabs on a few of the Washington Post reporters who we believe do not have the best interest of the country in mind when they write the stories they do. Specifically, Mike has been tailing Bob Woodall.

Are you acquainted with him?" Anderson asked as they sat down in the Chief of Staff's office.

"I know who he is." Larson said, "But I don't think I've ever met him." Shit! Larson thought. What are they getting at?

"Hmm. That's interesting sir," Malloy spoke up. "Since you had a couple drinks with him at the bar at the Mayflower Hotel last night."

"Was that Woodall?" Larson backpedaled. "He didn't introduce himself. We just struck up a conversation over a couple of drinks. Seems the gentleman went to the same high school I did back in Pittsburgh. There wasn't much to it."

"You are aware of course that he took care of your bar tab." Anderson said. "You need to be careful with that Gary. You could get into an ethics issue by letting outsiders pay for your expenses."

"Yes, of course I'm aware of that." Larson spoke the truth at least. "The guy left before I did and I didn't know he had paid until I asked for my tab."

"So you didn't discuss anything about a pending operation we are embarking on in Cambodia?" Anderson asked, "Nothing that would give him information for his article in the Post this morning?"

"No. Of course not." Larson replied. "In the first place, I'm not privy to anything we might be planning. I have not been included in the meetings where Dragon Savior has been discussed. And even if I was, I certainly wouldn't give it to some reporter."

Anderson's raised his eye brows when Larson mentioned "Dragon Savior." "Mr. Larson, how do you know anything about Dragon Savior? That term has not been out for public knowledge."

Larson was taken aback. He knew he was on thin ice. "Er, I don't know. The President must have mentioned it in passing sometime during the day. We have a lot of discussions about every topic imaginable."

"Ok Gary, thanks." Anderson said as he and Malloy got up to leave. "I'll make my report to the President. Be careful though about who you associate with and who you let buy your drinks."

"Sure. Thanks." Larson got up to see them to the door.

"God Damnit! Larson thought. That son a bitch is going to get me in real hot water. I've got to do something to salvage my job.

Later in the day a courier arrived at the Washington Post with a package for Bob Woodall. In it was a tape recording and a note. "Bob, you might be interested in this. If you use it though, I need you to do me a favor. Come up with someone else as your source. Maybe someone in the Pentagon. I'm already it hot water about this morning's story. Did you know the FBI has you under surveillance?" It was signed "Larson."

Chapter Twenty One

OPERATION DRAGON SAVIOR - THE GULF OF THAILAND

At midnight Wednesday the USS Virginia surfaced about 500 yards off shore near the South Vietnamese coastal town of Ha Tien. Twelve SEALs and four U.S. Army special forces men climbed into two large Zodiac rubber boats. They were all dressed in black and had painted their faces black and dark green. They loaded with them a couple large bags with their guns, ammunition, and a couple high powered radios. They pushed off from the Virginia and using very quiet battery operated outboard engines, headed in toward the shore. Before they were twenty yards away, the conning tower of the Virginia disappeared below the waves.

The waves were fairly calm and it was a moonless night, so the team made very little noise and were nearly impossible to see. As soon as they got underway, one of the SEALs unpacked a radio and Master Chief Johnson got on the horn to the AC-130 that should be overhead.

"Spectre, Alpha Team. How do you read?"

"Alpha, Spectre 01 has you five by sir and we have a visual." The gunship was overhead and with their infrared system were able to see the boats in the water.

"Roger, Spectre, got you five by as well. How's it look on shore?"

"Alpha, it looks quiet down there. We saw two vehicles on the road out of Ha Tien, but they stayed on the Vietnam side. There's nothing going on up north."

"Roger that Spectre. Have you heard anything from the airlift boys?" Johnson was inquiring about his truck delivery.

"Not yet Alpha. They're still a little over an hour out though. We'll let you know when they're inbound."

The assault team made their landing on the beach just north of a rock karst that stuck out into the water. They pulled their Zodiacs up onto the beach and quickly deflated and packed them up. A ten man Zodiac folds down to a package about 3 feet by 3 feet by 5 feet, and fits into a large bag with heavy duty handles. It weighs close to 200 pounds, but they had them ready to load onto the trucks. Then they scouted out the beach. They sited a stretch of beach that was about a half mile long with minimum curve to it. The sand wasn't too soft. Johnson assigned his men to their duties. Two of the SEALs positioned themselves at each end of the designated landing zone. Johnson and the rest of the team and the special ops truck drivers set up shop in the jungle at about half way along the drop zone. Now they waited.

Just before 0200 the C-141s checked in with the gunship. "Spectre 01, Penske 10 and Penske 11 on freq, how do you read?"

Penske! That's a hoot. The gunship pilot thought. I guess they are in the rental truck business. "Penske we have you loud and clear. Your target area looks clear and your rental customers are on the beach waiting." He responded.

"Roger that. We're coming in low and dark. Should be on target in 12 minutes." The lead C-141 pilot said. His wingman was about a mile behind him and a little higher. The flight lead had just turned off all his navigation lights, so flying formation was nearly impossible from a mile behind. They simply maintained the briefed airspeed and keep their altitude at about 700 feet, while the leader was supposed to be at 500. It was formation by deconfliction.

"Penske this is Alpha Team, How do you read?" Johnson had heard the first exchange and needed to give approach guidance to the C-141s.

"Alpha, we have you loud and clear. Understand you want to rent a couple of our brand new trucks."

"You betcha Penske." Johnson came back. "I just hope they are in good shape after the joy ride you're about to give them."

"No guarantees there Alpha, and I'm afraid you're going to have to take them as is. There's a no return policy on this delivery."

"Understand that. Ok, we've scouted out the drop zone. As you approach the coast, swing a little to the south and set up south to north along the beach. There's a large karst formation of rock that juts out into the water about 1/4 mile south of us. We'll pop two flares at either end of the zone, about a half mile long. Stick 'em as close to the middle of that as you can."

"Roger that Alpha. Penske 11, I'll drop in the first half of the zone, you plan on dropping long on us." The flight leader instructed his wingman. Johnson thought I guess that makes sense. We wouldn't want the wingman to be long on a delivery that aimed short of his leader's. Good chance of trucks piled on trucks.

"Alpha, Penske's commencing our turn up the beach." The lead C-141 declared.

"Roger that. Flares, flares." Johnson said both to the C-141 and on a hand held radio to his men on the beach. Four red flares blossomed out.

"Visual on the target, Penske 10."

"Visual, Penske 11."

The first big bird came in over the karst and then let down to about 100 feet off the ground. They had slowed down to just above a stall speed, in fact they had flaps down to help maintain a level angle of attack. The large back doors were open. Inside, the Loadmaster stood ready with his hand on a trigger switch watching for the green light from his pilot. The light went from yellow to green and he pulled the trigger. A bundle shot out the back end and immediately blossomed as a small parachute. At the same time, chocks were released under the pallets on the rails and the first truck on a pallet rumbled out the door. Attached to its pallet was the bundled chute for the second pallet and the second chute deployed. Out rolled the second truck. It all took about ten seconds. As soon as the pallets were free of the aircraft they started to fall and a large parachute deployed from the top. Each truck on a pallet got one swing under a parachute and then slammed into the sand with a crunch.

"Bombs away." Yelled the Loadmaster over his intercom to the pilot, and he initiated the closing of the ramp and doors. The pilot added full power, retracted the flaps, raised the nose about ten degrees, and started a climbing left turn out to sea.

Penske 11 came in a little high and hot. When his leader's trucks passed under his nose below he initiated the green light sequence. This one wasn't as pretty. Because he was a little high the trucks on their pallets hung up in the air a little longer and were approaching the north end of the landing zone. In fact, the SEALs holding the flares up there had to scramble to keep from getting "Trucked." Penske 11 cleaned up his configuration and turned left to look for his flight lead for their return to Clark Air Base in the Philippines.

The SEALs and truck drivers scrambled from their jungle observation point and began to strip down the pallets and get the trucks off the beach. One problem right off the bat. Neither of the first two trucks had the keys in them. "You're shittin' me!" Johnson said when his truck drivers informed him. "God Damnit! Can you hot wire them?" He asked the nearest driver. About that time the second truck fired up.

"Yeah." The sergeant said. "Just like that." He climbed aboard and his steed and fired it up in about two minutes.

The second delivery of pallets hit the beach a lot harder and a little off mark, so that the second pallet actually bounced off some hard ground or rocks. The truck had a broken axle. There was no way it could be fixed, so the team quickly unloaded it and spread the goodies among the other three. They were able to hook up to the lame truck and drag it off the beach into the jungle a little bit. Then they covered it and the a pile of all the pallets with branches and palm fronds. An hour or so later the convoy was ready to move out. They stayed on the beach where it was clear and headed south toward the border fence.

"Spectre, this is Alpha Team. You still up there?" Johnson checked in with the gunship. He could hear him up there, but of course couldn't see him. Spectre had all his lights off.

"Alpha, roger that. We see you moving now." The pilot replied. "Looks quiet ahead of you although we can't tell from up here where the actual border fence is. Suggest you turn on your roof lights so we can track you." The trucks had been outfitted with strobes on their tops that were shielded from the side and only visible from above. That way only someone airborne could see them.

"Copy that Spectre. Strobes on. By the way, there are only three trucks now. One busted axle on landing." The team leader responded. "Pass that on to the command center please. And if you still have those airlift guys on freq, you might ask the first pilot to have his Loadmaster check his pockets for some truck keys."

"Oops!"

"Yeah - no problem though. These special forces guys were ex-car thieves and they hot wired their charges in a New York minute. We'll keep the chatter down now unless you see something we need to know about." Johnson signed off.

Chapter Twenty Two

WASHINGTON D.C.

Bob Woodall at the Washington Post was beside himself. Here was an exclusive story with all kinds of implications. He and the Post had been locked in battle with the Gatewater Administration from before the President was even inaugurated. Of course, Gatewater was a staunch conservative Republican and the Post was about as far left as the New York Times, careening off the left side of the news waves constantly with as much opinion in their stories as fact. The fact that the President was going back on his promises to the Congress and the American people, and was going back into Southeast Asia with another invasion was for sure not going to be popular. So what if there are American lives at stake? That's what those career diplomats and CIA agents signed up for. Woodall drew the line though on blaming another source for his information. He owed no loyalty to Gary Larson, and in fact if the story was written correctly - or at least to the slant he wanted it, Larson would be toast just before the President would.

The Headlines in the early morning edition of the Post on Thursday read, "Invasion of Cambodia Underway! U.S. Mounts Military Strike!" The entire operation was exposed, from the SEAL landing that had supposedly already happened to the infiltration of the river convoy and the take over of the Phnom Penh airport. Very little was said about the reason - to rescue the embassy staff, but a lot was said about the forces to be used. The source of the story was described as a "high level person within the White House staff." Since only the President within the White House was in on the planning, it became fairly obvious that someone privy to his office was the leaker.

The Chairman of the Joint Chiefs and the Secretary of State both got word of the story early Thursday morning. By 7 AM the whole planning team and the Director of the FBI were aware of the article. The President was sleeping in, and Gary Larson was not about to wake him up early for what he knew would be at the very least, a severe ass chewing. Larson was beside himself. He didn't know whether to shit or go blind. He put in a call to Bob Woodall at the Post.

"Bob, what the fuck? You've hung me out to dry. I thought you were going to name someone at the Pentagon as your source. What are you doing?" Larson pleaded.

"Sorry Gary, but this was too big a story, and I'm not about to name my source. I'm certainly not going to name someone that wasn't the source. Besides, I didn't name you. Take it easy. Just play dumb. That ought to be easy for you." Woodall said.

"Screw you Woodall. The FBI is already on my case. I'll sue your ass if this blows up." Larson threatened.

"Heh. Heh." Woodall chuckled. "Gary, you forgot one very important thing. I've got the tape. Between it and the note that you sent with it, your ass is mine and I'm going to see to it that you and that trigger happy boss of yours both go down in flames."

"Christ Bob, don't you realize you are putting the lives of a SEAL team and the entire staff at the U.S. embassy at risk?" Larson was practically crying.

"Not me Gary boy." Woodall came back. "It's your boss and his henchmen that have done that. I've just reported the truth based on some information my source gave me. It is the truth isn't it Gary?"

"You're a real ass hole, Woodall." Gary was going on the offensive now. "You'd better tell your editor to expect the wrath of Kahn to come down on his head when the Joint Chiefs, the Secretaries of State and Defense, the CIA and the FBI get into this. Not to mention the President of the United States."

"You know Gary, I think you've got something there. I might just be put in for a Pulitzer for this story." and with that Woodall hung up.

No sooner had Larson hung up the phone than Admiral McLean was on the line demanding to see the President immediately. "Mr. Larson, you need to get the President up and in front of this morning's Washington Post. In the meantime, arrange an emergency meeting for as soon as possible with the National Security team." The Chairman demanded. Then he didn't even wait for an answer, he hung up and called Director Anderson at the FBI.

Larson figured he didn't have a choice. He sent word to the Secret Service to wake the President and he went about organizing a meeting in the Situation Room at 8 o'clock.

Director Anderson brought the Attorney General with him and they came into the Washington Post offices turning a bunch of heads. They went directly to the office of Ben Brady, the Post editor, and told his secretary to also "invite" Bob Woodall to join them. They determined the damage was done and there wasn't anything like a rebuttal or correction that could help. However, they leaned hard on Woodall.

"Mr. Woodall, I assume you understand from the seriousness of the operation you described in your story this morning, that it could be a compromise of our forces." The Attorney General stated.

"Well, yes sir. I suppose that's possible. But all I did was transcribe what I heard on this tape recording to paper in the form of a news story." Woodall responded, waving the tape recording in front of them.

"I don't suppose you'd like to share with us who gave you that tape?" Director Anderson asked.

"No. That would be a breach of confidence. Besides, like I said in the article, he is a high level member of the White House staff. I would think that with all your investigative experience, the FBI could uncover the source." Woodall said. Ben Brady squirmed a little in his chair and basically let his reporter hang it all out to dry.

"Ben," the Attorney General directed his comment to the editor. "You and I have been friends a long time. I assume you know what kind of political damage this story can do to the Administration? I think you'd better prepare yourself for some repercussions."

Brady smiled. "Is that a threat Mr. Attorney General? All I can say is 'Bring it on!' This is just the kind of story we need to bring your precious President to his knees. Now, you gentlemen know your way out, I presume?"

The two visitors left and went directly to the White House.

Chapter Twenty Three

SOUTHERN CAMBODIA

The road beside the border fence between Cambodia and South Vietnam was barely passable. It obviously hadn't been used in years, and it was likely only constructed to bring equipment in to erect the fence in the first place. It was better than driving through the deep jungle just beside it, but not much better. Several times along the way the team could see the more serious road that paralleled the border on the Vietnamese side, and every once in a while there was traffic on it. The team would bring their convoy to a halt whenever they encountered nearby traffic, and since they had their lights completely off - even their brake lights disconnected, as long as the traffic was moving on, they felt fairly safe. The big diesels though were noisy and belched a lot of smoke. If the traffic was still, there would be a good chance of discovery. Because of this problem, and the fact that the terrain was steep and rough, it was a slow going trek. They had hoped to get up to abeam of Chau Doc and meet the CIA agent whose name was Minh, while it was still dark. As it panned out though, they pulled in there right at sunrise.

In the meantime, at about 0500 hours, Pete Trask arrived on scene over the convoy and relieved the Spectre gunship. Pete checked in with the Alpha Team.

"Alpha this Nail 48, OV-10 on scene. How's it going?"

"Nail, this is Alpha. We've made it to our rendezvous point, looking for our local contact. How's the traffic up there?" Johnson replied.

"It's quiet up here. I've got two flights of fighters inbound for support. Let me know if and where you need it." Trask said. "We'll be maintaining an orbit over the Cambodian side until you start down river."

The team waited for almost an hour. They had no way to contact the CIA agent. He supposedly had a radio and would be on the operational frequency. Johnson and Trask both tried to raise him to no avail. Pete contacted the ABCCC to relay back to Colonel Parsons for guidance. Parsons came back with a request. Could the Alpha team and convoy break through and make it to the barge by themselves? Trask relayed the question.

"I was thinking you'd say that." Johnson replied. "Yeah, we've found a spot in the fence we can cut and be in Chau Doc in probably a half hour. Then I suppose we just keep going to the river and look for a barge and a tug looking for a job."

Trask relayed back through the ABCCC, and Parsons soon came back with a "Go!"

"Roger that, Geronimo!" Johnson decreed, not that Geronimo was any kind of code, it just sounded good. The SEALs and special forces guys had a hole cut in the fence down one side and across the top in about 5 minutes. Then they simply grabbed hold of the chain link and pulled it back to create a hole for the trucks to get through. When they were through the fence was pulled back into position and zip tied in enough places to hold it in place. The convoy rumbled into Chau Doc while the city was waking up to another boring day.

I had been listening to the radio chatter as I flew south and I arrived on station at about 0645 to replace Trask. "Nail 48, Nail 32's about three miles at your 9 o'clock, visual on you." I told Pete I was there and had him in sight. About that time two flights of F-4s showed up.

"Nails, Buick flight is up with four phantoms, CBU, and about 30 minutes play time." The first flight of bombers said.

"Roger Buick. I'm smokin' now. With a good visual, orbit over my position at 14 thousand. We're just getting started." Pete directed.

"Buick copies. Visual your smoke. Three, deploy back." The F-4 flight lead had a visual contact on Pete and directed his second element two ship to set up in the orbit a mile or so behind him.

"Nail 48, Shogun's up with two F-4s loaded for bear and 40 minutes of play time." It was the first Udorn flight of air to air tasked fighters in case we had any airborne threats.

"Roger Shogun. Maintain above 20 thousand. All is quiet so far, but we'll rely on you to tell us if we have any company. Break. Break. Nail 32, you ready to shake the stick?" Pete directed the air patrol jets to stay above the fray and keep their noses (and radars) pointed toward the potential threat - South Vietnam. Then he called to pass the baton to me.

"Roger. Nail 32's ready. I'm at your 7 o'clock level." I responded.

"Ok. Nail 32, it's all yours. Alpha, new baby sitter is Nail 32. Four Eight's off and we'll see you tomorrow."

"Alpha copies. Nail 32, we're in the city now. No resistance. Just a lot of puzzled looks." Johnson called.

"Roger Alpha. I have a visual on you and what looks like a barge about three miles on your nose tied up at a rickety looking pier." I passed on to the truck convoy.

"Nail FAC, this is Malloy, flight of 4 A-7s, five miles south with Mark 82s and 30 minutes of play time." The Navy's first support bombers showed up.

"Roger Malloy, Nail 32. Maintain orbit between 16 and 19 thousand. Flight of four F-4s below you at 14 thousand and two above you at 20 thousand. No action yet, stand by." I radioed back. In the mean time, my cockpit plexiglass was getting busy. I had Buick, Malloy, Shogun and the ABCCC all annotated and stacked with my grease pencil.

"Uh, Nail 32 this is Alpha, looks like we have a small problem here." Master Chief Johnson called. "We're coming up on a road block. Three jeeps and about 6 or 8 of what looks like South Vietnamese soldiers. They're beckoning for us to stop."

"Copy that Alpha. I'm moving over top to get a closer look." I said. "Tally ho!. Doesn't look like any more of them around. Maybe just the local gendarmes?"

The Alpha team stopped, and Johnson and one of the special forces drivers got out. The driver spoke Vietnamese. He asked the apparent leader of the road block, what the problem was. They were holding an oriental man in the background, under guard. While the driver was conversing with the soldier Johnson called, "Mr. Minh?" The oriental looked up and nodded his head vehemently.

"Tell them we were to meet a guide here and we are taking supplies to the army down river." Johnson directed the driver.

The soldier frowned and looked at the trucks, at his prisoner, then at Johnson. In broken english he said. "Where you come from? What supplies? You come from across border?" As he asked he moved toward the first truck.

"Yes, we stole these supplies from Americans in Cambodia for the Vietnamese army." Johnson lied.

The Vietnamese sergeant in charge laughed and then said, "You come through fence. You lie. No Vietnamese army near here."

Johnson moved back to his truck and the radio and called me. "Nail 32, looks like we may have a stalemate here and these guys have got our Mr. Minh. How about a noisy show of force?

"Aha! Good idea Alpha. Standby" I said, and then on the UHF radio, "Buick, we need a bit of a noisy fly by down in the middle of the town. Our truckers are being held up by a nervous gomer. Follow me down. I'll put down a smoke. When you see it and pick up the convoy and jeeps, blow by them at the speed of heat and spill their coffee." I cleared the Ubon F-4s to do a shine-your- ass fly by on Chau Doc.

"Buick copies. Buick in trail, follow me." The flight lead directed.

I rolled in to about a 45 degree dive and fired a Willie Pete rocket. I rolled up on one wing and looked down. The smoke landed about 50 yards short of the trucks. "Just a little long of my smoke Buick, do you see the trucks?"

"Roger that. Buick's in dry and fast." The leader said. The F-4s went blowing over the group of trucks and personnel at about 50 - 100 feet, doing close to 500 knots, then one by one they peeled back up and to the west to join up and wait.

Down below the Vietnamese scattered. They ran for cover and the guard watching Mr. Minh abandoned him. Johnson ran over, grabbed Minh and they piled back into their truck. The trucks drove down to the pier where the barge and tug were waiting. Minh jumped out and signaled the tug crew who pulled out a couple ramps and set up for the trucks to clamor aboard the barge. Within about 20 minutes the barge was pulling away from the pier.

However, the sergeant in command of the Vietnamese roadblock had changed his underwear and ordered his men to the pier. They drove up and started shooting at the barge and the trucks. The SEALs were just pulling out their gear and couldn't defend themselves yet. Johnson called for more help.

"Nail, we're taking a little incoming here from the pier. Any chance we can get something a little more destructive than noise from you boys?"

"Roger that Alpha." I replied. "Buick cleared in hot on the pier with guns only."

"Buick copies. Buick green 'em up. Guns one at a time, One's in." The F-4 rolled in from the south and parallel the pier.

"Buick flight, you're cleared hot." I said and watched as the F-4s chewed up the pier and the men on it with their 20 mm canons. After number four went through it was real quiet and even the pier was gone.

"Good shootin' Buick. Cleared back to orbit." I directed.

"Good show Nail." Johnson said, "I guess you flyboys can shoot straight sometimes."

The barge moved on down river toward the junction where the spur of the Son Wau River that they were on merged with the main channel that came down from the north. There they were to take that channel back upstream to Cho Vam where they would merge with the Mekong and hopefully the main convoy.

Buick, Malloy and Shogun flights all ran out of play time and had to head home for fuel. They were replaced by others, but for the rest of my time on station there was no activity. The squadron Operations Officer, Lt. Colonel Mike Majors came on at about 0830 and relieved me. I headed back up north to an uneventful mission termination at Ubon.

Dragon Savior had begun.

Chapter Twenty Four

WASHINGTON D.C.

At 8 AM Thursday morning they were all there. The National Security team, the FBI Director and the Attorney General. The President came into the room in a sour mood. He marched to the end of the table to his seat before he even told the group to sit down. "Well, well, well. We seemed to have uncovered a hornets nest." The President said to no one in particular and looked at all of them. "I've had calls from the Prime Ministers of Thailand, Canada and Japan asking me what in the world we are doing in Cambodia. I basically told them all to bug off, that we'd let them know as soon as we could. Now - how did Bob Woodall get this information?"

"Sir, with all due respect, I agree that we need to ferret out this leak, but right now we need to decide what to do about Dragon Savior and whether to proceed." Admiral McLean offered. "The mission is on going as we speak, and so far there have been only minor setbacks, but I'm afraid this story in the Post will spur the Vietnamese to action and embolden the Khmer Rouge."

"Do you propose we abort the mission?" The President asked.

"I don't think we can at this point Mr. President." The voice came from a speaker phone on the table. It was CINCPAC

Admiral McMaster. He, General LeCroix (PACAF Commander), General Tobin (Commander of 7th Air Force), and Admiral Ages (Commander of the 7th Fleet) were all piped in on the phone. "The trucks are on the barge and moving down the river toward their rendezvous with the river convoy. They lost one truck on beach landing, but were able to load all its equipment onto the others. They encountered some minor resistance in the city of Chau Doc, but with some Air Force help, were able to press on."

"Sir, I think if we abort now, not only will we leave the embassy and our folks in Phnom Penh in the lurch, we'll have a team of SEALs and special forces floundering around deep in Apache territory with no way out." Admiral McLean said. "I believe we need to keep going but be prepared for a lot bigger threat and more action."

The President and his staff kicked the subject around for a few more minutes and finally Gatewater asked SECSTATE Crittendon, "Henry, what do you think? Will the Vietnamese react to this incursion into their country? Can we tell them it is only temporary and we will be north of their border with the convoy probably tomorrow?"

"We can tell them whatever we want them to know Mr. President, but they will do whatever Hanoi directs. My guess is they will try to stop this convoy and our plans."

Finally the President made a decision. "Ok Admiral McMaster, get word to your forces and the command center you have set up to press on but to be ready for significant resistance."

"Yes sir." CINCPAC responded. "We'll keep you advised sir." And the Pacific warriors signed off.

"Now what in God's name are we going to do about this leak?" The President asked. He looked at Director Anderson. "Did you have your conversation with my Chief of Staff?"

"Yes I did sir. He denies having anything to do with it, but he also seemed to know that we had an operation named Dragon Savior in the wind." Anderson replied. "We also visited the Washington Post this morning and had a discussion with Ben Brady and with this reporter Bob Woodall. They were not very helpful, and in fact all but said they are going to use this as a springboard to try and bring you down sir. Woodall flashed a tape recording in our face that he said had all the specifics that he put in his story, and that you and most of the folks in this room were on it."

"Mr. President, that recording could only have come from our meeting in your office where we discussed the operation." Secretary Crittendon offered.

"Well I certainly didn't tape our meeting. Did any of you?" He looked at the others in scorn.

"Sir, I believe that tape was provided to Mr. Woodall by Mr. Larson." Anderson said. "Woodall all but specifically named him when he told us the tape was provided by a 'senior person in the White House staff.' Who else would have easy access to the Oval Office?"

"I suppose someone in the cleaning crew could have planted a recorder in the office." The President was trying to defend his friend and colleague.

"Sir, if I may be so bold. Why not call Mr. Larson in here and ask him?" The Attorney General jumped in.

"All right." The President punched onto the intercom on the phone and told the operator to have his Chief of Staff join them in the Situation Room.

The President and his staff sat for 15 minutes talking about other issues, but he was getting frustrated. Just as he was punching up the phone again, the head of his Secret Service detail knocked and came in. "Sir, I understand you are looking for Mr. Larson. He..."

"Yeah we are. Where the hell is he?"

"He just left the building sir and he seemed to be in a big hurry."

The President hung his head for a moment. The others sat patiently. The President looked at Director Anderson and said, "He's all yours Andy. Go get the son of a bitch," And he got up to leave.

Gary Larson drove straight to his condo in Georgetown. He quickly packed a bag and before he went out the door he went to his safe and took out the Glock 9 mm automatic he kept in there, along with a box of shells. He went back out and basically spent the day in his car, driving around, staying off the radar. He parked down the block from his condo about noon for a while and saw the FBI come and go. They posted a D.C. black and white across the street and it was obvious he was a hunted man.

Chapter Twenty Five

UBON RTAFB, THAILAND

General LeCroix contacted Colonel Parsons at the Ubon Command Center about 0900 Thursday to tell him about the compromise to the mission generated by the Washington Post story. By then four of the Nails had already launched, and in fact, Pete Trask was already back from his mission. Parsons contacted the ABCCC C-130 though and had them pass the word on up the line to be heads up for more activity from the other side.

"So what does this mean General?" Parsons asked LeCroix over the phone. "What kind of Rules of Engagement (ROE) are we to follow if we encounter heavy defenses, and especially an air threat?"

"It means do whatever you have to do to protect yourselves from anti-aircraft fire or missiles." LeCroix answered. "As far as an air threat goes, I guess I'll have to run that up the chain. As far as I'm concerned you can wade into them guns a blazin,' but I'd better clear that. You know how it was the last few months of the war."

"Yes sir." Parsons came back. "That's why I'm asking." During the last year of the war in Southeast Asia pilots were severely restricted when reacting to a MIG threat. They basically could only fire when fired upon. That pissed off a lot of pilots, and even got a few shot down. By the time a MIG gets into position to fire at an American aircraft it was invariably too late to do anything about it. The superior radars and tactics our pilots had at their disposal meant they could usually detect an inbound threat BEFORE it gets into shoot parameters, and could shoot first. But the ROE wouldn't let them.

"OK. Let me get back to you." LeCroix said, hung up, and immediately got on the horn to his boss, CINCPAC Admiral McMaster. The question ran up the ladder and eventually SECSTATE Crittendon, wearing his National Security Advisor hat, took it to the President.

"Mr. President, I don't think we should burn our bridges in the area just because an American reporter turned loose a hornets' nest. I believe we should not fire on anyone not a direct threat to the convoy and our people as they evacuate Phnom Penh." The Secretary said. It seems he was really wearing his SECSTATE hat after all. "We should limit the activity and any damage to a minimum. We should also be sure there are no collateral civilian casualties."

"I suppose you're right Henry." The President said. He was still in a tizzy about his Chief of Staff going AWOL and not thinking about much else. "Pass the word on to the military." Neither the Chairman nor any of the Joint Chiefs were ever even consulted.

CINCPAC passed the ROE on to the 7th Fleet, and General LeCroix called Colonel Parsons. "Just as I suspected Howard," He said. "The powers that be have levied even more restrictions on us. We are not to fire upon an enemy aircraft unless fired upon first. We are not to attack anything on the ground that is not a direct threat to the convoy. Also, we are to limit any civilian casualties to a minimum of none."

"God damnit sir!" Parsons came back. "That sucks! We're putting a lot of fighter pilots' lives at risk. You mean to say if they are attacked by a AAA site or a missile, they can't react by destroying that site? We're going to have some pissed off aircrews."

"I understand your frustration Howard." LeCroix said. "So hear me out. As far as I'm concerned, have your pilots do whatever they have to do to defend themselves. If that means drawing their pistols faster and blowing the other guy away, so be it! If we have any problems with this guidance, it's on me."

"Yes sir! And thank you sir." Conversation over.

Chapter Twenty Six

CAMBODIA - THE SON WAU RIVER

The operation ran smoothly and without any hiccups for most of the day Thursday. The SEALs set up shop on the barge with their variety of "artillery." They had a mortar set up going off each side, a couple of machine gun "nests," some rocket propelled grenades spread strategically around, and all cleverly camouflaged or covered with tarp. They also re-inflated their Zodiacs plus one more that had been loaded on the trucks. The trucks had three 50 hp Mercury engines on them to beef up the Zodiacs' speed. In the end, the barge was a disguised "gunboat" or miniature destroyer. Lots of firepower.

The going was slow. Big river barges aren't made for speed, and the tug that Mr. Minh had commandeered had seen better days. It basically took several hours to make it back down the spur of the Son Wau River they were on to the main channel. Then they turned back upstream, north toward Cho Vam where they would merge with the Mekong. It was dark by the time they turned north and the Nails had turned the support back over to the AC-130 gunships.

The Air force had provided several flights of F-4 bombers and 12 flights of air cover, while the Navy had provided eight flights of A-7s. None of them were utilized and to their chagrin, the pilots had to return to base fully loaded. Although they don't like to do it, pilots can land on runways with a full load. It's just that they are heavy weight and there's always a slight chance the jarring of the wheels hitting the runway could knock something (like a bomb) loose on landing. For that reason, Air Force F-4 pilots worked hard at making it a smooth landing.

For the Navy it was a different story. They never landed on a carrier to snag the cable with bombs hanging. The procedure was always to release the munitions harmlessly out to sea. A waste of good bombs, but the price we pay for peace and diplomacy.

Close to midnight things started to heat up. There were several vehicle lights on the south shore of the river, and the SEALs could tell there were several dozen troops running around. That part of the Son Wau is not very wide - maybe 1/4 mile. The north shore seemed peaceful so Master Chief Johnson had Mr. Minh direct the tug captain to move the barge over closer to the port side. However, evidently the river is also not very deep except in the middle where it was regularly dredged, so the captain couldn't provide much more separation.

"Spectre, this is Alpha," Johnson radioed the gunship. "Are you seeing this activity off our starboard side?"

"Roger that Alpha and it gets even more crowded as you move up river. I've got heat signatures of dozens of personnel and several vehicles." The Spectre pilot came back. "To top it off, there's a bridge across the river around the next bend ahead of you and there's a lot of activity on it." Johnson figured it would be about

40 minutes before they got to that bridge, so he called up the ABCCC.

"Big Shot, this is Alpha, are you monitoring our calls to Spectre?" Johnson asked.

"Roger that Alpha, we copy and we're scrambling you some help now." The Command and Control supervisor said. This was a flaw in the planning. This bridge coming up was supposed to be the only one that would cross any of their route. The Mekong is too wide for a bridge on the Vietnamese side of the border, and on the Cambodia side the first one is just beyond Phnom Penh. Because there was no threat expected, the planners had only fragged a few night bombing missions. Of course that was before the shit hit the fan at the Washington Post. As a precaution, Colonel Parsons put both the 8th TFW at Ubon and the USS Enterprise on alert to be able to scramble fighter bombers in 10 minutes.

A flight of two F-4s from Ubon and two A-7s off the Enterprise were inbound, but the F-4s would take about 50 minutes to get on scene. The A-7s would be there in about 25 minutes.

"Alpha, this is Big Shot, can you slow down? We should get you some help within 30 minutes, but the rest won't be for another 20 or so." The Major in the back of the C-130 with all the communication gear asked.

"Christ man, this thing is barely moving now into the river flow." Johnson replied. "Besides, if we slow down now we stand a good chance of not making it to the Mekong in time to meet the convoy. Negative. Bring in what you've got and Spectre, can you handle this?"

"We thought you'd never ask Alpha." The gunship pilot said. "This baby has the new 105 mm howitzer and our standard 40 mm canon. I'm pretty sure we can help you out."

About that time mortar rounds were landing in the water just short of the barge and there were flashes of small arms fire from shore. A few of the rounds actually made the distance and the SEALs manned their guns. They lobbed a few mortar rounds of their own and they raked the shoreline with machine gun fire. In the mean time the AC-130 opened up with it's 40 mm pom-pom like canon. It did some major damage on shore. Vehicles blew up and gomers were running for cover. The heat seeking capability of the gunship is amazing. They can even see the heat of a single man running in the jungle.

As the barge plied further up river, the action got even more intense. The barge was taking almost as much incoming as they were putting out. There were some old wooden pallets on the barge and the SEALs stacked them up around the front ends of the trucks to try and protect the engines from incoming fire. It wouldn't do any good to arrive in Phnom Penh with trucks that were shot full of lead. The AC-130 was busy with the 40 mm and let loose with a couple of howitzer rounds as well against vehicles.

When the bridge came into view Johnson could see it was teeming with soldiers and vehicles. They had started amassing on the north side of the river as well, on the approach to the bridge. Soon the barge would be under siege from both riverbanks and the bridge above. Things were looking grim.

"Houston check."

"Two."

"Spectre, this is Houston, flight of two A-7s about five minutes out, you need some help?" The A-7 lead pilot checked in.

"Roger that Houston, we've got bad guys on both banks up near the bridge and a slew of them on the bridge." The gunship pilot explained. "In the meantime we're raking the south bank where most of the incoming has come from."

"Houston, this is Alpha Team. What kind of fire can you provide?" Johnson wanted to know.

"Alpha, we have four CBU canister's a piece, and a hot gun." The A-7 had a 20 mm canon, the same as the F-4s.

"Roger that. For right now can you strafe the south shore a few passes to help keep their heads down?" Johnson asked. "It's going to be another ten minutes before we get to that bridge. I'm afraid to turn you guys all loose on it now and then give the gomers time to climb back on it as we get there."

"Can do Alpha. Spectre, we'll call in on each pass to deconflict with your canon." The A-7 lead said. "Houston, green 'em up guns."

The A-7s made three strafe runs apiece on the troops on the south shore, while the AC-130 kept pounding away with the 40 mm canon. Things got pretty quiet on that side. The SEALs shifted their focus to the port side and set up a machine gun to rake the bridge as well.

"Spectre, Houston, this is Alpha." Johnson had a plan.

"Go ahead." Spectre said.

"Houston's on."

"Ok guys, here's my idea. First off, Spectre, what kind of damage can you do to that bridge? Can you take it down on the approach ends?" Johnson asked.

"You betcha we can. This howitzer will put a hole the size of one of your trucks in that rickety bridge."

"Ok. Here's the idea. As soon as it really starts getting hot down here from that bridge, and I expect that'll be in about 4-5 minutes as we move closer, Houston, I'd like you to make one pass each, stringing two CBU canisters the length of the bridge. That should keep their heads down - hopefully permanently." Johnson explained. "Then Spectre, put two of your truck size rounds in both ends of the bridge so they can't reinforce it. Then, Houston, lay one more canister each on that north shore of gomers. Let's save the last two until we see what's on the other side of the bridge."

"Houston copies. Two set up singles, 100 ft spacing."

"Spectre copies. We're setting up now."

About a minute later all hell broke loose from the bridge. The bad guys had set up mortars on the bridge and were raining it down on the barge. One of the trucks took a direct hit. Two SEALs went down.

"Now, Houston. Now!" Johnson screamed and watched as the jets blew over the bridge from south to north at about 100 feet. It looked like the Fourth of July with fireworks popping off all over the bridge. A moment later the big gun went "Whumpf! Whumpf!" from the gunship and the north end of the bridge basically collapsed Spectre moved over to the south end and "Whumpf! Whumpf!" London Bridge was falling down. The SEALs were hootin' and hollerin,' but not for long.

As the barge cleared the bridge it was obvious there was more resistance on the south side. The SEALs re-configured their defenses to take on incoming and spewed what they could from the barge.

"Houston, if you're still up there do what you can with the gomers on the south shore." Johnson pleaded.

Roger that, Houston's in from the west then we'll be 'Winchester.'" The fighter's made their pass west to east and spread what death and destruction they had left on the troops on shore. Then they were off for the ship with no more munitions to give (Winchester).

As the second A-7 pulled off from his run a shoulder fired surface to air missile flamed up from the opposite shore. Johnson saw it first.

"Houston, break break! Missile at your six." He yelled. It was too late. the missile went right up the tail pipe of the fighter and the jet exploded right in front of the barge about 1000 feet up.

"Shit!" Johnson yelled. "Houston lead your wingman took one. We're looking for a chute."

"Copy that." A somber flight lead radioed back. "I'm about out of gas. I've got to get to the ship." About then the familiar Beep! Beep! of a pilot's locator beacon went off on the guard frequency and one of the SEALs pointed out a parachute.

"Houston, we've got a visual on him." Johnson said. "I hope he has the sense to drop in the river. We're launching our boat to get him."

"Praise God. Thanks guys. Good luck. Houston out."

"Chevy check."

"Two"

"Alpha, this is Chevy, flight of two Fox Fours inbound as fast as we can. We heard the beeper and your last transmissions. Can we help?" The flight lead of the Wolfpack F-4s checked in.

"Roger that Chevy." Johnson replied. "First off, be advised these guys have got SAMs and maybe anti air guns. Break. Break. Spectre do you have a visual on the chute?"

"Negative Alpha and we've put on a little more altitude for safety. I think I saw where that SAM came from though and were in hot there." The gunship opened up on the jungle north of the river.

The SEALs immediately launched one of their Zodiacs and were beating feet toward the 11 o'clock of the barge, keeping an eye on the parachute. It appeared the pilot did have the right idea and he was steering his chute toward the river.

"Chevy, what kind of ordnance you got?" Johnson asked the F-4s.

"Six Mark 82 five hundred pounders and a hot gun each with about 20 minutes of play time. We burned a lot of fuel getting down here at the speed of snot." The flight lead came back.

"Ok. Use your guns first on the south shoreline but watch your ass. That SAM was a surprise and there's probably more out there." Johnson had not been briefed by any of the airborne support about the likely change in the threat level.

"Copy that. Chevy's in hot from the west." The F-4s made three hot passes each and ran out of ammo. Then they made a couple dry noisy passes just to try and keep the gomers' heads down.

The pilot from the A-7 managed to plop in the water, but then he just about drowned. Turns out he had wrenched his back in the ejection and was not able to get out from under his chute when it fluttered down on top of him. The SEALs were there in a heart beat though, and as they roared up in the Zodiac, one of them rolled off the side and swam under to cut the pilot loose and bring him out from under. The Zodiac came back around and scooped the two swimmers up and started for the barge.

Just about then, out from a small cove in the river came two gunboats high tailing it toward the Zodiac. The SEAL at the helm called to Johnson on his hand held radio. "Hey boss, we got company here, and they're coming in hot." Master Chief Johnson saw it all unfolding in front of him about 100 yards.

"Spectre and Chevy, we got visitors down here." He said. "Two gunboats closing in on our Zodiac."

"Chevy's got the gunboats, but I can't see your Zodiac." The Zodiac is a low, black, rubber boat on a dark river at night. Tough to see at 400 knots per hour, or without night vision goggles.

"The Zodiac is between the gunboats and the barge. See what you can do to slow the gunboats down."

"Roger, Chevy's in from the east. Two, go to singles and 50 foot spacing." The fighter lead rolled in and laid his string of six 500 pound bombs 50 feet apart on a diagonal along the gunboats. His bombs missed completely. Hitting a fast moving boat that's only about 30 feet long in the dark is no easy task. However, number two's second bomb was a direct hit and one of the gunboats went down.

"Alpha, Spectre's got this." The gunship pilot announced. He rolled the big beast up on its left wing about 45 degrees, and "Whumpf!" the howitzer belched, and the gunboat disintegrated.

"Good shootin' Spectre." The gracious F-4 flight lead said. "Alpha, we're outta here. I think the bosses were generating more support for you ASAP. I'll relay whatever I find out."

"Thanks. Good shooting to you as well." Johnson replied. "Things seem to be quiet right now. Spectre, how are you doing for gas and ammo?"

"We're just about out but our replacement is 5 minutes away."

"Copy that. You're cleared off and thanks for all the help." Johnson signed off.

The SEALs got the A-7 pilot aboard and they were able to make him comfortable. All of the SEALs have some medical training and one of the special forces truck drivers was a Medic, so he was in good hands. The second AC-130 showed up and stayed on station until the FACs arrived at sunup. There was minimum activity. Some light ground fire here and there, but when it was all met with 40 mm and 105 mm cannons from the sky, the bad guys kept their heads down.

Slowly but surely the barge and tug made their way down to the confluence with the mighty Mekong River.

Chapter Twenty Seven

WASHINGTON D.C.

Gary Larson spent most of the day just driving around. He ditched his Mercedes early, figuring the cops would be looking for it. He thought that since he was already up for treason or whatever they would call giving the tape recording to the press, he might as well go all in. He decided to steal a car. He watched as a young mother left her minivan running outside a Day Care school as she ran in, probably to pick up her kids. He slid in behind the wheel and took off down the street. He figured he'd be invisible driving a regular "Mom Mobile."

Larson found a parking spot across the street from the Washington Post building and watched and waited as reporters and staff came and went. Finally, about 5 PM he saw Bob Woodall come out and hail a cab. Larson fired up his new found steed and followed the taxi as it made its way across town to of all places, the Mayflower Hotel. That figures, Larson thought to himself. The son of a bitch must have another story on the hook at his old hunting grounds. He got out of the car, slipped his gun in his belt, zipped his jacket up around it, and went inside.

Gary forgot that the FBI Director had told him they had been following Woodall for months. Special Agent Mike Malloy, on surveillance at the time, was just about to go into the hotel himself when he spotted Gary Larson. He made a call into headquarters and then went in to watch both subjects.

The bar was crowded. After 5 PM it always seemed that half the folks that wanted to be seen on the D.C. scene frequented the Mayflower's bar. Larson snuck in quietly, hoping that no one recognized him, and settled into a booth near the door with a good view of the bar. He spotted Woodall there talking to a very attractive woman. He thought she looked familiar, but it took him a while to recognize her. She was Justine Miller, the news anchor of the local NBC affiliate TV station. I'll bet they're talking about me and that damn story of Woodall's, Gary thought. He ordered a double Black Jack on the rocks from the waitress. He needed to get his courage up for what he was about to do.

About a half hour and another double later it looked like Justine was getting ready to leave. She stood up from the bar and Woodall stood to shake her hand. Larson decided now was the time. He stood quickly, pushed through the crowd and confronted the couple about 20 feet away with his Glock in his hand.

"Hang on there Miss Miller." Gary yelled. "You can get an exclusive on this story." He pointed the gun at Woodall. A woman on the next barstool screamed and everyone around them started pushing and shoving to get out of the way.

"Woodall, you're a son of a bitch. And you're a traitor as well." Larson accused. "Your story will probably mean dozens of American lives will be lost, not to mention my career. Get on your knees." Woodall was shocked, and he was also a coward. He grabbed Justine Miller and held her in front of him and started backing away.

Justine gasped and yelled, "Let go of me you bastard!" She turned and buried her fist in Woodall's crotch and broke away. Woodall bent over with a loud "Oooof!"

"Hold it Larson." A voice said from behind him. "Drop the gun." Gary turned to see FBI Director Anderson standing there beside four of his agents, all pointing their weapons at him. He turned and moved off to the side so that he could see everyone, but he kept his gun leveled on the Post reporter.

"This son of a bitch deserves it," he yelled. "His story not only ruined me, it put a lot of good folks in danger."

"Look, I just…" Woodall tried to say. He had recovered quickly from his blow below the belt.

"Shut up! What you 'just' did was betray me and your country." Gary raised his gun to shoot.

"Don't do it Gary." Anderson stepped forward and said. "You're right. He's an asshole, but you can't do this. Now put the gun down."

Gary looked at Anderson and lowered the gun, but he didn't drop it. He looked perplexed. Woodall breathed a sigh of relief. Gary stood there for what seemed like forever. It was really only a few seconds and the FBI agents had managed to move to surround him.

"Drop the gun Gary." Anderson ordered. Larson looked at him and broke down sobbing. Woodall laughed.

"Hah! Big man!" He said.

"Shut up Woodall!" Anderson ordered.

Gary Larson looked one more time at Bob Woodall, then at Andy Anderson. Then he quickly raised his gun, stuck the barrel in his mouth and pulled the trigger. The back half of his head exploded in blood, brain and bone all over the folks behind him. Anderson had taken a quick step forward when he realized what was about to come down, but was obviously too late to do anything. He caught Larson's body as he fell. The gun went sliding across the floor and came to a stop at Justine Miller's feet. She bent over to pick it up.

"Don't touch that gun." Anderson ordered as he slowly lowered Gary Larson to the floor. "Well, I guess you Ms. Miller, and you Mr. Woodall, obviously have a juicy exclusive story to tell. But I swear to you, if you sensationalize this anymore than the sad situation it was, I personally will make your lives miserable."

"I'm sure you've heard of a thing called the First Amendment, haven't you Mr. Anderson?" Woodall gloated. "And the freedom of the press?"

"Sure I have Woodall. Otherwise your ass would have been in jail for that story you wrote this morning." Anderson came back. "What I'm saying is your story is what initiated this whole sad affair. If I were you, I would start off writing about this one with an apology, an apology to Larson's family, and an apology to the nation."

"Yeah, Right!" Woodall sneered and started to walk out. "Don't hold your breath." He left the bar as did Justine Miller, still very shaken up.

Chapter Twenty Eight

THE MEKONG RIVER - SOUTH VIETNAM

We expected that Friday would be the most intense day of the campaign, even before it was highlighted in the press. After all, we were operating in South Vietnam. The convoy wouldn't cross into Cambodia until late in the afternoon or evening. The Viet Cong and North Vietnamese were much better equipped than the Khmer Rouge, and we had already seen that there was anti aircraft weaponry in their arsenal.

Pete Trask arrived on scene as the sun came up and the Alpha team's barge was approaching the confluence of the Son Wau and Mekong Rivers. The main river convoy was already about halfway through the confluence. Master Chief Johnson had the tug captain push on out into the Mekong and parallel the main convoy, to look for an opportunity to merge into the traffic. Meanwhile Pete was gathering his forces. He had two flights of four F-4s and one of A-7s stacked up waiting for trouble.

Trouble came in spades. The Viet Cong or North Vietnamese, knowing we were coming, had clamored aboard one of the main convoy barges. They set up mortars, machine guns and had at least 20 soldiers onboard. They had covered themselves with tarps so that to Trask and Johnson the barge looked like all the rest, loaded with cargo under cover. As the Alpha team's barge slid back towards the rear of the convoy they came up abeam the trap. All of a sudden all hell broke loose. The SEALs were taking fire from almost point blank range.

Pete had stayed up at about 7000 feet so he didn't see the attackers right away.

"Nail 48, Alpha, we're under attack from the barge next door. Can you help?" Considering the intensity of the incoming Johnson sounded remarkably calm.

"Roger that. Break, break. Buick flight follow me down. Target's the barge lined up with the main convoy. Good guys are on the barge beside it out in the water. Hit my smoke." Pete directed while he rolled in, close to a 90 degree dive.

"Buick's in. FAC in site. Green 'em up Buick, string 3 singles, 50 foot." The flight lead came back and directed his flight to drop three of their bombs in a string, 50 feet apart.

Pete directed the flight to hit his smoke even before he had laid it down. He always was a little cocky, but he was also a good shot. At 2500 feet he let 'er rip, pulled up out of the dive and rolled off to his left to see that his Willie Pete hit dead center on the gomer barge. The F-4s of Buick were each carrying 6 Mark 82 500 pound bombs, and released three of them.

Buick Lead's first bomb hit the water just short of the barge, but his next two walked from aft to bow with direct hits. By the time all four Buicks had pulled off the target, they had five bombs directly on the barge, one on its tug and three in the water. The enemy soldiers who survived the blasts dove into the water and started swimming toward the Alpha barge. About that time the northern bank of the river lit up with artillery and mortar fire.

"Good shootin' Nail, but now we've got incoming from the north shore." Johnson said, again very calmly.

"Tally ho Alpha," Pete responded. He knew the flight of A-7s were carrying CBU, so he called them in next. "Boxcar, Nail 48, do you have a tally on the north shore of the river? Need you to wade into them, spill their blood!" Pete quoted George C. Scott in the movie "Patton." He rolled off his perch in about a 25 degree dive and put one Willie Pete short, and one long of where he wanted the strike. "Between my smokes!" He ordered.

"Boxcar copies." The flight leader said. "Got your marks. We're in from the east." The A-7s spread their little bomblets in a pattern about 50 yards wide and 200 yards long, doing a lot to suppress the incoming fire.

In the meantime, Master Chief Johnson had a decision to make. He had 6-8 gomer soldiers in the water swimming toward his barge. They weren't armed. They were obviously looking to be rescued. His SEALs wanted to blow their shit away, but he knew that wasn't real kosher. Obviously, if they had a white flag to wave it would indicate they were surrendering. The problem was the Alpha barge sat pretty high in the water. Their trucks didn't weigh all that much compared to the heavy weight most barges carried with a load of coal or other cargo. It was close to eight feet from the gunwale to the water. Johnson quickly made up his mind. He had his men heave one of the the Zodiacs overboard and tie it down, and waved to the swimmers to swim to that side. All but one made it. That one basically got run over by the barge. There were two SEALs in the Zodiac and they grabbed the remaining gomers and rolled them aboard.

Meanwhile there was still sporadic incoming from the north shore. Trask continued to lay down fire along that bank. During all of this, two gunboats had emerged from the south bank and were quietly gaining on the convoy from behind. Since the Alpha barge had merged into the parade about three barges from the rear, the SEALs didn't see them. But Trask did.

"Alpha, looks like two gunboats are trying to sneak up from the rear. Heads up!" He said. "Boxcar, you have anything left?" He queried the A-7s.

"We've got one can apiece and a hot gun Nail. I have a tally on your boats out for a Friday cruise."

"Ok. See what you can do. Break, Break! Buick, you still with me?" Pete asked the F-4 leader.

"Roger that Nail, and we each have three bombs and a hot gun." Buick Lead replied.

"Nail 48, Olds is still here as well. We have two Mk 84 smart bombs a piece" The other F-4 leader was feeling left out.

"Copy that Olds. Standby." Trask came back and rolled up on a wing so he could watch the A-7 attack. They managed to get one of the gunboats, but the other one was savvy and he started weaving and pouring the power to it when he detected the threat. He came through unscathed and was now about two barges back from the Alpha barge. "Boxcar, you got one of them, but the other has moved up abeam of the second to last barge. Cleared in hot guns."

"Boxcar roger. Boxcar, one pass each. Use it all up! Nail, after this pass we are bingo fuel and headed for the ship." The leader passed on.

"Copy that. Good shootin' so far." Pete said and he rolled up to watch their strafe run.

As the third A-7 made his turn over the shore at about five hundred feet, another shoulder fired missile came up. Number four of the flight saw it first. "Boxcar three break right. Missile at your six." The A-7 broke off his run and made a hard right turn to increase the angle and reduce his heat signature for the missile. It worked and the missile went ballistic. Boxcar Four adjusted his run and strafed the jungle where he thought the missile had come from.

The lead two A-7s were able to at least disable the gunboat and the four of them headed south to return to the Enterprise.

"Ok, Buick, did you see where that shot came from?" Pete asked the F-4 driver. He didn't get a good tally himself. He was watching the gunboat attack.

"Negative Nail. All I saw was the smoke trail. Came from the north side though." Buick Lead answered.

The convoy was still taking fire from the north shore and now they were shooting at the whole convoy. It was obvious they wanted to stop its progress north.

"Ok, Buick, let's lay your bombs down along the shore where the fire is coming from. Nail 48's in for a mark." Pete rolled in again and put two rockets about 200 yards apart. "Between my marks and a little longer north, Buick."

"Roger that. Buick's in." The leader came back and the four of them spread their remaining 500 pounders along a swath about 300 yards long on the shore. In the pull off, Number four's back seater saw a missile flash and a smoke trail tracking. He directed his pilot to break hard and came up on the radio. "Buick Four's breaking left, missile away." He too was able to put enough angle on the missile and had pulled his power out of afterburner to reduce the heat signature. The missile exploded harmlessly about 200 yards behind them.

"Buick, I got a tally on that one." Pete said. "On me, guns a blazin'" He rolled into a deep dive and pickled off two quick Willie Petes. He rolled up on a wing and said. "Hit my smoke." Three of the F-4s emptied their 20 mm guns on the area where Trask's smoke was and peeled off for a join up. Number Four was still floundering, and simply turned to rejoin his formation heading home - probably ready for a change of underwear.

Chapter Twenty Nine

THE MEKONG

I had arrived on the scene about 0645 and witnessed the proceedings from about 10,000 feet and offset out of the way. I was monitoring some significant activity up river and on the north shore. It appeared to be some sort of port with several boats tied up. A closer inspection with the binoculars showed that three of them were gunboats. But it was two of the others that got my attention. They were speedy little power boats, no more than 15-16 feet long and outfitted with good size outboard engines. They had just shoved off from the pier and were headed toward the lead barges of the convoy. Since they weren't a threat to our guys I didn't think much about it. Big mistake.

After Buick flight left the fight I called to Pete. "Nail 48, Nail 32s on station and ready anytime."

"Roger that 32, I've been eating up the gas and need to head to the house. You've got it. You have Olds, flight of 4 F-4s with smart bombs, and Pepper, flight of 4 A-7s just pulling into orbit. Break, Break. Pepper, say again your load." Pete called to the A-7s.

"Roger Nails, Pepper's got CBU and a hot gun."

"Nail 32 roger. 48 I'm at your 8 o'clock two miles."

"Roger, Nail 32. Shake the stick. You've got it. You also have Shogun and Zorro, two F-4s each for air cover." Pete said as he headed northwest.

I had a Weapons Systems Officer (WSO) in my back seat and a Pave Spot pod under the belly. Olds flight's two thousand pound smart bombs were meant for our use.

The shelling was continuing from the shore, and I decided to put the A-7s in first. Their cluster bombs would be much more effective on troops in the open and the small arms fire.

"Pepper, let's lay your CBU down along the north shore there to see if we can keep their heads down. Follow my smoke." I called to the A-7s as I rolled in with about a 30 degree dive and put one smoke short and one long. "Pepper string 'em out between my smokes and a little longer. Cleared multiple passes, but save one can for me later." I cleared the pilot to lead his charges around in a wheel and they made three passes each with one CBU canister on each pass.

"Copy that Nail. Pepper's in from the east."

All of a sudden the lead barge came to a stop. I guess it wasn't "all of a sudden." Those things don't stop on a dime, but the tugs pushing the first two barges had stopped pushing. I looked through the glasses and sure enough, the power boats I had seen earlier were tied up to the two lead tugs and there were soldiers on the decks of the tugs.

"Alpha, looks like your barges are stopping. You might want to steer around them if you can." I was worried that if the Alpha barge was too close to the tug ahead of them they wouldn't be able to maneuver around it when it stopped.

"Copy that Nail. You think it's a highjacking?" Master Chief Johnson asked.

"Could be. Two fast boats came out from a marina like affair just up to your north a mile or so. They're tied up to the lead tugs now and there are gomers with guns on board the tugs." I replied.

"Well, I'm not about to stop this thing." Johnson declared. "We might be a convoy of one, but we're heading on."

About that time the dam burst. The convoy was taking fire from both shores. Fortunately the river was over a mile wide and the small arms wasn't effective. However, the gooks had come up with some sort of artillery. I knew the North Vietnamese had a lot of Soviet equipment, including tanks, mobile rocket launchers, and heavy artillery. They weren't very accurate, but they were splashing up the waters around the Alpha barge.

In the meanwhile, the gunboats in the port where the power boats came from were launching. I quickly told my WSO to green up the Pave Spot pod.

"Olds. We've got three gunboats getting ready to leave port on the north shore, about a mile ahead of the convoy. We're armed up with Pave Spot. Follow me in one at a time. Let's see if we can light 'em up." I directed the F-4s with the smart bombs. I rolled in and lofted a rocket out near the boats, but mainly pointed that way so my WSO could lock on with the laser.

"Olds one copies. Got your smoke and the boats. Which one are you lazing?"

"The closest, most southern one." I said as I made a lazy turn to the left while the WSO kept the laser highlighting the gunboat.

The F-4 rolled into about a twenty five degree dive, put his pipper on the boat and released his bomb. The Mk 84 glommed onto the laser beam and rode it right on down to the target. Two thousand pounds of serious destruction turned the gunboat into a smoking hulk. I rolled off onto the right wing and pointed at the second boat, which was doing about 10 knots away from his smoking buddy.

"Olds two I'm highlighting the runner." I said to the F-4 wingman. "He's the one further out in the river."

"Olds Two copies, in hot." Unfortunately the gunboat captain was a wily old coyote. He weaved and jinked, and although we were able to keep the laser on him, the bomb couldn't make the corrections." He missed.

The third boat had made a fatal mistake. He was trying to pick up his comrades from the first boat out of the water. I was at a pretty low altitude by now, but we were able to lock on with the laser and I started a climbing left hand turn so the WSO could keep it illuminated. "Olds Three, the third boat's the charm. We've got him illuminated but it's a pretty shallow graze angle. Cleared in hot."

"Olds Three copy Nail." The pilot said. "I'm in from your 10 o'clock, passing close aboard to capture your beam." He basically needed to put his bomb in a basket formed by our laser beam, so he came in close to do it." I got a face full of F-4 as he pulled off the delivery. "That was close!" I said to my WSO. The gunboat went up with a huge fireball.

By now two more F-4 flights and one more set of A-7s had checked in. I put the CBU loaded bombers up and down the shore line to basically keep the gomers' heads down, and used the boys with 500 pounders on point targets - gun emplacements, vehicles, and artillery pieces. I was designating targets with the laser when I got a call from Big Shot, the ABCCC C-130. He had been monitoring the radio and communicated with Colonel Parsons back in Ubon.

"Nail 32, Big Shot. Word from home base is to unload on those two lead tugs to hopefully get the remaining convoy back underway." That made sense I guess. If the tugs were no longer threatened or under guard, maybe they could get moving again and make it to Phnom Penh with their precious cargo.

"Roger that Big Shot. Break, Break! Olds, this oughta be ducks on the pond. Target is the two lead tugs. I'm in on the second tug, cleared hot." I rolled in and put a smoke right behind the transom of the second tug, and rolled off to an easy turn while my WSO burned his laser.

"Olds one, copies. In from your 5 o'clock Nail, Two to follow." As soon as the first bomb went off I saw it was a direct hit and started to roll back in on the lead tug. We illuminated it and I started a climbing left turn. "Olds Three and Four you're cleared hot on the first tug."

"Olds Three's in hot." He responded and that tug was toast as well. About that time we had company.

"Nail 32, Shogun. We have traffic inbound about 10 miles north at twenty thousand. Looks like four of them. Shogun's engaged on the lead pair. Zorro, you got the trailers." The air to air boys were on their own. I wasn't about to get into their business. Hopefully they would be able to keep the bad guys out of our fight.

"Roger that Shogun. Happy hunting. Keep us informed." I said.

"Alpha, Nail 32." I hailed the SEAL team chief. "Looks like we took care of the lead tugs. Anything you think you can do to get the convoy moving again? Our Mother hen wants us to get as many of them to Phnom Penh as possible."

"We'll see what we can do Nail, if you can keep the gomers' heads in the sand we'll pay the tug captains a visit." Johnson replied.

Johnson dispatched two of his Zodiacs, each with three SEALs, and one with Mr. Minh on board, the other with the special forces truck driver who spoke Vietnamese. They hop scotched their way from tug boat to tugboat to "convince" the captains that it would be much better for their health if they kept going. All but one of the captains agreed. They had been on this convoy many times before, and until last week they hadn't had too much trouble from ashore. But the hijacking and destruction of the convoy last week had them all running scared. Not nearly as scared as they were of these big, ugly creatures in their black rubber boats pointing guns at them. The one captain refused to go on. The SEAL radioed back to Johnson for instructions.

"Shoot the son of a bitch, and put someone else at the helm." Johnson ordered. "One of his crew, maybe?"

"They're all scared shitless boss. No one wants to step up." The SEAL said.

"Ok. Shoot the captain anyway. Then rig that barge and the lead two that are floundering about up there without any guidance. Rig 'em to blow on command. Then drive that tug over to our position. We'll hook him up here and see if we can get some more speed out of this heap." Johnson was thinking ahead and he let me know what he was doing as well.

The main convoy started north again. By then the Alpha barge was in the lead, and with another tug working hard, it could easily outrun the rest. That wasn't the plan though, so Johnson had the tugs hang back so they could maintain convoy integrity.

Meanwhile, Shogun and Zorro each took a flight of what turned out to be MIG 19s. Shogun lead remembered what the ROE was supposed to be, so since they weren't being fired upon yet, he led is wingman in a swooping dive down to the MIGs' 6 o'clock and just sat there. The MIG 19 has no radar to speak of so they never even knew the F-4s were there. The rear element of MIGs however, saw the conversion unfold in front of them and warned their comrades up front, not knowing though, that they had their own playmates to deal with. Zorro converted form below and settled in about a mile behind the rear MIGs.

The lead MIGs reacted to the call from their comrades and made a hard left turn, staying together and cranking their necks to pick up the F-4s. At this point Shogun lead rightfully decided that what was an offensive position was about to decidedly turn defensive. The MIG 19 could out turn an F-4 and Shogun did not want to get into slow turning knife fight. He let 'em fly.

"Shogun One is Fox 2, Fox 2, Shogun Two clear to fire." An Aim 9 heat seeking missile came off Shogun One and found its target, the lead MIG 19's tailpipe. Shogun Two's missile missed. The MIG got too much of a turn in and had rolled back his power to decrease the heat. The MIG kept up his turn and basically met the F-4 180 degrees out, about 500 feet abeam. He continued his turn to try and convert to the Phantom's six o'clock. In the meantime, Shogun One had taken his steed straight up, stood it on it's end, and as the airspeed deteriorated quickly, stepped on the rudder and was able to get behind the MIG's three-nine line. He kept the nose down with full afterburner cooking and cut across the circle to achieve a guns tracking solution on the MIG. The MIG driver never saw it coming. He was so intent on getting to the F-4 wingman he never even looked back to see the big white belly of the leader's jet as Shogun slid into position. "BRRRRRTT!" the 20 mm canon belched from Shogun One and the bullets ripped a string across the lower wing and through the cockpit. The MIG driver died in an instant - never knew what hit him.

The trailing pair of MIG 19s saw this all unfolding in front of them and tried to maneuver to sneak up on Shogun flight. Zorro, watched and closed up to about 1500 feet in trail with Zorro one tracking the left MIG, Two the right. The growl of the heat seeker itching to fly was loud. "Shogun, Zorro. Continue your heading. Two more at your six, but two miles out. We got 'em"

"Shogun One copies, but don't wait too long." The F-4 pilot leading the parade said. "I feel the hair on the back …."

"Zorro, Fox 2, Fox 2." Two Aim 9s flew and both hit their marks dead on. There were two more MIG drivers in the silk, parachuting to hopefully a safe landing.

"Nail 32, Shogun and Zorro are back on CAP (combat air patrol), four dead bogeys." Shogun announced.

"Copy that Shogun." I said. "Likely more to follow."

"Roger that, and we have reinforcements on the way." Shogun said.

I spent the remainder of my time on the scene putting flight after flight in on the shore batteries that were trying to shell the convoy. The Mekong was at least a mile wide along this stretch, so the accuracy of the shelling was minimal. Every once in a while another gunboat would venture out to try and intercept the convoy, but Master Chief Johnson had his SEALs in their Zodiacs busy as well. Although they lacked the firepower of the gunboats, they were low to the water and fast. Twice the SEALs managed to maneuver up to inside the range of the gunboat's guns and using their own personal weapons, laid waste to the entire crews. The SEALs were able to board one of the gunboats and after tossing its crew overboard, brought it back to the Alpha barge. From there on up river, between our close air support and the SEALs self defenses, we were able to keep the gunboats at bay.

I was monitoring the three floundering barges that originally led the convoy. A new tug appeared and two of the fast power boats. They managed to hook up the tug to the lead barge and had a line to the trailing barge, very slowly moving them off toward the shore. I called the Master Chief. "Alpha, not sure what you have in store for those rogue barges, but now might be the time. They have a little help trying to get them to shore."

"Hey, roger that Nail. Hang on to your hat." I watched as Johnson set off a detonation string that blew the two barges to smithereens. It was quite a fireworks display. "Take that Davey Jones." I said.

I handed the scene over to Lt. Colonel Majors at about 0845. For the rest of the morning and into the afternoon the fight went on with FAC guided close air support along the shoreline, periodic anti aircraft fire and one or two more MIG intrusions.

Just south of the Cambodian line lies the city of Hong Ngu on the Mekong. It is a medium size South Vietnamese city with several marina like structures and piers on the river. There were also several barges tied up along the bank. It was a target rich environment and we wished the ROE would allow us to go on the offensive. There were just too many places for the enemy to hide and boats for them to use. To make matters worse, the river narrowed to about 1/2 mile as it passed through town.

Chapter Thirty

HONG NGU, SOUTH VIETNAM

Just south of Hong Ngu a major highway runs for about 5 miles on a ridge line overlooking the river from the east. Gomers were able to set up on the road and lob mortar and artillery shells down on the convoy. The good news though (bad news for the bad guys), is that sitting in the middle of the road they were easy targets. We were able to sit back and watch as the F-4s and A-7s had a field day spreading cluster bombs and strafing the highway. Two of the barges took direct hits though and they had to be pushed out of the way. Their tugs then caught up to the remaining barges and doubled up for more speed. By the time the convoy approached Hong Ngu it was down to nine barges, being pushed by 11 tugs.

From the FAC viewpoint from above, Hong Ngu looked to be a hornets' nest of activity. There were several artillery sights, mortar set ups, and more gunboats. Master Chief Johnson made an executive decision. The convoy was about an hour out of Hong Ngu and it was getting close to sundown. He called a halt to the convoy. They basically treaded water with the tugs simply pushing against the current to keep the barges straight and in position.

Johnson decided going through Hong Ngu at night, blacked out would be more prudent. Turns out he was right on. The last Nail FAC turned the war over to Spectre 02 at 1915 hours.

At that time there were still fighters in orbit with CBU and Mk 82s, but most of them were running out of fuel. The down time while the convoy sat idle ate up their on-scene time. Major Dave Hilton, the last FAC on scene decided to soften up Hong Ngu as much as they could and put the fighters in on the shore batteries in the city ahead of the convoy. Unbelievably, that decision got him in a lot of hot water later. It seems the desk jockeys back in D.C. who were monitoring the ongoing battle for the Administration, decided that since the convoy wasn't there yet and the shore batteries were not firing at it, that Hilton stretched the definition of defensive only operations. It probably wouldn't have mattered to a hill of beans if there hadn't been a major problem.

Edsel flight of four F-4s with CBU made several passes over the marinas and piers and shoreline on the north side of the city. They did some substantial damage too. But on their fourth pass a shoulder fired missile came up out of nowhere and nailed the number two Edsel. The missile went off under the fuselage and took out the right engine. The left one was still operating, but not at full power. The pilot had zoomed to altitude as soon as he was hit, trading airspeed for altitude. He immediately headed south toward the Sea of Thailand. His flight leader went with him and directed the other two Edsels to return to base.

Turns out Edsel Lead was the 497th squadron commander. Two was a new lieutenant on just his fifth mission in country. "Ok Two, keep her heading south." The calm Lt. Colonel said. "See if you can maintain about 250 knots, I'm coming up under you to check it out. You boys stow your gear and get ready to punch, but let's see what we've got first."

"Two copies. Two fifty knots. Lead, I've got a dim, flickering fire light on the left engine and it looks like we've lost hydraulics." The lieutenant was not so calm.

"Copy that. Take it easy. Break. Break, Big Shot, we're heading out towards the water. Roust the rescue boys. We'll likely have a crew down just north of the coast." The leader said to the ABCCC C-130.

"Edsel, this is Houston. We're four A-7s inbound from the south. Anything we can do to help?" A flight of Navy guys had launched off the Enterprise and was arriving on scene.

"Roger Houston," the commander said. "I'm going to try something I've heard about but always thought was stupid. I might need you to cap where we go down. I'm hoping to get us out to sea and as close to the Enterprise as possible." Now everybody airborne was really confused. Nobody had a clue what the Colonel was up to, but it soon became apparent.

The two ship was descending through 6000 feet when Edsel One commanded. "Two, lower your tail hook."

"Say again sir?" The wingy asked.

"Lower your hook. I'm going to push you out to sea." Major Hilton later told me when he heard this he about croaked. He thought the Lt. Colonel had lost his mind. I think everyone airborne up there at that time thought the same thing. But as the leader later said in his debriefings, he didn't want the aircrew to go down in South Vietnamese territory, and making it up north to Cambodia was just about as far as to out to sea. At least out at sea they had a chance of being rescued by good guys. The problem was though, that by pulling off this feat, he also was dooming his own jet. He would not have enough fuel later to get to a runway anywhere. Although he was later awarded a Silver Star for his actions, he was also fired for losing a perfectly good F-4.

The lieutenant lowered his tail hook and set up a speed of 250 knots. He was getting only minimum thrust out of the left engine and was losing altitude at about 500 feet per minute. His flight lead snuggled in close trail behind him and inched up so that the foot of the tail hook was right in front of him in the windscreen. He slowly inched up and contacted the hook at the base of the windscreen, then slowly increased his power. It was just like air refueling, basically flying a close trail formation, only this time the "boom" wouldn't be giving him any gas. He was able to stop the descent, but not climb any. He was burning a lot of fuel as well, and the Lieutenant noticed he was losing fuel quickly. It was obvious as the boss said, "It's streaming out from your right wing route. Just hang in there."

In the meantime, the Houston flight lead in the A-7s had called back to the Enterprise and the Admiral of the Fleet ordered the submarine Virginia to beat feet to the north as quickly as possible.

The two F-4s crossed the coast at 5000 feet in a slight descent. The wingman's left engine sputtered and then just quit.

"Boss, it just got real quiet in here." The lieutenant tried to sound calm.

"Ok, copy that. At three thousand feet I'm going to back out from under and up to your wing. When I say so, you guys eject. Copy?"

"Yyyes sir."

Passing 3000 feet Edsel Lead backed down, away from the hook and then quickly up to the right side about 100 feet out. "Ok boys, Take a hike. Eject. Eject." He said. "Boom, boom!" The canopy blew to pieces and the ejection seats fired up about 100 feet. Both crew members got a good chute and Edsel Lead set up an orbit around them as they settled into the water.

"Houston, this is Edsel. What frequency is your carrier on. I think I'll get in close to her before I go swimming."

"Roger that Edsel. We're on 324.6. The submarine Virginia is just now braking the waves. She's about two miles off at your 10 o'clock. I can hang around here until they get your boys aboard." The A-7 pilot said.

"Thanks, but if it's all the same to you, I think I'll stick around a little bit longer too." The Colonel said. The locator beacons of the downed crew went off and the pilots airborne watched as the two downed crewmen crawled into their life rafts. The WSO came up on Guard frequency.

"This is Edsel Two Bravo on guard. Anybody read me?" The back seater broadcast.

"Roger that Bravo, Edsel Lead here. How's your buddy? Come up channel Alpha." He directed the survivors to change their radio channel to get off the guard emergency frequency. You never knew who might be listening there.

"Edsel Two Bravo's up" The WSO said on the new radio frequency.

"Lead's up."

"Houston's up." The Navy pilot came up the same frequency to see if he could help. "The Virginia has surfaced and it looks like they are manning a Zodiac to come get your boys Edsel."

"Copy that. Bravo, how's your front seater? Can you get to him?" The leader asked the survivor. He could see both men in their life raft, but they had not heard from the pilot.

"I think he's ok sir." The WSO said. "He climbed into his raft, but he's not moving much." He tried to paddle his raft over closer to his pilot.

The two man crew from the Virginia showed up in their Zodiac and pulled both swimmers into their raft, and headed back to the sub. The pilot finally came up on the WSO's radio. "Edsel Lead, this is Two. Thanks for the push sir, but what are you going to do sir?"

"Well, I'm a bit skosh on gas, but I think I'll get closer to the Enterprise before we hit the silk. You ok?" The flight lead asked.

"Roger. Back's pretty sore. You know sir, I had a premonition about this mission when I saw the call sign they gave us. If I'm not mistaken, I think the Edsel was one of Ford's disaster cars."

"Yeah, you're right. I actually owned one back when I was a lieutenant. It wasn't a bad car, but I did manage to wreck it too." The squadron commander said. "You boys enjoy the Navy hospitality, I'm heading for the mother ship."

A few minutes later Edsel Lead came up on the Enterprise frequency. "Enterprise, this is Edsel. I'm five miles north at 3000 feet, looking for a wet landing."

"Roger Edsel, This is Captain Martin, Edsel's CAG. You sure you don't want to try to land that thing?" He was about half joking. The Navy certainly had F-4s in their inventory, but the landing gear were beefed up to take the hard landing that is required to squat on the deck and grab the cable. Chances are the Air Force jet would crump on collapsed wheels and could easily slide off the deck.

"It's tempting CAG," Edsel said, "But I never thought you guys were sane in the first place, landing on a pitching carrier deck. I think I'll just dump this thing in the water nearby."

"Copy that. We have two boats in the water off our port side." CAG advised. "Suggest you line up parallel the deck about 1/2 mile out and they'll scoop you up almost before you get your feet wet."

The Lt. Colonel did just that. He lined his jet up beside the carrier, descended to 2000 feet and slowed to 250 knots. Then he commanded his WSO to bail out first. As soon as he saw a good chute he pulled the handles himself for a quiet ride to the water.

That night things were a little somber around the Ubon Officer's Club. Half the folks were lamenting the loss of two aircraft and the harrowing ordeal their squadron commander and his flight had been through, while the other half rejoiced at the "save" their boss had pulled off with his little escapade.

In the meantime, back at the ranch called Hong Ngu, Dave Hilton put the rest of the flights airborne on the city and then turned the babysitting over to Spectre 02.

Chapter Thirty One

WASHINGTON D.C.

President Gatewater was down in the dumps. Gary Larson had been a good friend. They had been high school buddies and Gary had been his campaign manager both for the Presidential run, and when Gatewater ran for Senator in California. He'd just got off the phone talking to Gary's mother. Larson was divorced with no kids, and the divorce was pretty ugly, the President remembered. Although he put in a call to the ex-wife, he didn't expect her to want to talk to him.

The Security Council was assembled in the Situation Room of the White House. They had just been updated on Dragon Savior and the President put in a call to the

Enterprise and Lt. Colonel Jim Davis, Edsel Lead. "Glad to hear you're ok Colonel." The President said. "I guess I wish we were talking under different circumstance though. As you might imagine, there are several opinions about what you did around here and in the Pentagon."

"I understand sir. My immediate concern was for my wingman. I did not want them to go down in South Vietnam, or even Cambodia for that matter." Davis said. "I guess I didn't realize how much of my own fuel it was going to take to push him out to sea. But I have thought about it a lot, and I think I would do the same thing again. Sorry about that Mr. President."

"No need to be sorry," Gatewater said. "As it turns out, the civilians in this room think you're a real hero because we don't have to explain to Vietnam and the world what we were doing if we had dumped an airplane in one of their rice paddies. I think it's your military bosses you have to worry about." The President signed off and turned to his advisors for more updates.

"Mr. President, I agree to what you said about us not having to explain away an air crash in the country," if was SECSTATE Crittendon, but I have a problem with the bombing that flight and others were doing miles away from the convoy where there was no threat."

"Now wait a minute Henry," Admiral McLean waded in. "The convoy had taken an hour or so off to wait until dark and the Forward Air Controller on site made a good decision to soften up the city of Hong Ngu while they had a chance. Besides, obviously there was a threat. That missile that shot down the F-4 came from the city of Hong Ngu."

"OK gentlemen, let's let this one rest a while." The President said. "Bring me up to speed. It seems to me like there is a real hornets' nest out there. What do you give our chances of pulling this thing off?"

There was also a discussion about the shoot-down of four Vietnamese MIGs that weren't really threatening the convoy. General Robert Black, Air Force Chief of Staff took on this one. "Gentlemen, understand this. Those MIGs WERE a threat. If they hadn't been, they would have turned tail and run once they realized they were in our sights. Instead, they attempted to gain a threatening advantage. Shooting them down has obviously deterred any further air activity since. There have been three more formations of Vietnamese fighters detected and all turned around and ran once they saw that they were targeted. As far as the Air Force is concerned, the pilots of Shogun and Zorro flights are heroes.

"That may be General Black," the Secretary of Defense jumped in. "But we specifically passed on the Rules of Engagement that said we were not to fire unless fired upon. Has someone down the chain modified that ROE?"

General Curtis LeCroix, PACAF Commander was on the speaker phone. "Yes sir, that would be me, General Curtis Lecroix. I passed on your version of the ROE to the operational commander, and after hearing his reaction, I modified them to basically shoot first at any enemy aircraft that could be a threat to Dragon Savior." He let it all hang out there. "I will reiterate that modification to the war fighters, and sir, when this operation is over, you'll have my letter of resignation on your desk." The room was very quiet for several pregnant seconds. Finally the President spoke up and said, "Not so fast General. Let's get the job done here, and since you're closer to the fight than we are, we'll do it your way. We can sort out the 'Who Said What' later."

The team briefed the President on the status of the operation and had varying opinions on the outlook for success. It was decided that the man on the scene, Master Chief Johnson, was doing the best he could with what he's got. They also discussed the fact that with one truck left on the beach and one destroyed on the barge, they would not have enough transportation to the airport for the whole embassy staff. Director Butler was tasked to get in touch with his Chief of Station (acting ambassador) and have her commandeer some more wheels.

The Security Team briefly discussed the latest story in the Post by Bob Woodall and the TV coverage by Justine Miller. The President put a squash on any reaction at this time, directing his Press Secretary to say that the White House is mourning the loss of its Chief of Staff, and would have nothing to say about an ongoing operation. "In the meantime though," Gatewater said, "Neither Woodall nor his 'cupie-doll' will be welcome in the White House Press Room."

With that, the meeting broke up and the President went out to interview the Deputy Chief of Staff for the principle job.

Chapter Thirty Two

HONG NGU, SOUTH VIETNAM

Friday night turned out to be just as intense as we thought. As soon as he found out that Master Chief Johnson was waiting until dark to pass through Hong Ngu, Colonel Parsons tasked another AC-130 so that there were two gunships overhead. It also had started to rain though, and the gunships couldn't help much if they were in the weather up top. The rain helped to lessen the threat a little. At least that was the expectation. It seems though that a little rain doesn't hinder Vietnamese soldiers or the Viet Cong. They were still out in force trying to zero in on the barges as they came though.

The dark and the weather also helped to deter any air threat. The North Vietnamese Air Force never flew much at night anyway. Their fighters were almost all "day VFR," meaning they flew only during the day and not in the weather. It also meant they had to see their targets to shoot. Only the MIG-21 had any radar at all, and it was very limited. So for that reason, Parsons fragged four two ships of F-4 night bombers from the Udorn squadron. They were staggered at 30 minute intervals to deconflict overhead and also to stretch out the available support.

Johnson waited until almost 2100 hours to crank up the convoy, and then he doubled up the tugs on the first two barges. After determining what the barges were carrying, he moved the ones with food and medical supplies up front, so that the Alpha barge plus one more could make a "run for it," as much as a barge can run. The plan was to get through the main threat at Hong Ngu, and then slow down further north as they crossed into Cambodia to let the slower barges catch up. The plan was also to run completely lights out. Fortunately with the rainstorms, the moon was hidden, so the barges were tougher to see, thus tougher to attack. At least that was the plan. Johnson had also planted a SEAL on each of the first seven boats behind him. That left two healthy ones with him on the Alpha barge, plus the special forces guys.

As they approached the city, the Vietnamese and Viet Cong had been able to regenerate their forces from the bombing runs Dave Hilton had put in on them at the end of his time on station. Although they couldn't be real accurate with their mortars, the river had narrowed significantly, the gooks were able to lob their rounds out there going for the "golden BB." It worked too. All of the barges took some hits, and two were sunk or disabled.

The Spectres came down through the clouds and orbited around 1500 - 2000 feet, maintaining a circular pattern around the city and river, flying at opposite sides of the circle to keep the fire constant. They were hampered though by graze angle and visibility, and couldn't see where all the threats were. They also put themselves in harms way from any anti-aircraft fire and missiles. They basically supported each other. If a missile or AAA came up under one of them, the other one across the river would bring the wrath of howitzer or cannon to bare. The AC-130s also had flare dispensers, so that if they did see a missile shot, usually it was one of the gunners who spotted it, and he could punch out a couple flares to hopefully disrupt the missile's flight path.

"Spectre 01, 02, this is Dodge Flight inbound with two F-4s and CBU. Need any help?" The first flight from Udorn announced.

"Roger Dodger, this is Spectre 01, we are under the weather orbiting the city at low altitude." The gun shipper replied. "If you can come down below the weather we could use your load on either or both shorelines. Multiple mortar and artillery sites there."

"Copy that Spectre. We'll see what we can do." The F-4 flight lead said.

Dodge Flight split up, with Dodge Two dropping to a mile in trail of his leader and with his radar locked on. "Two, I'm going to make an easy descent through the weather to 2000 feet on a heading of 180. Follow me down in trail and hopefully we'll break out underneath."

"Two copies." Fortunately this part of Vietnam is very flat and not much above sea level. The highest hills in the area were no more that 400 feet in elevation. As long as the pilots didn't get spacial disorientation, maintained a slow but steady descent, and observed a strict minimum altitude, they would be ok.

Spacial disorientation is a real problem in piloting. Especially in single seat cockpits, it is not unusual for the seat of the pants to tell the pilot he was in one attitude, when in fact he was in another. It was especially dangerous when using slow and shallow bank turns. If the pilot wasn't watching and believing his instruments, his internal attitude indicator could tell him he was straight and level, when in fact he was in a banked turn and losing altitude. The record of night flying accidents is full of reports that the pilot got himself into a position or altitude he couldn't recover from, and bought the farm. The problem often had a bit to do with ego and the fact the pilot would swear the instruments in the cockpit were wrong, wouldn't believe them, and tried to recover by his own seat of the pants.

Fortunately the F-4 is a two seat aircraft. At night or in the weather most pilots made sure their back seaters were glued to the instruments, and if necessary, could read off the attitude, altitude, airspeed, whatever needed, to keep the pilot's head on straight. That was the case tonight with Dodge Two. He got a bit sideways in the descent following his leader, and the WSO had to actually take the stick to get them back to wings level flight. It worked and they came out of the weather a mile behind and a little offset the leader at 1500 feet.

"Dodge Two's clear, visual One." The pilot radioed rather meekly.

"Roger that. We'll keep it not lower than 1500 feet and follow me back to the north." The Leader directed. "Break, break. Spectre, Dodge is five miles south of the city at 1500 feet. No visual on you."

"Copy that, Dodge. Spectre One is in a left turn about 9 o'clock to the city if we call the river a north-south run. Spectre Two is about 2 o'clock on the other side. One is firing a flare now." The pilot told his gunner to pop a flare.

"Ok, visual your flare and radar contact on you. How would you like your gomer cooked?" A little humor never hurts in a tense situation.

"Can you string them south to north along the east shore? If so, cleared hot. Spectre 01 will follow your run."

"Copy that. Dodge Two green 'em up, three singles, 100 foot spacing. Dodge One is in hot from the south"

The F-4s were on target, stringing 6 CBU canisters along a two mile stretch of the Hong Ngu shore line. The bomblets blew away soldiers, vehicles, buildings, boats, and whatever else was down there.

"Good show Dodge." Spectre One said. "Now can you do the other side?"

"Oh yeah! Standby. Two, I'm going to make a right 270 and sling the last three down the west shore." He had turned off the first run to the left and was too tight to simply roll in on a north-south run that close aboard. He maneuvered off to the north and then,

"Dodge is in north to south on the west shore."

"Cleared hot." The gunship pilot said.

"Spectre, that's it for Dodge. We're Winchester. Break, Break, Two I'm taking it up at 30 degrees of climb straight ahead, rejoin on top." He directed his wingman.

"Good copy Dodge, and good shootin'. Have a good trip home."

"Spectre, this is Fiat, flight of two F-4s, 10 east with CBU." The next flight lead announced.

"Fiat roger. Did you monitor Dodge down here?" The gun shipper was hoping to not have to repeat everything.

"Roger that Spectre. We're in a descent to below the weather now." Lead Fiat said.

"Copy Fiat. Same drill. String half your goodies down each side of town. Maybe move it a little long on each pass. Might as well let all the little buggers in on the fun down there. Let me know when you're on approach. We'll spring a flare."

Master Chief Johnson was listening to it all and he and his men were enjoying the fireworks on shore. The lead four barges had made it through half the city so far. It was quiet - too quiet, and Johnson wondered what he was missing.

What the SEALs were missing were three gunboats that launched off after the convoy passed. They were blacked out and moved only a little faster than the barges so as not to put out a wake the gunships could see. They came up very slowly on the trailing barge from the side so that the tug captain couldn't see them. Two soldiers jumped on board the barge and then made their way back to the stern. When they got there, one of them zeroed in with a sniper rifle on the tug helmsman in the bridge of the tug, and fired three rounds. The first two busted the thick windscreen on the bridge and the third round found its mark on the helmsman's forehead. The soldiers then jumped onto the tug and killed the rest of the crew. Then they brought the tug to a halt and let the barge drift.

The two other gunboats moved forward to the next to last barge. Two crewmen did the same thing - jumped onboard the barge about halfway up ahead of the tug. There was a SEAL on board this one, and he noticed the barge behind him slowed and veered off to the side. He radioed Johnson on his hand held radio and about that time the windscreen of the tug exploded and a sniper round hit the captain who was at the helm. The SEAL reacted quickly and took up a position to defend the bridge of the tug. Two Vietnamese soldiers had jumped onto the tug and were running aft. The SEAL took out one of them, but the other one stopped coming and hid behind a lifeboat on the deck.

"Boss, Jake. I got company back here." The SEAL radioed his leader. "There's at least two of them and they shot the captain. I got one, but the other's got me in a stalemate." Jake ran into the bridge and saw that one of the crew had taken over from the captain at the helm. But he also saw that the tug had swung away from its barge, leaving the barge floundering.

"What are you doing?" Jake yelled at the helmsman. "Capture the barge." He said in hysterical english and pointed to the barge. The trouble was, the helmsman didn't understand calm english, let alone a raving lunatic wearing warpaint and pointing a gun at him. He simply let go of the helm and ran out of the bridge.

Jake took the helm and spun the wheel hard left to try and proceed up river. As he did a sniper's round pinged off the cabinet about two inches from his head. The soldier was out there and had the advantage.

"Jake, Alpha One. I'm sending you help. Zodiac heading your way. What's your status?" Johnson called.

"Looks like I'm large and in charge, but of what I don't know." The SEAL replied. "The helmsman took off, and I can't stay at the helm for incoming." He thought about it a minute and realized he couldn't go on like this. "I'm gonna tie this thing off and go hunting.'"

The SEAL used a line that was attached to a life buoy and tied the wheel to steer generally up river, then ducked down and exited the bridge opposite the side he last saw the sniper. He crawled forward to where he could see the area where he thought the gook was, but as luck would have it the little bastard had moved. Jake was hit in the right shoulder by an AK-47 round and he rolled off that way. He had held onto his rifle though, and swung around to lay three rounds into his oncoming assailant. The soldier went down in a heap. Jake looked around. It seemed all the crew had jumped overboard. He was wounded and alone on a tug being left behind. He made it back to the bridge and was able to man the helm and poured the power to the tug's engine. He headed up stream. He figured the barge they were pushing was a lost cause. She was already laying broadside in the river and sliding downstream.

The SEALs in the Zodiac made it back to their comrade's tug and one of them climbed aboard to help. He applied a temporary dressing to Jake's wound and then took the helm. The Zodiac stayed nearby. There were still three gunboats out here somewhere with Vietnamese or Viet Cong soldiers on board.

"Spectre, this is Alpha, we got some visitors down here." Johnson called the gunship.

"Copy that Alpha. Looks like two of your barges are taking a walk. What's up?"

"At least two, maybe more gunships snuck up from the rear and they're trying to pick the barges off one by one." The Master Chief said. "They got the last one and I had a man on the next to last one. They got into a gun fight. The good guys won, but the barge is gone. Tug's coming forward. Check for the gunboats next to the barges." About that time the SEAL on board the third barge came up on the handheld.

"Alpha One, this is Six. Two gunboats, one on each side just passed us and are heading up along side the barge."

"Copy, Standby. I'm calling for help." Johnson passed on the information to Spectre 01 and the gunship altered his flightpath to monitor the situation.

"Spectre 02, this is One. You maintain the orbit and control the bombers. One's going to help out the convoy."

"Spectre Two copies." Pontiac and Plymouth flights had checked in with the same CBU and the plan was to use them like their predecessors, to lay waste to the riversides of Hong Ngu.

The big AC-130 rumbled across the tail end of the convoy at about five hundred feet. They could see the two gunboats beside the barge that was now last in line. Soldiers were jumping onto the barge. The Spectre pilot maneuvered his big steed to roll up on the left wing while crossing behind the barge. The gunners inside highlighted the port side gunboat with the heat seeking target finder of the 105 mm howitzer, locked on and fired away. "Whumpf!" The big gun belched and the gunship seemed to moved sideways 50 feet in the air from the recoil as the gunboat disintegrated. Immediately the gunner manning the 40 mm canons opened up on the starboard side gunboat and quick as a wink there were two smoking hulls in the water.

There were still gomers on foot on the barge heading back toward the tug. The SEAL on board positioned himself in the prone position on the roof of the bridge and had a good view of the three bad guys heading his way. At the same time, the Zodiac with the rescued SEAL in it had come forward and from a vantage point off to the side, had a tally on the three apaches as well. SEALs all get a lot of small arms and sniper training in their business and it showed tonight. The SEAL on the barge made cadavers out of two of the Vietnamese, while his buddy on the Zodiac wasted the other one. What no one had noticed however, was where was the other gunboat?

She was at 7 o'clock to the last barge about 500 feet out. As the AC-130 flew over head on the next pass one of the crewmen on the gunboat let loose with a shoulder fired missile at the big airship. The pilot was looking down that direction and saw the flash the same time his gunner did in the rear. The plot rolled hard the opposite direction and the gunner punched off about four flares. They almost made it. The missile went off under the left wing and blew shrapnel through the left outboard engine. It caught fire and the crew got all kinds of red lights in the cockpit, not to mention a sudden loss of thrust.

The pilot of Spectre 01 immediately rolled wings level and the copilot went through the engine fire emergency procedures, cutting all fuel feed to the engine.

"Spectre One's taken a hit. Working on three engines, climbing out." The gunship captain said rather loudly.

"Spectre Two copies. You gonna make it?" The wingman knew that the C-130 will fly just fine on three engines, but he didn't know if there had been other damage.

"Roger that. Everything else seems to be fine. See what you can do to help the convoy. There's still at least one gunboat down there." The wounded duck pilot said.

"Spectres, Pontiac. We're just south of the city at 2000 feet. I saw where your lucky shot came from." The leader of the third F-4 flight said.

"Copy Pontiac. If you can get him, go for it." Spectre Two's pilot said.

"Copy, Pontiac Two, I can't see a distinct target, but I'll lay a string down about where I think they are. You hang back about two miles and as my bomblets go off, maybe you'll have something to aim at. Pontiac One's in from the southeast." The F-4 pilot rolled into a shallow dive and released his string to start just short of where he thought he saw the missile fire from. Sure enough the flash of the bomblets highlighted the profile of the gunship just off left of the string of lights.

"Two copies, tally ho the target, in hot from the southeast." The wingman's CBU were right on target on a line that cut a diagonal across the gunboat from the starboard stern to the port bow. The boat blew about 30 feet in the air when its cache of ammo ignited.

By now the lead barges had cleared the city to the north. The incoming hadn't completely ceased, but the river had widened and the barges were able to trudge on up stream just out of range of at least the mortar fire. Johnson slowed the convoy down enough for the final barges with one tug a piece to catch up. He got Jake on board and the medics were taking care of him. He also stationed a Zodiac at the convoy's six o'clock to watch for sneaky petes.

Spectre 02 put Pontiac and Plymouth in upstream of the city and the convoy to try and be proactive as they steamed up to the Cambodian line. In the meantime, Spectre 01 made it above the weather and up to about 10,000 feet and limped on to Utapao. As soon as Colonel Parsons heard about the issue he scrambled a third gunship to go in and help and relieve Spectre 02.

Pete Trask arrived on station just north of the Cambodian border and took over from the Spectres about 0630. The Mekong gets very wide from this point almost to Phnom Penh, so the fire from the river banks was nil. The only big threat were gunboats and presumably any air attack the North Vietnamese might have. They had not been known to fly ground attack missions before, but Parsons was ready. He kept sending out flights of F-4s and A-7s with bombs and CBU, and he maintained a constant air cap (combat air patrol) of F-4s from Udorn.

Chapter Thirty Three

THE CAMBODIAN MEKONG

Trask's morning was comparatively benign. There were two gunboats that made approaches and several fishing boats that seemed a little too curious. Although the keepers of the ROE might not agree, he assumed they were all the bad guys and had the bombers lay waste to them if they got within half a mile of the convoy.

The stretch of the Mekong from the border to downtown Phnom Penh is 20 miles. Most of it is very wide. However, it narrows down at the town of Neak Loeung, and lo and behold, there was a bridge there. We had been briefed that the only bridge left over the river was north of Phnom Penh, and that the one here at Neak Leoung had been destroyed just a couple months ago during one of the Americans' last missions in country. Obviously the Vietnamese ingenuity and voracity had been at work, and they had rebuilt the bridge.

I took over from Pete at 0730. I saw the bridge on my way down there and made a low pass to see if it was inhabited and being fortified. Of course it was, so I put a call into the ABCCC. "Big Shot, Nail 32. We've got a surprise bridge down here about

5 miles ahead of the convoy. Do you have any smart bombers inbound?" I wanted to be able to blow down the bridge and one ton bombs are just what the doctor ordered.

"Standby, Nail 32." He was checking. In the meantime, I took over the scene and Pete headed back to the house.

"Nail 32, negative sir. But Control says they can scramble some." Big Shot came back. Obviously Colonel Parsons and his planners had believed their intel folks as well. There wasn't supposed to be a bridge here, so there was no need for smart bombs, unless we were to use them for gunboats. As it turns out, the later missions in the day were to be loaded with Pave Spot and smart bombs, expecting gunboats about where the convoy two weeks ago had been hijacked. It didn't matter. The convoy only had 5 miles to go to the bridge and I knew that Alpha One did not want to stop or slow down while the Air Force caught up to his needs.

"Negative, Big Shot. No time. We'll work with what we have." I came back.

Ford and Jaguar flights of F-4s both had six Mk 82, 500 pound bombs. The way I figured it, four five hundred pounders in the same hole as a 2000 pound bomb ought to be a push, right? Well, not exactly. The pilots had to be awfully accurate on every pass to hit the same hole several times in a row. But I figured 24 to 48 five hundred pounders on a hastily rebuilt, rickety bridge should do the trick. As it turned out, it didn't take all their bombs. Ford flight alone was able to destroy the bridge with well placed bombs, and the threat from it was neutralized.

We still had fire from the shore where the bridge used to stand and the river had narrowed down to strike range for the gook mortars. In addition, just north of Neak Leoung was a large reservoir called Krong Prey Veng, and its dam was basically the starboard shore of the Mekong for about a mile along. As we expected in our preflight planning, the Indians used that as a place to ambush the cowboys on the river. I spent the rest of my time on scene putting the Air Force and Navy bombers in on the dam, trying to keep the indians' heads down. Fortunately, after Ford and Jaguar flight, all the attackers had CBU. One thing we didn't want to do was blow a hole in the dam with 500 pounders and have it spill into the river. That would have not only played havoc with control of the convoy, but probably put half of Phnom Penh under water.

I passed the gavel to our Operations Officer after the dam and headed to Ubon. I understand things went rather smoothly from then on until the point on the river where the previous convoy had been attacked and hijacked. There we had some help. It seems the Cambodian army wanted to do what they could to help our progress along. They had moved out of Phnom Penh with tanks, light artillery, gun mounted jeeps, and troops, and set up along the river on the port side. The only threat then came from Starboard, and it appears the Vietnamese and Khmer Rouge put all they had left into the fight at that point - about 5 miles south of the city.

Chapter Thirty Four

PHNOM PENH

Liz Montgomery got the word from Director Butler that the inbound convoy needed some help. She first sat down with the Marines and tasked them to help out where they could. She deployed an indigenous contact she had in the city to keep a watch for the convoy and let her know as soon as they were spotted. Then she tasked the Marine Guards to do a little vehicle "shopping." Basically they went out into the city and commandeered (stole?) a large truck to use to replace the destroyed one that the Alpha team was bringing in. Liz then gathered the whole embassy staff together and told them to pack up their things in nothing more than a small duffle bag and to be ready to go early Sunday morning. Finally, she then set about burning and shredding every piece of documentation in the compound.

About 8 PM Liz got word from her contact at the pier that the convoy was in sight, but that there was still some residual fighting going on - mostly shelling from the opposite bank of the Mekong. She tasked 6 Marines to take the new truck and go out to the pier to meet the convoy. Then she had the embassy chef prepare the best meal he could for about 20 folks.

As the convoy approached the city, the shelling from the starboard side got pretty heavy. However, with answering fire from the Cambodian army on the port side, and the air support the FAC and the AC-130 were able to provide, the incoming was minimal.

The last FAC left the station at 1900 hours, turning it over to Spectre 03. There were still two flights of Navy A-7s and one four ship of Air Force F-4s to use, and the gunship directed them against the north shore of the river. There were a couple more missile shots at the aircraft, but none were successful. In addition, two MIG 21s came blowing through the mix right at sundown, but more a pathetic show of force than anything else. They were no threat to the convoy, but were of great concern to the AC-130. There were two flights of Udorn F-4s in the CAP, but no one saw the MIGs coming. They must have come in from tree top level and the F-4 radars simply did not pick them up. That could have been a disaster. As it was, the MIGs made a high angle pass at the gunship, and were trying to convert to the big airplane's six o'clock when they were finally detected by the nearest F-4 flight - Buick.

"Buick, Spectre, we've got a MIG trying to convert to our tail." The gunship pilot said. "Can you shoo him away?"

"Roger that, Spectre. Buick's got a tally." The F-4 leader said. "Keep your turn coming hard, we're across the circle from you." The F-4 pilot pointed his nose at the MIG and the WSO locked him up on radar. They fired an AIM 7 radar guided missile from close range, more to scare the MIG pilot than to hit him. The MIG was right at minimum range for the AIM 7, and in fact it missed.

However, the site of that big "telephone pole" of a missile coming at him was enough for the MIG driver. He dove for the deck, turned north, and beat a stealthy retreat. The F-4s chased him about 20 miles, but then decided to retreat back to their CAP.

By 20 hundred hours the convoy had landed. There were several piers to tie up to but Johnson wanted to keep the barges as close together as possible. He had the tug driver run the Alpha barge up onto the shore and then had the others tie on to each other. He then took inventory.

There were two trucks that came off the Alpha barge with minimum damage. The SEALs quickly loaded all their goodies onto the trucks and made ready to launch off toward the embassy. The Marines arrived with their truck and excess equipment was stowed aboard it. There were six other barges out of a starting armada of 12. The ones with the food and medical supplies were being off loaded right away. It was a mad house. The word spread through the city that there was food to be had at the wharf and it was a stampede to get to it. The Cambodian army took charge, but were a little too rough about it. They basically beat the crowds back and set up a distribution center that was skewed heavily toward feeding the army first.

Johnson and the Marines didn't like what they saw, but they decided that it was best to stay out of it. They loaded up their wounded. Five SEALs had taken hits plus the A-7 pilot, and one of the SEALs wounded in the original battle when they had first reached the barge had died. The SEALs used a body bag and brought him with them, and followed the Marines into the city. Before they left they turned their prisoners from the gunboats and barges that had been swimming over to the army. The Spectre gunship stayed aloft monitoring the truck convoy's progress and sure enough, the battle was not over yet. About two blocks from the embassy compound a panel truck was parked in the middle of the road. The Marines were in the lead truck and they didn't like what they saw. They stopped a half block short of the panel truck, and sent two Marines forward on foot to check it out. They got maybe 50 yards out when they came under fire from the building in front of the truck. The Marines retreated back to their truck and they and the SEALs set about returning fire.

"Spectre, this is Alpha." Johnson called. "Can you get rid of this little problem for us?"

The gunship pilot had been watching the activity, and "Roger that Alpha. Standby." He rolled the big AC-130 up on its left wing and "Whumpf," the howitzer hit the panel truck dead center. It was the biggest explosion any of them had ever seen. Obviously the panel truck was rigged to blow and the blast leveled buildings on both sides of the street. Even the lead truck in their convoy took some shrapnel, and the cover over the back of the truck peeled completely off. One more SEAL and one of the Marines were wounded. With that, the route was cleared to the embassy.

The trucks and personnel made it into the embassy compound and the SEALs went about organizing their loads for tomorrow's run to the airport. Then they enjoyed a great steak and potatoes dinner and got some much needed sleep. The Spectre gunships stayed aloft all night, just in case there was an attack on the embassy. Fortunately they were not needed.

Chapter Thirty Five

UBON RTAFB

Colonel Parsons and his mission planning cell were busy most of the night Saturday. The gunships were on station over Phnom Penh and the embassy, but the scene was mostly quiet. The Khmer Rouge rebels who had taken over the airport were lobbing mortar rounds here and there, but it was difficult to pin them down from the AC-130. The mortar crews would launch one off, and then pick up and move. So, even though it was easy to see the detonation when the round struck, it was almost impossible to detect the specific source. Based on the Rules of Engagement, the gunships weren't aloud to just indiscriminately fire on the airport area. There were still civilians living very close in, and although they were obviously living in rebel held territory, they couldn't be labeled as bad guys. The gunships got off a little fire here and there with the 40 mm canon when they could detect a heat source fleeing from a suspected mortar launch site. But for the most part, their night was uneventful.

The best thing about having the aircraft overhead was that Master Chief Johnson and Liz Montgomery could use them to relay calls to and from the embassy. Otherwise there was no communication. Phone lines had been cut and even the hard line crypto communication system was disabled.

"Alpha One, this is Spectre 01, how copy?" The gunship pilot radioed in.

After a few minutes, "Spectre, this is Alpha, go ahead." Johnson had been called into the communications center by the Marine on duty there.

"Roger Alpha. Big Shot has info from the Command Center about tomorrow's activities. Does the embassy have secure voice capability?" The idea was to not alert the entire world what their plan was, and if there was a secure radio they both could use it would help. Unfortunately, the embassy didn't have that kind of comm capability.

"Negative Spectre. No such luck." Johnson replied.

The gunship relayed by secure voice back to Big Foot, the ABCCC C-130, and they in turn talked to Colonel Parsons at Ubon. It was determined that they would only pass what was absolutely necessary and even then, use whatever imaginative code the gunship and Johnson could come up with. The plan was to launch out of the embassy about an hour before sunrise on an indirect route to the airport. The hope was to make the Apaches think the Cowboys were heading back to the river to continue on up the Mekong to relative safety. The gunships would be on station and soften up the river and the area around the convoy at the start of the trip, then switch to a route into the airport via what intel had deemed to be the least threatening route. They needed to be in the airport complex by 0730 hours, set up a perimeter to initially protect themselves, then widen it as quickly as possible to allow for the evacuation aircraft to come in. Those C-130s would be on alert at Utapao Air Base and when called, could be on approach into Phnom Penh within an hour. Parsons was shooting for about 1000 hours for them to be on the ground at Phnom Penh. FACs, fighters, and bombers would be overhead for close air support, air superiority, and C-130 escort.

"Ok, Alpha, Spectre here. Anyone there speak Spanish?" Major Miguel Gonzalez, gunship aircraft commander asked.

"Standby Spectre, let me check." Johnson checked with his men and the Marines and he had two that were fluent in Spanish. "Si, Señor Spectre, yo hablo espanol. Que pasa?" The Marine selected to interpret said.

"Ah, muy bien Alpha, ..." and the gun shipper relayed the instructions in Spanish, hoping no one out there listening was a multi-lingual gomer.

Master Chief Johnson and Liz Montgomery discussed the operation and they determined that just the three trucks wasn't going to be enough. They had 40 embassy personnel, 12 Marines (one of them wounded), 12 SEALs (5 wounded and one in a body bag), and one injured Navy pilot. That was 64 souls, two of them on stretchers. That would be 21 or 22 per truck. There would be no room for the equipment and arms the SEALs and Marines would need to take the airport and hold it. Mr. Minh, the CIA liaison, had come with them to the embassy, and he had some contacts in the city. Johnson sent two of the Army Special Forces drivers out with him in the middle of the night with an escort of four Marines and a big wad of money from the embassy safe. They were able to procure two panel trucks of medium size, enough to stuff ten people or a lot of gear in each. In addition, Montgomery suggested the use of the Ambassador's armor plated limousine. That was enough they decided, and went about designating who was going to ride where.

Back at Ubon the schedule was skewed a little. Parsons and Lt. Col. Majors wanted Pete Trask and I overhead during the bulk of the action and until the C-130s were wheels up on the way out. It was determined that Major Hilton would take the first shift until about 0700 on station, Majors would relieve him until 0845, Pete would have the third shift, and I would take the last, but arriving on station about 0945 to double up with Trask and split the area of responsibility.

Pete and I divided up the air support we would get and have them orbit separately - Pete's aircraft southwest of the airport, and mine northeast. What we didn't know was that Colonel Parsons had another Ace up his sleeve. The next morning, as we were getting breakfast at the officers club, he came in and sat down with us. Hilton was already airborne and on his way, and Majors was just stepping to his Bronco.

"Mitchell, Trask, you're gonna have some company up there." Parsons said. I thought he had intel of some bad guy air coming to threaten the ops. That's why we had the Udorn and Wolfpack boys armed with missiles, I thought.

"Yes sir," Pete said. "What's new?"

"I'm going to launch off between the two of you and hover overhead monitoring the fight." He said. "I'll make the decision if and when to launch the evacuation aircraft from Utapao. I need you to get me a seeing eye instructor for my back seat though. I'm a little out of landing currency and I haven't had much sleep in the way of crew rest." His landing currency issue was a laugh. The man had over 3000 hours in the OV-10 and he knew it inside out, but he was right, to be legal he should have an IP with him. The crew rest thing was a real issue however, and although legally it didn't matter whether he had an IP or not, he was not supposed to fly without adequate (12 hours) crew rest. Neither one of us was going to tell him that though. More curious to me was the loiter time he would have on station.

"No problem sir, we'll get you an instructor, but sir you won't have enough gas if you get there that early to make it back here." I said.

"You let me worry about that. You guys just get down there and do your thing. I want rockets and bombs on target." Parsons said. As it turned out, what he had done was have the maintenance guys load and rig up a bladder in the back of his OV-10 with about another two hours worth of gas. We had been experimenting with the bladders back before all this shit hit the fan in preparation for our deploying the OV-10s out of Thailand.

Chapter Thirty Six

PHNOM PENH

By 0400 Johnson and Montgomery had everyone up, fed, accounted for, and standing by their mode of transportation. Most of the embassy personnel loaded in the back of the trucks. There was a special forces soldier at the wheels, and SEALs riding shotgun. Three Marines were in the back of each truck amongst the sheep. The Ambassador's regular driver was at the wheel of the limo. Johnson rode shotgun, Montgomery and the Ambassador were in the back with two Marines. Liz convinced Ambassador Mondavi that the safest place for him was in the way back with a big Marine beside him. He gratefully agreed. The rest of the people were in the panel trucks along with about half of the equipment. Food, arms, and other equipment was loaded in all six vehicles, so that if they lost one or two, they wouldn't lose all the goodies.

At 0530, "Spectre, this is Alpha One. We're ready to go." Johnson called to the gunship.

"Roger that, Alpha. Let 'er roll!" The gunship pilot answered. The limo led the way, then a big truck, followed by a panel truck, big truck, panel truck, and big truck caboose. They moved fast down toward the river with the gunship overhead looking for any heat signatures of bad guys. As they got close to where the barges were still being downloaded by the army, they took ground fire from a building off the left side. The Marines in the lead truck immediately swept back the canvas siding, had shooed their passengers down onto the floor, and opened up with rocket propelled grenades into the building. At the same time, the AC-130 let loose with 40 mm cannon fire and the building basically crumbled around a bunch of dead gooks. The Cambodian army guys that were downloading the barges basically ran for cover, not knowing what was going on.

About that time, the American Embassy in Phnom Penh went up in flames after a series of huge explosions detonated on a timer set by Liz Montgomery before they rolled out. The entire compound was on fire and the destruction and rubble left looked like it had been hit by several bombs.

The convoy made a hard right turn and made a beeline for the airport. The airport in Phnom Penh is situated in the southwest part of the city, only about three miles from the wharf. The Spectre gunship laid down a path of destruction along their route, trying to make sure he didn't block their path with debris. In the meantime, Dave Hilton had called in on scene and had A-7s and F-4s with CBU almost carpet bomb the whole northeast quadrant of the airport zone, laying to waste anything that moved or even thought about it. No doubt there were significant civilian casualties, but there also was very little resistance, at least from that direction. The convoy was stopped three times, and the SEALs and Marines deployed out in front to clear roadblocks and sniper fire. At the third location, only about a half mile from the airport terminal, the resistance was significant. Johnson basically circled the wagons - in this case, trucks - and had everyone get out and take cover behind them. The SEALs and Marines were doing their best to break through, but the gooks just kept reinforcing. One SEAL took a round in the head and went down for the count. One Marine took one in the leg, and another was gut shot. The embassy personnel played nurse maids while the fight went on.

"Nail 67, Alpha One. We're pinned down here, can you put in some air support?" Johnson called Hilton.

"Roger that Alpha, break break, Houston flight do you have a visual on the convoy?" Hilton asked his orbiting flight of A-7s.

"Roger Nail. Looks like fire from their 10 o'clock?"

"Roger that. I'm rolling in for a mark. Make your approaches from the right or left - not directly over the convoy, and cleared hot. Call the trucks in sight." Dave wanted to be sure the fighters each actually saw where the good guys were and that they didn't drop their bombs directly overhead. He rolled in and put a Willie Pete rocket through the sandbags the KR fighters were firing from. "Hit my smoke and on back behind it."

"Houston One's in, trucks in sight." The leader said as he rolled in at about a 10 degree dive getting down low. Each wingman called in with "Trucks in sight" and put their CBU in a blanket covering close to 100 yards around the blockade. The site went quiet and Johnson had his charges pile back into their vehicles.

The convoy pressed on into the airport complex and halted 50 yards short of the terminal buildings. The idea was to not level those building if possible, so the fighters bombed all around it, trying not to make a direct hit. Unfortunately that meant the KR fighters in the building were relatively safe and the SEALs and Marines would have to rout them out.

Johnson deployed a standard "V" formation of SEALs and mixed the Marines in with them. Three Marines were held behind with the four Army special forces guys to protect the civilians. They had two machine gun positions there and two Mortars set up to help out when needed.

The formation moved in slowly and got to within a hundred feet of the main terminal building when the place lit up with defensive fire. Johnson deployed RPGs and the Americans charged the building. At the doors they tossed in flash bang grenades to stun and smoke out the occupants and then burst in. It was room to room and hand to hand fighting, but after about thirty minutes the airport was secure. The trucks and personnel were brought up and the folks were secured inside. Johnson was ready then to expand his perimeter. Specifically they needed to secure the runways and taxiways and the approach to the runway from the southeast.

"Nail 67, Alpha. We're ready to move out in a larger perimeter and then skew it toward the runways." The Master Chief hailed the FAC.

"Copy that Alpha. We got the brief. We'll put CBU in a general circle around you for at least a half mile and then on anything we see moving on the runway complex." Hilton called back. "And be advised Nail 02 is now on scene and will take it from here. You guys take it easy and I hope to see you at a bar sometime soon."

"Roger, thanks for the good work, Break, Break - Nail 02 we're moving out now."

"Nail 02 copies. Rolling in now from the west. Houston you still with us?" LTC Majors called for the A-7s.

"Roger Nail. We've each got two cans of CBU."

Morgan rolled in and put four rockets in an arc about 200 feet apart. "Ok, Houston spread 'em between my first two smokes west to east. Buick, if you see Houston and my smokes you're cleared hot between the second and fourth smokes." He called in a flight of F-4s to follow. Majors continued on a circumference around the terminal complex, smoking and putting the fighters' CBU in a swath that no one could survive in. It was an impressive sight from the ground. This went on for an agonizing 45 minutes until Majors was satisfied there was nothing alive out there within a half mile of the airport. By then he was about out of gas and he had expended all of his rockets when Pete Trask showed up. Pete took control and starting reconnoitering the runway/taxiways.

In the meantime, Colonel Parsons was overhead watching and monitoring. He had Captain Doug Walker, one of our newest instructors in his pit - basically along for the ride. Parsons had greased up his canopy with all the call signs, weapons loads, station times, and seemed to have them all identified as they rolled in to deliver their bombs. He was just about to call Big Shot to have them launch the evacuation C-130s from Utapao when Shogun Flight of F-4s came up on frequency.

"Nails and fighters heads up. Shogun's got a flight of four bogeys inbound from the north about 20 miles. Shogun pincer. You go up and left, we've got down and right." The air CAP F-4s went after the incoming threat.

"Nail 48 copies. Happy hunting Shogun. Buick, you're cleared hot on my smoke." Trask didn't miss a beat. He kept on FACing.

Nail 01 (Parsons) looked to the north, not expecting to see anything but just to realize where the threat was coming from. He decided not to call in the lifeboats just yet.

Shogun flight of four performed a classic pincer attack, splitting to the sides and also vertically to intercept the inbound targets. Since they had no clue if it was inbound bad guys or Vietnamese planes out for a Sunday ride, they wanted to visually ID the threat. The targets were four bogeys, two by two with about two miles separation. The lead Shogun WSO locked up the lead bogey and called for a conversion. The pilot bent the Phantom around and started a climb in mid afterburner to come in from about the bogey's 8 o'clock. Unfortunately Shogun Three's radar had gone tits up on them, so they were relying on a rookie WSO in the number four jet to call their turn. They swooped down from the left converting to about 4 o'clock to the rear two ship of bogeys.

Shogun Two's front seater made the first visual ID. "Bandit. Bandit. Bandit! Fishbeds." He yelled, identifying two MIG 21s.

"Roger, Take the right one, cleared to fire." Shogun Lead said while leading the first bogey and firing his own AIM 7 radar guided missile. The Lead MIG must have been looking out and probably saw the tell tale black smoke trail an American F-4 makes, because he broke into the turn and defeated the missile. His wingman though didn't see the turn right away and the AIM 7 fired by Shogun Two hit home, blowing the MIG into several big chunks.

The trailing MIGs saw and heard their leader react to the F-4 sighting and turned left as well. That was a big mistake, because they basically turned tail to the incoming trail F-4s. The Phantoms were doing about 600 knots coming downhill from the left and were closing on the MIGs quickly - too quickly. Shogun Three managed two switch to heat missiles and fired an Aim 9 heat seeker at the lead MIG. It went straight up the tailpipe from minimum range and detonated. Two down. They were going too fast for Shogun Four's reflexes and he went blowing by the trailing MIG without getting off a shot.

In the meantime, the lead MIG had decided to unload and accelerate out of the fight directly toward Phnom Penh. Shogun One and Two turned hard after him, but were too far away for a shot in a tail chase.

"Nails and fighters one MIG 21 heading your way. We're too far behind to get him soon. Heads up." Shogun announced.

The trailing MIG that had been scared out of his wits by a huge F-4 screaming by him close aboard turned tail and ran north for home. Shogun Three and Four turned back to chase, but again were too far back. However, what they did see when they turned toward the north stood their hair on ends. Six to eight more targets inbound, all moving fast and descending through 20,000 feet.

"Shogun Four's got multiple bogeys inbound, 20 miles north moving fast." The element leader squawked.

"Shogun One copies." The flight lead called. "Zorro, Saber, you up?" He called for help from the other F-4s in the CAP.

"Zorro's up. Heading your way." The first flight of the stack reacted.

"Saber's got the rogue bogey coming south. We'll be with you guys in a bit." The third flight lead had radar contact on the lead MIG 21 that had escaped Shogun's fight up north. They swooped down from his 2 o'clock and Saber One fired an Aim 7 missile. "Fox 1, Fox 1, Saber One. Nail 48 heads up, he's at your five o'clock about two miles." Pete heard that call, broke off his orbit and turned into the threat. About that time Saber's missile detonated just off the wing of the MIG and the Fishbed went into a death spiral. Trask turned back to the fight.

"Good shot Saber." He said.

Zorro and Saber headed up north to join Shogun who were still split up with Shogun Three and Four closest to the incoming bogeys. Shogun Four's radar was showing targets all over the place. "Shogun Four's got multiple targets, all incoming fast."

"Shogun One copies and contact multiple bogeys." The flight leader said. "Shogun Three, take it down and go for the rear targets. One and Two are at your six, 4 miles. Break, Break, Zorro, Saber, you seeing all this?"

"Zorro's contact, showing at least 6 hits, targeting the lead pair."

"Saber's still ten miles out, several contacts."

"Roger, Saber. Maintain a CAP between us and the FAC. Shogun and Zorro will wade into this. You take anything that gets through." Shogun took command of the battle.

In the meantime, Pete was putting in bomber after bomber with CBU, keeping the perimeter clear. The SEALs and Marines had swept the area around the terminal. They had jumped into the Ambassador's limo and one of the panel trucks, and they were reconnoitering the taxiways and runway. Overhead, Colonel Parsons was getting nervous.

"Shogun, Nail 01," Parsons called to the fighters. "We need to get this show on the road and the evac aircraft in here. You gonna be able to control that fight up there?"

"Nail 01, Shogun, I think so sir. There are 12 of us, and so far only 8 bogeys inbound." The flight lead didn't really seem all that optimistic, especially since he already had let one MIG get through.

"Copy that. Just let us know if any get through you." Parson said and then switched to his VHF radio.

"Big Shot, this is Nail 01. Launch the evac aircraft. I repeat, launch the C-130s." The ABCCC copied the message and immediately called the Utapao command post to scramble the launch. The crews of the C-130s were in their aircraft ready to go. They were airborne within 5 minutes.

"Nail 01, Big Shot. Freedom birds inbound." Parsons got the word and passed it on to Pete and Master Chief Johnson.

"Expect them here in about 40 minutes. Alpha, are your folks ready?" Parsons asked.

"We will be sir." Johnson replied. "We're still encountering a little activity off the south end of the runways. Soon as we're satisfied the landing pattern is safe, we'll head back to the fort and round up the herd."

Flight after flight of fighter bombers checked in and Pete stacked them up south of the airport, using one flight after another to keep the perimeter clear of anything that moved. More air CAP arrived too, and Shogun held them back overhead the airport, watching for more threats. I was inbound, about twenty miles northwest of the city, listening to all the chatter.

Chapter Thirty Seven

FURBALL

The dogfight to the north was what fighter pilots call a "furball," a big circle of good guys and bad guys going round and round, trying to achieve a firing solution on whoever was in front of them while reacting to attacks from the rear. I didn't know it at the time, but Shogun One was Captain Scott Perkins, a classmate of mine in pilot training. We were also together after that in instructor school while plowing back to be pilot training instructors. I certainly didn't know it then, but Scotty and I would be stationed together four or five times later on in our careers. Anyway, as Shogun Lead he basically took command of the fight for the American side.

The three flights of four Phantoms split up into six elements and fought in twos, working to get a 2 vs 1 scenario whenever possible. They flew a "fighting wing" formation for the most part. The wingman would fly in a cone about 45 to 60 degrees back of the leader and 1000 to 1500 feet out. It was a very maneuverable formation. The wingy could slide to the outside and inside of the turn in his cone. It was for sure an offensive formation, the six o'clock coverage was limited, and usually covered by the wingman's back seater. His pilot was flying formation and looking out front for the targets, while the lead aircraft crew were on the offensive, visually and on the radar. The plan was to maintain element integrity and not go splitting off alone into a target rich environment.

The idea for the F-4 pilots was also to keep their airspeed up. They did not want to get into a slow speed knife fight with a MIG. All of the MIGs in the North Vietnamese inventory could out turn the F-4. So the plan was to target a bogey across the circle, take an intercept angle, keep the speed up, and hopefully lock him up with the radar and fire an AIM 7 radar guided missile. Failing that, and finding themselves in the rear quadrant of the target, they could take an intercept that would put them crossing the plane 1000-1500 feet behind the MIG, and firing an AIM 9 heat seeker. If it got down to a gun fight, it had to be quick and dirty, and then get out of Dodge, which meant a high angle, limited success shot.

The first set of targets were a flight of four MIG 21s and a flight or four MIG 19s. They basically waded into the fight as single ship attackers, with maybe some wingman support at the beginning. However, once they got to turning with old "Big Ugly" (a friendly nickname for the F-4), they were on their own.

Although it seemed like an eternity, the first furball of 12 vs 8 lasted about three minutes. When it was over, six MIGs were down and the other two were running for home. About the time that happened and the F-4s were joining back up, another small wave of MIG 19s blew through. They were chased down and two were nailed, while the other two retreated north. By then, Shogun and Zorro were "Bingo" fuel and headed northwest for Udorn. Saber joined up and headed back to the CAP above the airport. Swordman and Knife were there keeping watch.

The fighters had basically set up their CAP so that it was a race track pattern generally oriented north-south. Each four ship formation split into two elements and were at opposite ends of the race track. That way they always had two radars sweeping north. The result of that was soon seen as a mistake. Fortunately, in the turn back to the north, Swordman Three's back seater spotted inbound bogeys from the east, the direction of Saigon. They were MIG 21s - four of them, and they were on the scene so fast the CAP couldn't react in time.

"Nails and fighters, heads up. Multiple bogeys inbound from the east." Swordman Lead announced. He led his two flights down from the 20,000 foot perch and tried to cut the Fishbeds off before they got into the bombers' shorts. Two of the MIGs had targeted an A-7 flight laying in CBU on the perimeter of the airport. The other two took on a flight of F-4s just rolling in for their turn. Both Pete Trask and Howard Parsons were more or less in the middle of a vertical furball that was about to ensue. I was just west about ten miles.

The A-7s broke off their attack and turned hard into the threat. The A-7 could turn about as well as a MIG 21, but they had only a gun to shoot. The Fishbeds weren't about to turn with four aircraft, so they blew through and swooped down in the dirt heading back east. Swordman saw them and gave a tail chase. The Phantom pilots traded altitude for airspeed and were pushing the speed of snot when they caught up. Swordman Lead got off an AIM 9 and watched the MIG disintegrate over the Mekong. The trailing MIG saw his leader die and made an unbelievable decision. He bailed out of his perfectly good, though threatened jet. No telling how successful he was, but he was doing over 500 knots when he ejected, and that usually doesn't turn out too well. It wasn't the first time a MIG pilot had hit the silk rather than fight. During one of the Israeli wars, they told stories of Syrian pilots bailing out when threatened.

The MIGs attacking the F-4 bombers achieved only one objective. They stopped the bombing run the Phantoms were making, because the F-4s jettisoned their load before they went into their defensive turn. The Phantom doesn't turn all that well anyway, and having an extra 2000 pounds onboard doesn't help, so getting rid of the load is standard practice when under attack. The good news though was that the F-4s were also loaded with AIM 7 and AIM 9 missiles, as well as a hot gun. So they immediately turned from being defensive to an offensive threat. Again the MIGs saw the angles and blew through towards the east. The F-4 pilots saw it coming and pulled up and around in a hard turn, and although they burned a lot of airspeed doing so, and they couldn't give a chase, two of the WSOs locked up the fleeing MIGs and hosed off an AIM 7 each. One found its mark and blew one Fishbed away. The other missed, but by then Swordman Three and Four were in the chase and catching up.

This MIG driver didn't give up and bail. He saw the Phantoms converting to his six o'clock and coming on fast, so he waited until he saw a missile fly off one of the attackers and he racked it into a hard turn to defeat the missile and met the F-4s heads on. He put the closest F-4 in the center of his windscreen and tried to actually ram the Phantom. This was Swordman Four, a young lieutenant. His WSO had locked up the MIG on the radar, and the lieutenant was waiting for a heat seeking missile growl. He didn't get one because it was a head on pass and the MIG driver had rolled his power to idle. With about a second to spare the lieutenant rolled hard right and pulled as hard as he could. The two jets passed within 50 feet of each other. In the meantime, Swordman Three saw what was happening and positioned himself for a high angle gun shot on the MIG who was now slow with his power in idle. The Vietnamese pilot saw the big white belly of the Phantom coming and pulled into the vertical hard to avoid the shot. He was at about 1000 feet altitude and when he went vertical at low airspeed, he stalled his jet and it rolled off into a spiral, hitting the ground near the runway of the airport.

About this time we heard "Nail 01, this is Freedom One and Two, ten miles out." It was the inbound C-130 evac aircraft.

"Roger Freedom. This is Nail 01. Keep coming, but be advised there are airborne threats up here and although the airport seems secure, you might still encounter ground fire. Recommend a high angle, short field approach. Shoot to touch down about halfway down the runway." Parsons replied. Then...

"Alpha and Nail 48, the Freedom birds are ten miles out. Let's make this quick."

"Copy that, Boss. Nail 48s got two more flights with CBU. We'll lay it down short and parallel the runway."

"Alpha copies. We're returning to the terminal to herd the cats now." Master Chief Johnson said.

Chapter Thirty Eight

NAIL DOWN

Trask was low on gas, but he didn't want to give up the scene yet. He turned it over to me and made one last rocket pass to put his fighters in on the closest threat to the airport. When pulling off from that run he called to me, "Nail 32, 48's got a suspicious couple of vehicles just south of the airport perimeter fence, going down to take a look, then I'm off to find a gas station."

"Nail 32 copies. Good trip home." I said and turned my attention to the area west of the airport. I had two flights of F-4s and one of A-7s stacked up in the holding pattern, all with CBU cluster bombs. I didn't see what Pete was looking at until he was pulling out of his dive. He had descended down to about 500 feet and was climbing out and heading west when the tell-tail smoke trail of a shoulder fired missile streaked up toward him. I saw it but had no time to warn him when the missile impacted his right wing, about where the engine is mounted.

Nail 48 was blown into a hard left turn, and although he had lost his right engine, he had enough airspeed and control to zoom for more altitude and turn to the south, away from the city. "Nail 48's taken a hit. Heading south at 4000 feet. Losing airspeed." Pete said, remarkably calmly.

"Nail 32 copies. Visual. Looks like you're trailing fire." I reacted and immediately turned toward him. About that time the two C-130s started their spiraling approach from about 5000 feet.

"Freedom One is overhead, wheels down for landing." The second Freedom bird pilot made the same call about 30 seconds later. I watched as they flew a right spiraling descent, staying over the airport as much as possible to avoid ground fire. One by one they swooped down on their last turn to roll out at 200 feet just above the end of the runway. They continued a slow speed dive down and touched down with about 3000 feet remaining on the runway. Then they rammed their four big engines into reverse and came down hard on the brakes, slowing enough to turn off the runway with 1000 feet to go. I had seen enough, and decided at this point that I needed to help out my roommate.

"Nail 01, Nail 32, you got this sir. I'm going to head south to monitor Nail 48. You've got three flights of four with CBU in the stack. Looks like some sort of activity near the southwest corner of the perimeter. That's where the shot came from that nailed 48." I didn't ask him, I just told Colonel Parsons that he had the air support control of the main show.

"Roger that, Nail 32." Parsons said. "Let me know if you need help."

Pete Trask was in trouble. He was flying just above a stall speed and his Bronco kept wanting to turn right on him. Not only had he lost that engine and had asymmetric thrust, the missile must have damaged the flight controls as well. The OV-10 will fly on one engine, assuming everything else works. Obviously, that wasn't the case. I was about 6 miles away now and pouring the gas to it trying to get to him.

"Nail 48, how're you doing? 32 is about 5 miles north." I said.

"Not good. This bugger doesn't want to fly straight." He responded. "I'm at least out away from the city. Lots of jungle down there."

"Copy that. I'll be with you in a minute." I said, then, "Big Shot, this is Nail 32. Scramble the Jollies. We may be losing a FAC down here about ten miles south." I called the ABCCC on the VHF radio and told them to scramble the rescue helicopters out of Ubon. It would take them close to an hour and a half to get to us.

"Big Shot copies Nail 32"

I caught up to Pete in his flailing Bronco and it was not a pretty sight. Not only was the right engine nacelle barely hanging on, he had a huge gash in the right boom toward the tail. That probably was his flight control problem. By now all he could do was make a right hand turn, and was losing altitude. I relayed the info to him about what I saw.

"Copy that. I'm going to have to leave this thing. I'm basically in a death spiral." He said, again very calmly. I looked out ahead of us and saw a fairly large clearing a few miles further south.

"Copy. Looks to be a clearing south ......" My call was cut short as his ejection seat came rocketing through his canopy and he was in his chute. The OV-10 tightened up its spiral and impacted below us in a medium size explosion. He must have lost a lot of gas too. There wasn't much of a fire. I set up a pattern at 5000 feet offset from the chute a bit so as not to pinpoint his location to anyone curious below.

Colonel Parsons was in the midst of putting his fighter bombers in on target around the airport. I broke into his radio calls with "Nail 01, Nail 48 has bailed out about 10-15 south. I might need some of your fighters. I've got plenty of gas for about an hour and a half. I'm setting up for SAR control. Jollies on the way."

"Nail 01 copies. Break, break... Waco flight, chop to Nail 32 for SAR support." Parsons sent his A-7s over to my control for Search and Rescue (SAR) support.

"Waco copies. Nail 32 we're heading your way at 10,000." the A-7 leader said.

"Roger Waco, Nail 32s smokin' now. Maintain your altitude and set up an orbit east of my position. Survivor is touching down now in the jungle, but not too far from a clearing about 5 miles west of my position.

"Waco's got your smoke Nail. Copy all."

I got down as low as I could to try and tell if Pete's chute had hung up in the canopy of the jungle. I could see some orange color down there, but couldn't see much else. The beeper from his locator beacon was going off loud and clear. As I was climbing out from my look see a lot of ground fire came up at me from a small clearing to the north. Obviously Pete was in indian territory. I climbed out to 5000 feet to stay above the fire.

Meanwhile, back at the ranch, the Alpha team was herding their sheep onto the two C-130s who hadn't even shut down, just opened the back ramp and let the folks scurry aboard. They were taking some sporadic gunfire from the perimeter, but as soon as something came up, Nail 01 made that guy wish he had kept his head down. Two flights of four F-4s carrying CBU cans spread their death and destruction all around at Nail 01's direction.

The two C-130s taxied out quickly and took off in about thirty second trail, climbing out quickly and in a steep, spiraling climb to at least 5000 feet before heading west toward Thailand. Nail 01 followed them out for a while and called the air CAP F-4s.

"Bowie flight, Nail 01, you still in the CAP?"

"Just coming back in Nail. We've been playing tag up here with a few MIGs, but seems to be quiet now." The lead F-4 pilot responded.

"Roger that. I want you to catch up to Freedom Flight, two C-130s currently climbing through 12,000 feet heading out southwest. Escort them until they get to Utapao or until you run short of gas." Parsons directed the combat air patrol (CAP) jets to be escort fighters.

"Copy that Nail. We're radar contact on Freedom, heading their way."

"Good. Now, is there anyone else up in the CAP? We've got a SAR situation going on down here and may need some air cover." Parsons asked.

"No one's here yet Nail, but Shogun is inbound." Bowie Lead said. Udorn especially kept using the same call signs over and over. It made sense though. They were sword fighters or jousters and the bombers were car makes - Buick, Edsel, Fiat, etc.

"Nail 01 this is Shogun. We're twenty minutes west at 20,000. feet. We were the last fragged for the mission, but they can scramble more from Udorn." Parsons was kicking himself. He planned and tasked plenty of air support and air cover for the duration until the evacuation was complete, but he hadn't thought about the need for more help.

"Roger Shogun. Contact Nail 32 this freq. He's running a SAR situation south of the city." Parsons said, then switched to VHF. "Big Shot, this is Nail 01. Scramble more air cover from Udorn and more A-7s from the Enterprise. Looks like we're going to be here a while."

"Big Shot copies sir."

Pete finally came up on the radio. "Mayday, Mayday. This is Nail 48 on guard down about 12 miles south of Phnom Penh."

"Nail 48, we have you loud and clear. Switch to channel Bravo." I directed. We didn't want the entire aviation world knowing where he was, so the standard procedure is to switch to another frequency on his handheld radio. He came up on the Bravo frequency, 331.0. "Nail 48's up."

"Nail 32s up. We've also got a flight of A-7s, Waco flight, and Shogun for air cap." They all checked in on the frequency. "You have any trouble on landing?"

"Yeah, I hung up about thirty feet high and had to cut my way out. Bunged up my right leg in the fall pretty good. I can move, but I'm not joining any running races any time soon."

"Ok. Copy that. Can you fire a flare up through the canopy? I want to pinpoint your location and get you moving toward a decent looking pick up point. And Pete, be advised, there are some gun totin' indians not too far from you to the east. They took a couple pot shots at me when I was down there looking for your sorry ass."

"Roger. Stand by for flare."

Pete fired a flare that cleared the canopy close to where I had been looking. I figured he was about a half mile from the clearing I had seen before he went down.

"Ok. Got your flare. If you can, move southwest about one half mile. There's a decent size clearing there. If you can get to the edge of it and dig in, we can bring the Jollies in to pick you up." I said.

"On my way. I'm hearing some thrashing around and voices yelling to my east."

Things quieted down for a while as I hoped Pete was limping toward the clearing. I thought about putting the A-7s in on where I had taken a shot from, but I decided it was best not to let the bad guys know for sure we had something going down there. I flew over top of the clearing. It was about three clicks (3000 meters) long by a click wide. There were a couple of roads going through it from the jungle. It looked like it was once a forest that was probably cleared for its lumber, and then was being cleared of the stumps to turn into farm land. I got down low and cruised up and down the edges to look for any ambushes. I guess I'll never learn. Sure enough I took some small arms fire, and a couple of dozen gooks ran out into the clearing to get a better shot. I was able to jink and get low over the trees, putting some jungle between them and me, and then I climbed on back to 5000 feet.

"Waco, we've got small arms fire coming from the southwest corner of that clearing down there. I need to clear it for the rescue choppers. Follow me in with one can apiece." I rolled over on my wing, took up about a 45 degree dive and plugged a Willie Pete dead center where the gomers were mingling around. "Hit my smoke, Waco!"

"Waco copies, in hot, FAC in site." The A-7s came in screaming and the Khmer Rouge never knew what hit them. Four canister's was probably overkill, but what the heck! Crispy critters!

About then we got the bad news. "Nail 01, Nail 32, Big Shot." The ABCCC calling.

"Go ahead." Both Colonel Parsons and I reacted at the same time.

"Sir, the Jollies had a problem coming in. Jolly 01 had an engine failure and went down about 50 miles west of Phnom Penh. Jolly 02 landed and picked them up and they're heading back to Ubon. Their unit says they don't have any more Hueys operational." The primary rescue helicopter in Southeast Asia was the HH-53 Huey, a real workhorse that had seen better days. The squadron had sent half their fleet home already and they only had these two that could fly - now just one.

"Nail 01 copy" Parsons acknowledged. I immediately called Waco.

"Waco, we just lost our Air Force choppers. Does the Enterprise have anything capable?"

"We have UH1B Seawolves Nail, but It would be a while before they could get here. The boat's about 100 miles off shore." Waco One said.

"Copy that. I'm hoping to get Big Shot to scramble them anyway. They're our only hope right now." I responded.

"Roger that and you might get them to scramble more replacements for us. Dallas, flight of three, is inbound, but that was all we were planning on."

"I'm hearing all that. You guys aren't painting a real rosy picture here." It was Pete Trask. He had made it to the edge of the clearing and was monitoring the radio calls between the A-7s and me.

"Yeah Roger that. Glad to hear you're back with us. You got a good place to hide?" I called to him.

"Roger, flashing the mirror at you now." He had pulled the mirror out of his survival kit, figured the angle of the sun and flashed me a couple signals.

"Gotcha!" I said. "Ok, be advised there were some indians down on the other side of the prairie from you, but Waco turned them into charcoal. Be heads up for more. I'm working the cavalry issue."

"Big Shot, Nail 32. Contact the Enterprise and have them launch their rescue choppers. Ask them to generate more air support as well. This might take a while." I called ABCCC, then "And also contact the command center and have them scramble more FACs this way. I've only got about 45 minutes of fuel and Nail 01 will have less than that."

"Big Shot, Nail 01. I've already done that." Colonel Parson was way ahead of me. "Ubon is scrambling more FACs, as well as F-4 support. I've got about 10 minutes left." Parsons came up. "Nail 32, I'm gonna have to head out, but you've got relief and support coming. Hang in there."

"Roger that sir. Good trip home." I said. Just about then a line of Khmer Rouge soldiers came out into the clearing due south of Pete's position and moved toward him. Shit!

"Waco, bad guys on foot south to north. With a tally, cleared in hot. I don't want to smoke or have our survivor flare his position. Hopefully they don't know exactly where he is." I went ahead and described where Pete was hiding out in reference to the clearing and the roads through it.

"Waco copies. We're in hot from the north." Again they laid down a barrage, and again it got quiet. Although not so much for Pete.

"Nail 32, I've got chatter east of me. They're yelling back and forth, probably a half mile, getting louder."

"Copy that. Break, Break! Waco, more activity in the jungle I'm rolling in for a smoke. Run north-south just east of my smoke." I directed the A-7s. Then I rolled in and put down a smoke about 50 yards into the jungle from where Pete was. Then I rolled up to look. "Ok, nothing west of that smoke."

"Er Nail, Shogun here. Sorry to screw up your day, but we've got four bogeys heading your way fast. Shogun's engaged." Christ, I thought to myself. Just what we need right now, an air war in the middle of a cluster fuck.

"Copy that Shogun . Keep me advised."

Shogun, flight of four F-4s left the cap and ran a pincer attack on the four bogeys. Turns out they were MIG-19s, and they descended about 20 miles out to take advantage of the ground clutter on the F-4's radar. It almost worked. Well, it did work for one of them. Shogun One and Two converted on the front pair and took an Aim 7 radar shot apiece. The missile from Shogun Lead's shot got lost in the ground clutter and detonated well behind the lead MIG who was basically at treetop level. The number two MIG was a little higher and the missile from Shogun Two found its mark. One dead gook.

Shogun Three and Four ran on the trailing pair of MIGs and closed in behind for heat seeker shots. Shogun Three "splashed" his MIG, but the fourth MIG saw them coming and made a hard turn to defeat the Aim 9 from Shogun Four. He kept his turn going and accelerated, keeping it down in the dirt and ran north. One more dead and one chicken shit.

In the meantime, the lead MIG kept going as fast as the MIG 19 can toward where he was told there was a downed OV-10. Shogun One and Two were in a tail chase, but were not closing quite fast enough.

"Nail, you've got a MIG 19 about to blow through about 5 miles north on the deck." Shogun One said. "We're four miles in trail and closing." I cranked it around and looked to the north.

I couldn't see the MIG, but I saw the tell-tail black smoke of the trailing F-4s.

"Visual on your smoke, but no tally." I said. "Waco, bogeys should be about your five o'clock." I warned the attacking A-7s. Sure enough, as Waco Four was rolling in for his last pass on the jungle, the MIG came up from his four o'clock and shot a heat seeker at him. It missed because there was too much angle off the tail for the missile to see enough heat. The MIG kept coming and was about to try a high angle gun pass when he exploded in mid air. Shogun One had splashed the MIG with a heater. Waco Four dropped his CBU, pulled up out of his dive, and decided he probably needed a change of underwear. Yikes! That was close!

"Ok, Nail. Waco's Winchester (out of ammo) and Bingo (out of gas). Dallas is on station." Waco One said as they joined up and headed for the carrier.

"Copy that Waco. Good shootin'" I said. "Dallas standby. It's getting a little too hot out here. Maintain your orbit and heads on a swivel."

"Nail 48. How's the air down there?"

"It stinks. Gomers close. I need to go off radio." Pete whispered.

Chapter Thirty Nine

BERNIE WHO?

The scenario was just too hot. We had a lame pilot down, surrounded by Khmer Rouge bad guys, rescue choppers way too far away, airborne threats, less fighter support than we needed, and I was running out of gas to make it back to Ubon. Fuck it! I thought. I'm not leaving my roommate down there. I'm sticking around until I can't stand it and then head south to feet wet and visit the Navy's hospitality. After all, that worked for two F-4 crews so far.

I didn't want to call Pete because it sounded like his "visitors" were too close and he wanted to keep radio silence. But I couldn't just do nothing.

"Dallas, Nail 32. Did you see where my smoke hit for Waco's attack?" I called the new A-7s on station - three of them. They must have lost one on start up.

"Negative Nail. Can you smoke again?" The flight lead asked.

"Roger that. I'm rolling in from the west. Plan on keeping your passes north-south, or at an angle, but not directly west-east. Survivor there." I rolled in with about a 60 degree dive and plunked one in the same hole as before, about 50 yards into the jungle from where I hoped Pete was still hiding. I rolled up to take a look.

"Dallas hit my smoke. One can at a time, multiple passes until I say so." I ordered. The A-7s made one pass north to south, then bent around and made one southwest to northeast, and were coming around for a third pass when Pete came up on frequency.

"Nail 32, 48. Hold off." He said. "These guys are real close and I can't hear them with the bombs going off. I'm pretty well dug in here and they don't know where I am. I can actually see a few of them through the bushes." Shit! I thought. That means they are closer to him than my smoke rocket hit, so all the bombs are missing them wide.

"Copy that. Dallas, hold off. They're getting too close." I called to the fighters. Just then I caught a wing flash of something behind and to my left 8 o'clock. I turned that way and got a face full of MIG 21 right in my snot locker.

Holy shit! I cranked it hard to the left to avoid hitting him. I don't know if the son of a bitch even saw me, or if he did and wanted to ram me.

"Shogun, you still up there? Where'd this guy come from?" I frantically asked our CAP F-4s.

"Shogun's in the CAP Nail, what the... Ok, tally now. He snuck in from the east. Shogun's engaged." I had to give it to the F-4 driver. He didn't waste any time swooping down and getting in the fight. The MIG saw him coming and they went into a bit of a furball until the MIG bugged out east. Shogun One sent his trailing element in a tail chase while One and Two stayed on the scene to look for more intruders.

That was it for me. I next made probably the dumbest decision in my Air Force career, but I've got to say that given the same deteriorating circumstances, I would do it again. After all, that was my best friend down there. The air support was down to only what I had on station. The cavalry would be at least another 30 to 45 minutes away. We had no rescue choppers inbound - at least none we'd probably see today.

"Nail 48, hold on. I'm comin' to get you." I called to Pete.

"You're what? Are you outta your friggin' mind? It's a shootin' gallery down here." He came back.

"Nail 32, Nail 01. Mitchell, what are you trying to pull? A Bernie Fidler?" Parsons was half way to Ubon but he heard my radio call.

"Yes sir. I think it's the only way to get him out alive." I said.

"Not only no, but Hell no! Mitchell, this is a direct order. DO NOT go in there. We don't want two of you as guests of the Khmer Rouge." The Colonel was livid. I decided not to argue with him, just do it!

"Dallas, Nail 32. I'm going to put this thing down in the clearing and pull our survivor out." I explained to the A-7s. "Dallas One, you have command of the scene. Put down all the cover you can. CBU, guns, whatever it takes to keep the gooks heads down in the jungle."

"Dallas copies Nail. You sure about this? Oh never mind. Your call. Dallas is ready." He said.

"Nail and Dallas, Shogun's up here with hot guns guys. We can help as well." The CAP F-4 lead offered.

"Shogun, Dallas, Roger. We'll do what we can until Winchester, then it's over to you."

For some reason right about then I reached down to my right hip and felt for my 45 automatic slung there in a holster. I assumed Pete had his gun as well. We were all issued little 38 revolvers that fit in the holster sewed into our survival vest, but most FACs opted for something with a little more firepower. I had a Kimber 1911 45 strapped to my hip like a cowboy. It fit nicely in the bucket of the ejection seat. I think Pete's was a Colt. We actually had one FAC in the squadron who flew with an AK-47 in the cockpit. I never asked him how he was going to carry it during an ejection. I guess he'd just hold it between his legs pointing up and boom - away he goes, ready to spread fire on the welcoming party as he descended in the chute. We had all talked a lot about saving one round for an emergency as well. The Khmer Rouge were known to be brutal and ruthless - even the North Vietnamese looked like pussycats compared to the KR when it came to the treatment of prisoners. We had said we wouldn't be captured alive. I was afraid that was what Pete was thinking right about now too.

I took a good look through the binoculars from about 3000 feet. I couldn't see any movement around where Pete was, but obviously they were there. I looked at the surface for impediments to landing and taking off. There was a basic north-south running dirt road - more like a double wide trail. Unfortunately it wasn't straight and it looked like dirt mounds or curbs on either side. If

I landed on it, I wouldn't be able to stop before it curved and I would probably have a problem with those side "bumpers." The east-west road was straighter, but short and nowhere near where Pete was hunkered down. There were also a few ditches crossing the clearing that would create a problem if I ever buried the nose gear in one. The wind didn't seem to be a big problem. What there was seemed to be west to east based on the smoke trails of my rockets and the fighters' bombs. I decided I'd land from south to north about 2000 feet from Pete, taxi up to abeam him, and hopefully he'd be able to limp out and jump in. I'd need to shut down the left engine to keep the prop from beheading him. The OV-10 has a "set ready to taxi state" system that is a parking brake. I'd be ready to use it if necessary to help Pete into the rear seat.

Chapter Forty

WASHINGTON D.C. - THE WHITE HOUSE

The President and most of his National Security team were in the White House Situation Room. The Chairman of the Joint Chiefs, along with the Air Force Chief of Staff and the CNO of the Navy had been there throughout most of the operation, from the delivery of the trucks on the beach. Others, including the President, had stopped in from time to time to get an update on the progress of Dragon Savior. But now, everyone was there and had been since the early morning hours Cambodia time. They were most interested in the evacuation plan. They had a direct connection to CINCPAC Admiral McMaster, who in turn had communications with Big Shot, the ABCCC C-130 over HF radio. Basically that meant the White House was getting near real time info. When the word was passed that the FAC on station was going to attempt to land and rescue the downed airman, the reaction was mixed.

"Jesus. Isn't that a bit risky?" The President asked.

"Yes sir. It's very risky." Said the Chairman. "In fact his commander, the Colonel heading up the entire operation told him directly to not even think about it."

"What are his chances?" SECSTATE Crittendon asked, presumably wearing his National Security Advisor hat, although it was always questionable what his interest was.

General Bob Black, the AF Chief of Staff answered. "Sir, I'd say his chances are less than 50%. Something like this was done a few years ago when Captain Bernie Fidler landed his A-1E Skyraider on a dirt field and his downed wingman jumped in. Fidler took off, took a lot of ground fire, and successfully recovered at Danang. He's been put in for the Medal of Honor for it, but there were those who would rather have had him court martialled."

Crittendon put on his Secretary of State hat. "So chances are we're going to have two pilots and two more aircraft down in Cambodia, a country where we're not supposed to be in the first place. Can we stop this guy?"

"Not without shooting him down ourselves." Said the Chairman.

"I hope you are being facetious Admiral." Said General Black.

"Of course I am Bob. At this point I think we need to just wish Captain Mitchell good luck and we can deal with the consequences later - one way or the other."

"Tell me about this Captain Mitchell, General Black" The President asked.

"I can take that one General." It was General Curtis LeCroix, PACAF Commander. All of the Pacific senior players had gathered at CINCPAC headquarters in Hawaii and were monitoring things both ways. "Brad Mitchell is a 27 year old captain in the Air Force.

He is relatively low experienced in the FAC business and the OV-10, but he is a flight commander. His roommate over there is Captain Trask, who happens to be the downed pilot."

"OK. Thank you General." The President responded. "Now, how are we doing on the evacuation?"

"Sir, the C-130s are out of Cambodian airspace and approaching their destination, Utapao Air Base. Everything went as planned on that front. We just didn't prepare for this much resistance on the ground, and especially the airborne threat." Admiral McMaster answered.

"I guess we have the Washington Post and my late Chief of Staff to thank for all of that." Gatewater said. He got no response from anyone.

"Mike, have you got extra support inbound to help out this extra curricular activity?" The Chairman asked Admiral McMaster.

"Sir, we have another flight of A-7s inbound from the Enterprise. They are probably 30 minutes out. We also have launched three four ship flights of F-4s from Ubon and Udorn. They're probable 45 minutes to an hour out. Colonel Parsons also ginned up two more FACs from Ubon, hopefully to get on scene and coordinate the rescue. The first one is at least an hour away." CINCPAC replied.

"So let me get this straight." General Black said. "The soonest we can get any support overhead is 30 minutes, and then only one flight of bombers for another 30 minutes? How much time on station does the flight overhead now have?"

"Not much sir." General Lecroix jumped in. "The A-7s have expended at least half their bombs. They will have guns to strafe with, as will the air to air F-4s. But that's it, and they are all getting low on gas. To be honest sirs, I believe that is why Captain Mitchell is doing what he plans. It sounds like it's getting real hot down there and he knows he's not going to have any support for a while."

"Well, all I can say is 'God Speed.'" President Gatewater said.

Chapter Forty One

HERE GOES NOTHING!

I dropped down to about 1500 feet and offset the clearing by about a half mile west and picked out what I thought would be a good touch down point just long of one of the ditches, and with what looked to be a relatively smooth rollout to where Pete was dug in. I put the landing gear down and lowered the flaps, turned a tight base leg 90 degrees to my final approach, and descended to about 500 feet. Then I rolled into a steep and short final leg, aiming for the ditch.

I flared right over the ditch about 5 feet high and let her settle in softly, not wanting to crunch anything. Once the main gear were on the dirt, I rammed the engines into reverse and came up on the brakes. I had landed. Everything seemed to be working. It was a rough ride across the field, but I was able to keep her moving.

As I taxied up to abeam where I figured Pete was I started taking some ground fire from my 2 o'clock position, short of my destination.

"Dallas, ground fire abeam my position now." I yelled to the A-7s.

"Roger Nail, copy that, we're in from the southwest." I came up to abeam the bushes where I thought Pete was, stomped hard on the right brake, and powered up the left engine to swing around the other direction and get closer in. About that time the three A-7s came screaming across releasing their CBU. I figured they had one more pass left.

"Pete, you in there?" I called for him on the radio.

"Yeah, but so is a whole war party of Apaches. Soon as I move they've got me." He whispered. With the engines running I could barely hear him.

"Ok, copy. Dallas, use your guns in close to our guy. Nail 48 pop a flare so they see where you are and then come runnin,". I said.

"Dallas copies. In hot looking for a flare." The A-7 leader said and rolled in pointing right at where I thought Pete was. This was going to be close.

"Hey Brad, I can flare, but I can't run. Here goes." Pete said, again remarkably calmly. His flare came up out of the bushes a little further south than I thought he was.

"Flare's in sight. Guns, guns guns!" The jet came blowing through at maybe 100 feet, 20 mm blazing. Two and Three were right behind him.

I shut down the left engine and set the parking brake, unstrapped and went over the side. As soon as I hit the ground I rolled to under the wing and then got up, 45 in hand, and ran toward Pete's position. I could see him just coming out of the jungle. He was limping badly. He also had his sidearm in hand, and took a couple shots back into the jungle. I hoped that Dallas was watching, because I had no way to talk to him now. I had kept my helmet with boom mic on, but I obviously was disconnected from the radio.

I got to Pete and threw his arm around my shoulder, and we ran a three legged race back to our trusty horse. We took several rounds of gunfire from further down the clearing, but most hit the dirt around us. We both fired a full clip of our 45s. No time to reload. Fortunately Dallas kept coming. They put in one more strafe run and then shed their last cans of CBU. That gave us time to climb aboard. I helped Pete up and he dove in the rear seat. I climbed into my perch and quickly hooked up my comm first.

I began the engine start process right away on the left engine and went about strapping back in, and closing the canopy, hoping Pete was doing the same. We took some hits. I could see gun fire coming in and it looked like some hit the left wing and engine nacelle.

"Dallas, I assume you're Winchester. How about you Shogun?" They were way ahead of me. About then an F-4 went screaming across in front of me guns belching at the jungle.

"Shogun's in from the west. You ready to roll Nail?" The phantom driver asked.

"Roger that." As soon as the left engine was back up I rammed them both into reverse while holding the brakes and then back out of reverse. That released the parking brake just like it was supposed to. Then I started to roll.

I quickly got her up to full power, had lowered the flaps before I shut down, and in that configuration proceeded with a short field takeoff - the first time I'd ever done one on a real short field. In the meantime, Shogun made pass after pass strafing the east edge of the clearing. It kept most of the heads down out there, but a few were still able to unleash in us. I could hear and feel the "pings" of bullets impacting the fuselage and wing. Just as I raised the nose to lift off, a rocket propelled grenade came screaming out of the jungle at us. I pulled her off the dirt into the air just as the grenade exploded beneath us. I felt the Bronco shudder, but she seemed to hold together. However, when I raised the gear handle, the wheels would not come up. The grenade must have blown something loose in the wheel wells. I still had three down and locked indicators.

After I passed over the end of the clearing at about 400 feet I turned toward the west - the direction of home. I climbed out as quickly as I could until passing 3000 feet, then settled into a more gradual, speed inducing climb.

"Nail 32, Shogun's Winchester. We still have some loiter time." The F-4 leader said. "You want an escort?"

"That would be great Shogun. Looks like the gooks got my underbelly. Wheels won't come up. Can you come take a look?"

I didn't want to overspeed the gear, but I also wanted to be able to let the F-4 saddle up and take a look. The Phantom driver came around to my six o'clock and slowed down in a hurry. He wallowed around out there at a speed the F-4 doesn't like much, lowered his landing gear and flaps, and taxied up beneath me. We were climbing through 3000 feet at about 220 knots.

"Er Nail, yeah. You've got a bunch of wires and cables hanging loose from the right wheel well. The gear themselves look ok." Shogun Lead informed me. "However, looks like you are leaking fuel from the right wing route." I took a quick look at the fuel gauge, and immediately looked again.

Shit! I thought. I'm down to about forty minutes of fuel. No way we'll make it out of Cambodia, much less to Ubon. I started a left turn and called Shogun,

"Shogun, roger that. We're losing petrol. Already down to about 30 minutes or so. Can't make Thailand, I'm turning out to sea. If you can stick around great. But bug out when you have to."

"Shogun copies. We can give you about 15 minutes." They still had air to air missiles on board. It was a good thing too.

"Shogun Three's got two bogeys, left 7:30, two miles and closing. Four, hard left." The trailing element of the air to air guys were doing their duty - checking six. And sure enough, old man Ho Chi Minh hadn't quit yet.

"Shogun One copies. Two, 90 left." The flight lead acknowledged the threat call and brought his two jets left to a 90 degree angle from the incoming bad guy to look for the threat and support his wingmen. "Nail 32, looks like we're going to have to leave you alone for a while."

"Copy that Shogun. Good hunting."

Through all of this it was obvious I could not communicate with Pete. He didn't have his helmet or headset to hook up to the radios and intercom. So I quickly scribbled out a note on the back of a piece of map and passed it back over my shoulder. He was able to reach it. "Gear stuck down. Losing gas. Heading to feet wet." Then I called the ABCCC C-130.

"Big Shot you still out here?" They had been real quiet ever since Parsons had told me to abort the rescue try.

"Roger that Nail. We're monitoring. What's your status?" They wanted an update to pass on to the powers that be.

"Airborne with the survivor onboard. Landing gear stuck down. Took some ground fire and leaking fuel. I can't make it home. Heading out to sea to go for a water bail out. Can you get the Navy to help? Shogun engaged with air threat." I listed the issues.

"Copy that Nail. We'll pass it on. Good luck." Big Shot seemed to be signing off on us.

The flight control stick shook in my hand. At first I thought it was a spurious control problem. Then after the second time, I realized it was Pete trying to get my attention. I looked in the mirror and saw he was trying to pass me a note. I reached back and grabbed it.

"You are a complete fucking idiot.... But I love ya."

I laughed and gave him a thumbs up.

Shogun managed to splash both bogeys - they were MIG 21s, but Three and Four used up a lot of gas doing so, probably in afterburner for a while. "Nail 32, Shoguns are back aboard, but we're sending Shoguns Three and Four home for gas. One and Two can give you another ten minutes max." We were just coming up on the coast and I figured that once we were feet wet we would probably be relatively safe. We were a long way from any MIG base in Vietnam that I knew of.

"Copy that Shogun. Head on out when you have to. We'll be looking for a nylon letdown near the Navy soon." I said.

"Nail 32, Big Shot."

"Go ahead." I replied.

"Sir, not so good news. The submarine Virginia is nestled up with the Enterprise, too far out to be of service early. But the Enterprise is steaming at full speed toward you. Sir, what's your position to the coast and airspeed?" Big Shot asked. I assumed they were going to predict a join up with the Navy for us.

"We're crossing the coast now, doing 250 knots. Can the Enterprise get her chopper airborne?" I asked planning for us to bail out and be rescued by the UH-1 Navy rescue helicopter. There was pause while Big Shot checked with the cavalry.

"Roger Nail. Chopper's lifting off now. We predict you'll be intercepting in 20 minutes."

"Ok, sounds good." I signed off for now and wrote up a note for Pete.

"Navy chopper inbound. 20 mins. How's your leg for bailout?" A couple minutes later he shook the stick and passed me his answer.

"Can't eject. No harness. Can't strap in. Leg's ok, but…?" Oh shit! I thought. I didn't think of that. But now I remember.

He had obviously shed his harness and everything when he cut himself out of his parachute. This was not going to work. He would never survive an ejection, much less have a way to hang on to a parachute.

"Copy. Plan B, or is it C? D?" I wrote back, not knowing what that would be.

"Big Shot, Nail 32. We cannot eject. Survivor in back seat has no harness and cannot connect to the parachute. I'll need to ditch this thing I guess." I called to the AB CCC.

"Roger, I'll pass it on."

"Tell you what, Big Shot. What's the carrier's frequency? We need to get you out of the middle here." I wanted to be able to get in touch with the Enterprise myself.

"Copy that, Nail 32. Contact the Enterprise on 324.6"

I sat and thought about it for a while and passed Pete a note to see what he thinks. "Not sure about ditching this thing. Not recommended from what I remember."

"Yeah, especially with the wheels hanging. Easy to ground loop. Water loop?" Pete came back. "I think you should set it up to splash down and bail out just before. I'll fly it in from there." He was trying to save my ass, knowing his was grass.

"No fucking way Jose. We be in this together."

I looked in the mirror and he flipped me the bird.

"Enterprise, this is Nail 32, wounded OV-10 in the blind, heading your direction." I called the mother ship.

"Ahoy Nail 32. This is the Enterprise CAG. We have you radar contact. Keep your heading. Looks like we're about 20 minutes out. What's your fuel state?" The captain in charge of flying operations asked. I looked down and saw that we had just about that much gas left.

"Nail's got 20 minutes if we're lucky. Losing it overboard pretty fast."

"Copy that. Understand you want to ditch that beast? Our chopper is up. He has you in sight. Should be at your one o'clock a little low."

"Nail 32, Big Shot. Nail 01 advises not to ditch with the gear down. He says tech reps concur, ditching will cause a ground loop." Colonel Parsons had contacted North American Rockwell and their gurus advised we not get our feet wet. They built the OV-10 and had put it through lots of trials, probably including a simulated ditching.

"Copy that." I was on edge now in a shitty. I knew the best would have been a bail out, but Pete would never survive that. Trying to land it on the water evidently was not a popular option either. My only other option would be....

"Nail 32, CAG. Think you can put that thing on our deck? After all, the Bronco was designed for the Marines to do just that, and from what I understand, you've already made one short field landing today." He came up with that idea at the same time I did. I had always thought Navy guys were crazy, landing on a postage stamp size airport that was pitching and rocking in the sea. Now it apparently was my only chance.

"Great minds must think alike sir. Or is it warped minds?" I came back. "Sorry - no offense CAG. I had just realized that is probably our only option as well, and I must say I'm thinking I must be crazy."

"Ordinarily I'd agree with you, but there are those all the way to the top that think you might already be a little nuts based on what you've done today. You can do this. We'll talk you down." The CAG said, giving me a little bit of a warm feeling. Or was that because I had just pissed in my pants?

I passed a note to Pete to tell him what I was going to do. As I expected, he too thought I was crazy. "Mitchell, you have completely lost your mind. But if you pull this off, I'll see to it you never have to buy another drink in the bar." He wrote back. I smiled and gave him a thumbs up in the mirror.

I picked up the Enterprise in my windscreen about five minutes later. She was turning into the wind, the standard procedure to accept landing aircraft. Every bit of headwind a pilot can have the better. As it turned out, I wasn't the only one due to land.

"Nail 32, CAG. I've got 4 A-7s I want to get on the deck before you if we can. They had headed off to support you at the fight, but you left town early. Head on in to overtop the boat … that is if you think you've got the gas." I didn't have a clue how much gas I had. The gauge ready empty, but the needle was bouncing around a little, like the probe could be sloshing in a gallon or two. Obviously though the CAG wanted to get his chicks on board before I came in and crumped his deck. I couldn't argue with that.

"Copy that sir. Got you in sight. I'll maintain 3000 feet. I have no clue on how much fuel is left in this thing."

Watching the recovery of the flight of A-7s from above was amazing. They hit the deck, hooked the cable, and before they could even throttle back the guys in Yellow Shirts were all over the place. The Navy uses color combos on the deck for their crewmen that tend to the planes. There are Red Shirts for fire and emergencies, etc. The Yellow Shirts are the guys who move the planes around, get them set up on the catapult for launch, and move them out of the cable after landing. They released the tail hook and vectored the pilot to taxi out of the way, he folded the wings, and they had it parked and out of the way almost before the next one landed. The whole recovery couldn't have taken more than 5 minutes and then...

"Ok. Nail 32. You ready to do this thing?" The CAG called.

"Ready as I'll ever be, sir."

"Roger that. Go ahead and descend to your normal downwind altitude. No need to configure. Obviously your wheels are down, but lower what flaps you want. Plan on a steep, short final. Shoot for the first 100 feet of deck. Don't worry about the cable. We're disconnecting it since you don't have a hook. We'll leave the throttle technique up to you. I assume you'll reverse thrust?"

"Roger that. Soon as my main gear touch. Should take less than 500 feet of roll out." I said.

"That's good, cause all you've got is about 400 feet depending on how close to the approach end you land." CAG cautioned.

Oh great, add to the suspense!"

I rolled off the perch onto base leg at 1000 feet and started a steep descending turn.

"Nail 32, base, gear down, full stop." What a joke! The Navy probably got a good laugh out of that too. Of course my gear was down, and of course it would be a full stop - one way or the other. Just a habitual radio call. I rolled out on a short final, took a look at the deck rockin' and rollin' in front of me, and took a quick look in the mirror. Pete was there grinning with a thumbs up. I hoped he settled back into the seat and grabbed onto something.

We hit the deck (and I mean that literally) hard and I rammed the engines into reverse, lowered the nose to the deck and came up hard on the brakes. I could see the ocean at the other end coming up fast. I brought her to a screeching halt actually short of where the cable would have been otherwise. I looked out and the yellow shirt guys were all clapping and giving me the thumbs up.

"Outstanding Nail 32." The CAG said. "We'll make a sailor out of you yet." And here I thought I was a sailor, just not doing it for a living. The Yellow Shirt in the front waved for me to follow him over to the side by the superstructure and then shut down.

We were down and we were alive. The only question now was how much trouble was I in?

About this time Nail 01 was crossing the border back into Thailand. He figured everyone else was out of the Cambodian skies.

"This is God on guard. Last one out turn off the lights.…. Again!"

Chapter Forty Two

USS ENTERPRISE

I quickly climbed out of the cockpit and helped the crew get Pete out and onto a litter. He high fives me and they whisked him off to Sick Bay. I walked around the airplane and marveled at the number of bullet holes in the fuselage and engine cowlings. There were a couple just below the canopy on the left side that if they were a few inches higher .... Anyway, I got around to the left side and noticed a small but steady stream of fuel leaking out of a small crack at the wing root. I figured that was not good.

One of the young Yellow Shirts on the deck came over and saw what I was worried about.

"I can fix that, sir." He said and then he went about taking a big wad of chewing gum he'd been gnawing on out of his mouth and stuffed it into the crack. Problem solved - no more leak. I didn't think there could be much more fuel in there to leak anyway, but his solution was ingenious.

"Good job. And thanks for helping us out after landing." I said.

"No problem sir. That's my job." I shook his hand and asked what his name was. "Carter Duthie sir."

"Well, good to meet you Carter Duthie, and thanks again." I said. He saluted me and said.

"Good to see you too, Gramps." And he walked away. Gramps? I thought. Jeesh! I might be a little older than him, but Gramps? Before I could say anything else, the Captain of the Enterprise walked up.

"Good landing Captain. Welcome aboard. I'm Captain Pete Paradime, Skipper of the Enterprise" He said. I saluted him and replied,

"Thank you sir. It's good to be here." I was about to say "on dry land," but that wouldn't have worked.

"Come on down below. We've got you set up in an officer's room with one of your fellow Air Force types." The Captain said, referring to the two crews from Edsel flight, the F-4s that dumped in the Gulf and were picked up by either the Enterprise or the Virginia. "Feel free to get cleaned up and join us in the Officer's Mess at 1730 for chow."

I first went to look in on Pete. They had him sedated and were about to work on him. Evidently he actually broke his leg in two places. It was amazing that he had been able to move at all out there in the jungle. The doctor on board was optimistic though. They were going to set his leg and he would only need a boot or a soft cast.

I found my room after a long search. All the rooms and decks look alike on a ship the size of the Enterprise. I got some help and had someone point me in the right direction. Captain Dan Jake, Weapons Systems Officer from Edsel One, was my roommate.

He and his front seater, Lt. Colonel Jim Davis, Edsel One and the squadron commander of the 497th TFS, had been on board a couple of days. The Navy had been treating them well.

I got cleaned up and put on a Navy flight suit the CAG, Captain Jon Martin dropped off for me, and Dan and I headed for the Officer's Mess. Chow was good. Not exactly four-star restaurant good, but substantial. I met Lt. Colonel Davis and his wingmen, the F-4 crew he had pushed out to feet wet. The submarine Virginia had picked them up and transferred them to the Enterprise the day before. I also met half the officer force of the Enterprise. The other half was on duty.

On Monday the Navy loaded the six of us Air Force types onto a C-2 Greyhound, two engine prop job used for transport, and flew us to Ubon to meet up with our squadrons. The medics had patched Pete up pretty well and issued him some crutches. They ended up parking our Bronco in a tight corner of the deck, and when they got to Subic Bay in the Philippines, the next port of call for the Enterprise, they off loaded her by crane and towed her to a hangar. Later on I know our maintenance folks at NKP sent a team of mechanics and specialists to Subic the patch her up and get her operational again.

My reception at Ubon was mixed. The squadron guys were all high fives and party down. Colonel Parsons was a bit reserved. He let the celebration go on for a day or so and then called me and Lt. Col. Bastione into the office they had arranged for him at the Ubon Command Center. The conversation went something like this:

"Mitchell, I gotta say what you did took a lot of balls and you are commended for saving your roommate's life and your own." Parsons said, and I waited for the "But…"

"But you disobeyed a direct order and came way too close to losing us two FACs and another good OV-10. I have half a mind to court martial your ass."

"I understand sir." I didn't want to say anything more like "I'd do it all again," or "I didn't have a choice under the circumstances." I figured he probably knew all that.

"I don't know what the brass and the civilian hierarchy are going to do, but I'd suggest you find your dress blue uniform and get it up to snuff. You'll for sure be on somebody's carpet one way or the other." Parsons wrapped it up and escorted us to the door.

I tried to salute him, but he just blew that off. When I was about to pass him at the door, he held out his hand and said. "God Damn Shit Hot, Brad. Good job." He was smiling and I shook his hand, a bit puzzled. I figured he felt he had to chew my ass first, but he really supported me. We'll see.

General LeCroix came in the next day and a meeting was held in the base theater. Every pilot and WSO on Ubon was there, as well as representatives from Udorn, Utapao, the rescue squadron, the gunships, and the Navy. The SEALs had been picked up from Utapao by the same C-2 that delivered us to Ubon, and delivered to the Enterprise, and the army guys were leaving by commercial air to go back to their stateside units. Master Chief Johnson was once again on the phone and piped into the theater.

Lecroix entered with Lt. General Tobin, Commander of Seventh Air Force, Admiral Ages, Commander of the 7th Fleet, and their aides, trailed by the Wolfpack wing commander. "Be seated." LeCroix commanded as he strolled down the aisle to the podium. He looked out over the crowd and smiled. "You folks have reinforced my faith in our military forces and what we are capable of. Colonel Parsons," The general said, looking at Nail 01, "You put together a good show. I have reservations about your personal participation, but I guess I should have known you'd find an excuse to get back in the cockpit. As it turned out I guess it was a good thing you were there when your young captain decided to go over the side. Good job, Howie.

"As for the rest of you, well done! I understand Master Chief Johnson is on the horn. You there Chief?"

"Yes sir. Read you loud and clear." Johnson broadcast.

"Good. Well hear this loud and clear. You and your men are true heroes. A bunch of people owe their lives to you and your ingenuity and perseverance. I understand you have a date back in Washington. Seems the President wants to meet you, as well as Colonel Parsons here." LeCeroix said, glancing again at Nail 01, whose reaction was in surprise.

"I thank you sir, but we couldn't have come close to accomplishing our mission without your folks and the Enterprise. We're just glad we had a chance to do our job the way we were trained." Johnson replied.

LeCroix finished up the meeting, congratulating everyone again. Then before he left he said, "Lt. Colonel Davis and Captain Mitchell, I want to see the two of you out at my aircraft before I takeoff." Lt. Colonel Davis was the 497th TFS Commander. He and I met up outside the theater. He had a squadron truck, so he offered me a ride to the flight line.

The General took Colonel Davis onboard his executive style T-39 jet first. I waited on the tarmac with LTG Tobin and Colonel Parsons, who'd come along to see the General off. Obviously I wasn't in the meeting, but I understand it was short and not so sweet. LeCroix congratulated Davis for his innovative action to save his wingman by pushing him out to sea. But he also relieved the Lt. Colonel of his command for losing a perfectly good F-4 in the Gulf of Thailand. As he came down the stairs from the jet, Colonel Davis looked dejected and I didn't get a warm fuzzy feeling as I climbed the stairs.

"Sit down Mitchell." LeCroix said after accepting my salute. "I understand Colonel Parsons has already had a piece of your ass for your heroic stunt down there, so I won't drag it out any further. What you did was over the top. I understand why you did it. I understand that you didn't think there was enough time to continue the SAR operation and get your buddy out by chopper. But you took a helluva big chance. Let me ask you this, before you went in there to pull him out what did you think your chances of success were?" I had to think about that a minute.

"I don't think I did ponder that question sir. I just decided to go and didn't really think about the 'what ifs.'" I said.

"That's the kind of thinking - or not thinking - that will get you killed someday." The General came back. "I don't know how this is all going to play out up the chain. I personally am going to recommend to the Pentagon that they just drop the whole thing - don't call you a hero, and don't call you an idiot. But like I said, I don't know what the reaction is with the brass." General LeCroix dismissed me after that, but as I stood to leave he said, "Mitchell, you've got balls, I'll give you that. But let me ask you this, how'd you like landing on the carrier?"

"Not something I'd want to do again sir. My balls were feeling awfully small about then." I left again not knowing if I'd been reprimanded or congratulated. I went to the squadron building and pitched in to pack for our trip back to NKP the next day.

We flew our steeds back to their barn at NKP and proceeded to party for a couple days at the Nail Hole. Pete was true to his promise. I drank free from then on if he was around. Over the next few weeks and months we continued our training on Chandy Range from Korat or Tahkli, and also continued to say goodbye to departing old guys, with no newbies to replace them. For the 23rd TASS it soon became obvious that not only was the war over, there was also no future for the squadron.

EPILOGUE

Over the next few months the FACs of Southeast Asia became history. In fact, most of the US Air Force in SEA became history. The F-4 squadrons from Ubon and Udorn were slowly withdrawn. The Jollies continued their draw down. They broke down and packed up some of their helicopters and shipped them out in giant C-5 airlifts, and gave the rest to the Thai Air Force. By early 1974 the 23rd TASS was the only operation in country. Oh, the C-130 Klong kept up its regular, though reduced schedule, base hopping around the country, but there were no fighters or bombers in the area. JUSMAG, the Joint US Military Assistance Group was still there, headquartered at NKP, and as it ended up, I'm sure glad they were there.

The Air Force personnel system kept up its program of handing out dog shit assignments to the FACs. We were used as filler pilots, sending us to jobs nobody else wanted. Some of the guys who hadn't already spent a tour as pilot training instructors received their assignments there in T-37s or T-38s. Some of us got transport assignments.

My assignment was to a C-5 out of Dover, Delaware. I swear that airplane doesn't fly. It's so big it just scares the ground away. I had decided it would be my last assignment, and that I would get out in three years and try for the airlines. At least with big heavy flying time, I should be attractive as an airline pilot. Pete got clobbered even worse than me. He was assigned as a missile control officer at Grand Forks, North Dakota. Overall, not one of us got an assignment that was anywhere annotated on our AF Form 90 - our assignment "Dream Sheet."

By April of '74 we had only 18 pilots in the squadron, and we all were just biding our time on our one year, remote tour. Finally about then, the Air Force decided to open a FAC squadron in South Korea, and we were to deliver them their aircraft. In late May Pete Trask and I were assigned to lead 12 OV-10s to Osan AB, Korea, via Utapao, Saigon, Clark AB (Philippines), and Kadena AB (Okinawa). We filled all the cockpits with guys who were going to the new squadron as their next assignment, At least they were getting to fly.

It was to be a four day trip that took two weeks. Two Broncos broke down at Utapao and we had to wait so that we could all go through Saigon on time and together. The South Vietnamese were still fighting their war and we were to get in, get gas, and get gone in an hour and a half. So, we waited at Utapao until we had 12 good to go and we went in to Tan Son Nhut Air Base. Amazingly, no one broke down there, although we mysteriously had two radio failures right after take off. Our Broncos had been outfitted with fuel bladders like Col. Parsons flew over Cambodia, and even with that we got to Clark with just enough fuel and broke a couple more planes. In addition, we had sent one of the pilots to Subic Bay from NKP and he fired up my trusty Dragon Savior Bronco, patched bullet holes and all, and flew it up to Clark. Now we had 13 to ferry. We played a lot of golf at Clark, and then some at Kadena, either because of maintenance issues or the weather in Korea.

We eventually made it into Korea. Pete was leading the first 6 ship formation and I had the second seven. He orbited a couple times and waited for us to catch up and then we came blowing across Osan Air Base with 13 OV-10s, all with smoke generators smokin.' Here we thought we were the cat's pajamas, sort of like we were at NKP. Well, Osan was a fighter base and no one was impressed. We got our asses chewed for showing off at a base where a few generals reside, and then after a semi-rousing party at the Officer's Club, Pete and I were poured onto a C-130 for the long ride back to Thailand. We arrived on base just four days before we were to leave for our own next assignments.

When I got back to NKP, Lt. Colonel Bastione, our squadron commander, met me at the C-130 and told me to go get a haircut and get into my blue uniform. I had an appointment with General Timothy O'Reilly, the JUSMAG Commander. I thought, Aw shit! Either someone from Osan called him about our arrival, or my extraction episode had finally caught up to me. But fret for not, because when I got to the squadron, ready to go for my appointment, they handed me a list of names to take with me. It included all of the squadron guys who had gotten assignments over the last year, their place and plane of assignment, and their "Dream Sheet" druthers.

I marched into the General's office and smartly saluted. He sat me down, was very cordial, asked me about the trip to Korea, and then sat back and said "Ok. What are you here for?" I explained that just before he left, the General's executive officer, a colonel and fighter pilot, had stopped by the Nail Hole, and after hearing our sob stories about our assignments, had offered us a visit with his boss, General O'Reilly. Then I handed the General the sheet of paper and explained it. He looked it over and said, "Holy shit. How long has this been going on?"

"Pretty much as long as there's been FACs for the personnel system to use as fillers sir. It seems that the FAC business was only popular in this part of the world." I also pointed to the painting he had hanging behind him on the wall. It was of an F-15, the Air Force's newest fighter at the time. General O'Reilly's son was in the first F-15 training class. Anyway, I pointed at that and said "That's what I'd like to fly sir."

The General looked at the sheet a little longer and finally said, "I don't know that I can do anything for you. It's probably too late, but let me keep this and I'll make some calls. Maybe we can change a few of these later assignments." I thanked him and saluted, and went to the hooch to pack. I wasn't there ten minutes when the squadron called saying General O'Reilly's secretary wants my social security number.

Two days later, when Pete and I had two days to go, the personnel office called me and told me about a change of my assignment to an F-4 at Hahn Air Base, Germany. Man, I was one happy dude. No one had to buy a drink at the Nail Hole for those two days. Of course Pete bought mine, but I bought everyone else's. Unfortunately, the General couldn't change Pete's missile silo assignment, or any of the other guys heading that way. He did manage to change a couple more jobs to fighter slots though. And, after his three years at Grand Forks, when it was time for his next assignment, evidently Pete's records had been "red tagged" for special consideration. Pete got an F-15 to Bitburg, Germany. I never liked the way those things worked - you know…. "It's not who you know, but who you ...." Oh well, I certainly wasn't going to turn it down.

The 23rd TASS was deactivated that summer. The last 6 aircraft were boxed up and sent to Osan or back to the States by C-5. Gee, just think. I could have been their truck driver.

I was called to Washington when I was in Florida for F-4 school. Pete met me there and we were escorted to the White House by the Chairman and the AF Chief of Staff. In the Oval Office we were met by SECSATE Crittendon and a couple other new folks in the Cabinet. The President walked in and shook our hands. "Glad to meet you men. Captain Trask, how's the leg?" Pete told him he was as good as new. "That's good. Well, Captain Mitchell I don't know whether I'm supposed to thank and congratulate you or scold you. I've been counseled to do both.... by different members of my Cabinet of course." I could see the Secretary of State squirming.

"I suspect you have been talked to extensively by your immediate superiors, so I'm not going to add to the misery. If you gentlemen would stand up, my Chief of Staff will read a citation." The new Chief of Staff read citations for each of us and the President hung a Silver Star medal around each of our necks. He also presented Pete with the Purple Heart. That was it. Case closed.

That evening we stopped by the bar at the Mayflower Hotel. Just by coincidence the Air Force had put us up at the Mayflower for the night. Pete and I were sitting at the bar. I was enjoying a single malt scotch on the rocks - Pete's treat of course, when up walked a man with a notebook and a pen.

"Hey, you are the two Air Force guys who dropped in and out of Cambodia last year aren't you?" He introduced himself as Bob Woodall, reporter for the Washington Post. By now the Watergate crisis was loud and clear in Washington and we knew who Woodall was. We also were briefed that he wrote the article in the Post that almost got Pete killed, and a lot of folks either killed or injured. "I understand the President actually awarded you medals today for that fiasco. What do you have to say for yourselves?"

We both got up quickly and Pete stepped towards the little shit with his fists clenched. I stepped in between them and while looking at Pete and holding his one arm, I swung my other arm down and back, and hard - right into Woodall's crotch. He went down doubled over with an "Oooph!" I looked at him, smiled, and then told the bartender to give the man a Shirley Temple.

Pete and I left the bar and went on with our lives and our Air Force careers.

THE END

ABOUT THE AUTHOR

Colonel Dana Duthie's assignment as an Air Force Forward Air Controller is the basis for many of the experiences in "Convoy Cover" His Air Force career spanned 24 years, from pilot training in Georgia and instructor in Texas to the skies over Southeast Asia in the OV-10, and from the F-4 phantom in Germany to the F-16 Falcon in South Carolina, Korea and Germany. The theme of "Convoy Cover" spawned from his tour with the 23rd Tactical Air Support Squadron in Thailand and Cambodia. He also "paid his dues" with three headquarters assignments and professional schooling. Colonel Duthie retired in 1992. He lives in Broomfield and Steamboat Springs, Colorado with his wife, and two children and four grandchildren nearby. One grandson is currently assigned as a Yellow Shirt on the USS Carl Vinson, nuclear carrier in the Pacific.

FROM THE SAME AUTHOR

Convoy Cover is actually the fourth book by Colonel Dana Duthie, USAF (Ret), but the first in the career of Brad Mitchell, Air Force Forward Air Controller and fighter pilot.

Phantoms of the Shah is the third book published by Colonel Dana Duthie, USAF (Ret). It is actually the second of four adventures in the Air Force career of Brad Mitchell. In Phantoms, Brad Mitchell is a Captain flying the F-4 Phantom in Germany. The plot is based on a deployment of his squadron to Shiraz, Iran. There they encounter trouble with the radical Islamists and rescued hostages being held on the base with the help of F-15s and a SEAL team.

Tremble is based on the author's tour in Korea in 1985-86 and Mitchell is the squadron Commander of the 80th Tactical Fighter Squadron. North Korea has stepped over the line one time too many. The Air Force launches an attack on a suspected nuclear weapons site in the North, and attempts to rescue a team of international weapons inspectors.

Dark Rain centers on the last years of Brad Mitchell's career as he participates in quelling Iranian terrorist attacks on the U.S. An Iranian "mole" steals an F-16 fighter armed with a nuclear bomb and flies it to a base in Libya with the intention of using it in an attack on Israel. Dark Rain is the story of how the U.S. goes about recovering the jet and its weapon, and stopping the Iranian tourist attacks.

www.ingramcontent.com/pod-product-compliance
Lightning Source LLC
Chambersburg PA
CBHW020719130726
47899CB00011B/449